MW01043516

ALBATROSS
Hall

Jean Baker

To Chrystine with
best wishes,
Jean,

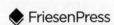 FriesenPress

Suite 300 - 990 Fort St
Victoria, BC, V8V 3K2
Canada

www.friesenpress.com

Additional Contributors:
Dr. William Brown, Professor of Neurology, McMaster University Hamilton Ont. (First contributor)
The Duke Of Northumberland, U.K. (Preface)

ISBN
978-1-5255-9239-3 (Hardcover)
978-1-5255-9238-6 (Paperback)
978-1-5255-9240-9 (eBook)

1. Fiction, Historical

Distributed to the trade by The Ingram Book Company

LIST OF CHARACTERS

Matthew Ponsonby, Heir to Albatross Hall

Lady Arabella Ponsonby, Mother

Lord Cecil Ponsonby, Father

Lieutenant Henry Ponsonby, Second Son

Lady Sarah Ponsonby, Daughter

Aunt Cassandra, Sister to Lady Arabella

Mrs. Hatchett, Housekeeper to the Ponsonbys

Gillies, The Gamekeeper

Hetty, Kitchen Servant

Molly, Scullery Maid

Tom, The Boot Boy

Everett, Tutor to Matthew

Hopkins, Manservant One

Bentinck, Manservant Two

Jed, Assistant Manservant

Dick Choke, Gardener

Mr. Tapper, Head Coachman at the Hall

Mrs. Dobson, Second Housekeeper, Sister of Jessie

Parson Bray, Rector of St. Mary's Church

His Wife, Emma Bray

Bess, House Servant to Mrs. Bray

Mr. Wick Sexton, at St. Mary's Church

Sir Charles Ponsonby, Brother to Lord Cecil

Life At Mulberry Court with Spinster Sister

And Religious Zealot, Miss Gertrude Gaunt

Matilda, Housekeeper at Mulberry Court

Feathers Family Lawyer Dr. Palliser, Family Doctor

Lady Charlotte Greville, Widow of Hon. Rupert Geville

Later Wife of Matthew Ponsonby and on his Death, Henry Ponsonby

Felicity, Lady's Maid

Edward De Lazlo. Marries Sarah Ponsonby

Colonel Billop, Military Companion of Henry Ponsonby

Sir Thomas Erskine Barrister

Sir Miles Standish, Companion to Matthew in Bath

Jakes, Third Manservant

Mrs. Fowey, Comic Companion of Jane Dean, both Widows

Quentin, New Companion of Mrs. Fowey

FOREWORD
BY DR. WILLIAM BROWN

Jean Baker has written a historical novel of fecklessness, dimwittedness, intrigue, humour, romance and murder spanning the decades between the American revolution and Napoleonic Wars. From cover to cover she has introduced a wealth of well-drawn characters, with accents to match their station in life and the times. Her book has pace and an eye for detail, whether high-born or low, manor houses or bawdy places.

Frankly once started, I couldn't put her book down-and for good reason, Jean Baker has written a rollicking story well worth the read.

CONTENTS

This book is dedicated in loving memory
of my late husband, Peter M. Baker.

CHAPTER 1:
THE RETURN FROM
THE GRAND TOUR

From school to Cam or Isis, and thence home;
And thence with all convenient speed to Rome,
With reverent tutor clad in habit lay,
To tease for cash, and quarrel with the day,
With memorandum book for every town,
And every post and where the chaise broke down,
His stock a few French phrases got by heart,
With much to learn, but nothing to impart;
The youth obedient to his sire's commands,
Sets off a wanderer into foreign lands ...
Returning he proclaims by many a grace,
By shrugs and strange contortions of his face,
How much a dunce has been sent to roam,
Excels a dunce that has been kept at home.

William Cowper (1731-1800)

Matthew Ponsonby, scion and heir of Albatross Hall, gazed listlessly through half-closed eyes at the endless raindrops spattering down in rivulets on the coach windows as it approached the village of Cobham, in the heart of the misty Kent countryside. Sheep grazed in sodden pasture and the ghostly forms of conical-roofed oast houses reminded the young lord that he was back on English soil. "Would Don Quixote have thought those oast houses windmills in disguise?" Matthew wondered, looking out at the forlorn landscape. The journey home from Italy he viewed as an unwarranted intrusion into his dissolute way of life, even if his father, the old earl, was on his deathbed. The sleeping figure of his tutor, propped against the faded red corded silk upholstery opposite, no longer inspired him as it had before Matthew's hasty departure from Oxford.

"You really are a disgrace to the whole family," Lord Cecil had said, pointing an angry finger at his son as he stood defiantly on the venetian marble floor of Albatross great hall. "I heard reports of your riotous living, drinking parties and fondness for the ladies. You have squandered a comfortable income in gambling and the horses. Because of your shameful profligacy, you have accumulated debts which I will no longer pay." The earl's voice had trembled. "I have appointed a tutor," he had continued. "You will be under strict supervision on your tour, sir."

Matthew had crossed over to the exquisite pietra dura table, a favourite piece of furniture cherished by his mother, Lady Arabella, and idly run his fingers over the fine interlaced marble set with semi-precious stones, purchased by a thoughtful ancestor from the Borghese palace in Rome. "Italy would be a welcome relief from the cloying atmosphere at Oxford and Albatross Hall," he had thought.

Like many a young man of aristocratic lineage and wealth, Matthew had fallen into ways of excess. Two noblemen, Lord Milleaux and Sir Francis Dashwood, achieved such notoriety that they were seldom sober the whole time they were in Italy. Sir Francis later formed the Hell Fire Club for debauched young men. As professor Adam Smith remarked, when he accompanied the third Duke of Buccleuch, "A young man who goes abroad at seventeen or eighteen and returns home at twenty-one, commonly returns more conceited, more unprincipled, more dissipated, and more incapable of any serious application either to study or to business than he could well have become in so short a time had he stayed at home."

Matthew's thoughts had not been on higher learning. He would be certain to meet more pretty women and wear the stylish clothes popularized by his idol, Beau Brummel. Like many of his forbears, he intended to enrich the walls of Albatross Hall with the purchase of landscapes: delicate scenes of Tivoli, and Busiri's admirable paintings of the Tomb of Cecelia Matella, with its unusual crenellated towers, or the artist's later masterpiece, the Ponte del Aqua stone bridge with rustic peasants tending goats in verdant pasture.

The coach lurched forward through the fog. Matthew closed his eyes and thought of Lady Charlotte Greville, a beautiful, young, wealthy widow—a brief encounter in Rome as Charlotte was leaving the studio of Batoni, the celebrated portrait painter, a favourite of the English aristocracy. He had stepped aside as she had swept by in a rapturous flurry of pink silk crinoline and ostrich-plumed pink velvet hat which had concealed her delicate, finely chiseled features. Charlotte had stepped into a handsome carriage drawn by two white horses and driven by liveried attendants across the Tiber bridge.

Matthew sighed as Everett stirred again inside his drab brown cloak, firmly fastened against the morning chill. His tutor was no longer a companion and confidante, but very tiresome, constantly reminding Matthew of his duty and the advice of his father to stay away from the gaming tables. In strict secrecy, Matthew had fallen into the bad habit of accepting loans from a certain Thomas Coutts, a Scottish banker known for his shrewdness in financial affairs.

"We have reached Cobham, my lord," said Everett as the panting and sweating brown bays rattled over the cobblestones to the door of the Three Jolly Rodgers at the end of the village street, bustling with tradesmen, hawkers, pickpockets, stray hens, and mangy ill-fed dogs. In the low-set bow window of the inn lay an untidy heap of dirty bottles, undisturbed for a century. Legend told of an evil fate awaiting anyone foolhardy enough to touch them. Tweedy, the stout, genial host, clad in brown leather jerkin and gaiters, lounged against the open sturdy oak door, placidly filling his pipe as Matthew approached, holding his green velvet cloak above the muddy, rain-soaked cobblestones.

"Good day to you, sirs," said Tweedy, noting Matthew's curiosity as he peered at the bottles. "Ah, them bottles is the talk of strangers in these here parts. Don't know how they got there," he continued, scratching his bald head. "All I knows is that two of the villagers came to a bad end arter they touched a couple. But that's afore my time here. But never you mind an old legend, genl'men."

He waved his hand in the direction of the cosy parlour, warmed by a blazing fire, crackling in an enormous ancient hearth above which was suspended an immense iron cauldron. Massive oak beams, darkened by the smoke and grime of centuries, supported the low ceiling and the deeply worn stone floor was strewn with reed mats upon which lay a black cat, indifferent to the approach of the visitors. "Ah, she's as good a mouser as ever I had," said Tweedy, as Matthew and Everett seated themselves into a comfortable oak settle lined with green cushions.

"Halloo there Snoggs. Halloo, I say." He called to a gaunt individual, who appeared immediately through a low stone archway bearing two steaming tankards of mulled ale and placed them on a low table nearby.

"Come far?" asked the waiter, tossing another log onto the fire.

"We have travelled from Dover and the continent," replied Matthew, warming his hands while Everett removed his wet boots and cloak. "The seas were rough, and our ferry had great difficulty in docking at the pier. We were glad to leave France though, as the country appears on the verge of revolution."

"Pity it's still such beastly weather," observed Snoggs, laying a large table on which he placed a cold fowl, hot roast beef, and a tureen of oyster soup.

"Good job you were not living in Cromwell's time," he continued, as he polished two wine glasses, holding them up to the window before setting them down before the newcomers.

"Why Cromwell?" asked Matthew, helping himself to a portion of soup.

"Why?" repeated Snoggs, crossing his arms. "Well, it's bein' a Sunday, we wouldn't have been able to serve you young genl'men such a feast."

"Ah," interrupted Everett, "quite the scholar I see. But what do you know about the bottles in the window?"

The waiter grew pale and his hand trembled as he poured Matthew a second glass of wine. "Them as cooked on a Sunday," he went on, ignoring the Tutor's question, "were sure to be reported by their neighbours and severely punished. Also, Cromwell wouldn't allow folks to gather in alehouses like this. They might be plotting a rebellion against him. Even the parents were punished if they failed to have their children baptized. Why Sir James Mallory, down in the next village, was accused of not keeping a bridge repaired because the road flooded. Ah them Puritans, they were so hard on the people."

"But how would the neighbours know if the landlord cooked on a Sunday?" asked Matthew.

Snoggs wiped his greasy hands on his white apron. "By the telltale smoke comin' out of the chimbley of course. You could always smell the cookin'. And afore Cromwell's time, in good ole' Queen Bess's reign, the Catholic priests would also be persecuted. They would seek hiding places in barns and haystacks and if they were found, they would go to their deaths on the scaffold. Then, before Queen Bess, there was that bloodthirsty ole' Queen Mary. She was alus taking away the property of the Protestants and giving it to them Catholics. If you ask me, there's not much difference between them." Snoggs stooped down and fed the cat some table scraps. "Did you ever hear of Sir Francis Englefield?" he continued. "Well he grew rich arter Lord Montagu died, you know. Ole' Queen Bess, she was a rum un. Tried to undo all that her sister Mary did." Snoggs paused and wiped his nose on his coat sleeve.

"Come to think of it," said Matthew. "My ancestor, Sir Thomas Ponsonby, entertained Queen Elizabeth. I seem to remember hiding in a priest's hole as a child. My family can trace its roots back to William the Conqueror. We've lived at Albatross Hall for hundreds of years."

"Indeed," said Snoggs, turning to Everett. "I will go and see if the fresh team of horses is ready."

Everett was relieved to be rid of the garrulous waiter. "Thank goodness we're not living in Cromwell's time," said Matthew, as Everett placed his cloak around his shoulders.

The landlord made a low bow as they entered the yard, now crammed with hay wagons, jostling drovers, and porters burdened with heavy boxes. The rain pelted down in torrents, filling the gutters to overflowing. It did not abate until the weary travellers reached Albatross Hall.

CHAPTER 2:
THE DEATHBED SCENE

"Never leave the young scoundrel a penny," Lord Cecil whispered hoarsely to his wife as she fluttered round the ebony tester bed, inlaid with ivory and supported by barley sugar posts, framed on all sides with rich damask drapery, and reputed to have been slept in by Lord Nelson. Albatross archives showed that it had been presented to Queen Elizabeth by the Earl of Leicester in 1575.

Lady Arabella pummeled the white lace-trimmed pillows in a futile effort to ensure his lordship's exit from this vale of tears was as comfortable as possible. Meanwhile she continued reflecting on the earl's desire for economy, outlined in a recent letter, and its impact on her husband's heir, whom the dying earl seemed determined to disinherit.

"It is impossible that we should continue our present mode of living. You must not purchase everything your eye is attracted to—no superfluous clothes beyond what is requisite for you to appear clean and decent—and, furthermore, you must be attentive to the bills of the children, especially Matthew; you are well aware that last year I found his extravagance most distressing." It was fortunate that Matthew had not been robbed of his "Batoni" portrait finery by Moorish pirates lurking off the Barbary coast of North Africa as the second earl had been.

Lord Cecil raised himself off the pillows once more. "And as far as Sarah is concerned," he said, "if she still insists on marrying Hopkins, you can cut her off as well." The angry earl had banished his wayward daughter to live with his brother, Sir Charles. A sharp-featured, humourless Ponsonby with stern demeanour, he could be relied upon to bring Sarah to her senses. Hopkins was a manservant in the earl's service. His lordship had expressed indignation that Sarah had had the misfortune to fall in love with a man well below her station, and she had further offended by rejecting all eligible suitors, despite the numerous balls given in her honour.

"No father", Sarah had said, shaking her golden curls, "I will not marry Lord Fitzwilliam Dolittle. He spends too much time closeted with the prince, and is much in debt. They play cards at Carlton House 'til the cock crows. Rumour suggests that he is actually defying his father and carrying on a relationship with a Mrs. Maria Fitzherbert, a devout Roman Catholic. If I can't wed Hopkins, I would rather marry an impoverished clergyman." Sarah had fled in tears.

"So the vultures are beginning to gather, are they?" said the earl irritably, as Lady Arabella smoothed the sheets closely underneath his chin, gently placing her hand on his brow.

"There, there, my dear," said Lady Arabella soothingly, "you mustn't upset yourself. Doctor Palliser and Aunt Cassandra will be here shortly." Lord Cecil briefly closed his eyes, as if warding off a vision of his vexing sister-in-law. Aunt Cassandra had always exerted too powerful an influence on his wife, encouraging her in extravagant habits distasteful to a man of frugal disposition toward his household and yet known to keep a good table for the local landed gentry.

Turning his head, he stared intently at a favourite portrait of the seventh earl by Sir Godfrey Kneller. This showed a charming, young, rosy-cheeked boy, dressed in a yellow silk coat adorned with oriental pearl buttons, lace cravat, and golden pointed shoes, carrying a dish of ripe apples, a King Charles spaniel at his feet. Like all the family portraits, the seventh earl was mounted in a heavily gilded frame, against a wall finished in fading green Chinese silk.

"Shan't be long following him," he observed morosely, as Doctor Palliser briskly approached the earl's beside, crossing the red carpet, on which the stained-glass armorial windows reflected the sun's splendour in pools of iridescence. Doctor Palliser was no mere country doctor in the role of village apothecary. He had studied with great diligence medicine and anatomy and was thus admitted to the College of Physicians and Surgeons in London, licensed to perform bloodletting with the aid of leeches and other primitive remedies fashionable in those days.

"How are you today, Lord Cecil?" he inquired, stooping to take his patient's feeble pulse.

"Not so good. Don't think I'm long for this world," whispered the earl hoarsely, sinking back again onto his pillows. "Blessings on my dearest wife."

Lady Arabella was weeping profusely, crumpled in a heap on the nearby crimson brocade sofa with a profusion of cushions sufficient to conceal or suffocate the family cat.

"Do try some of Mrs. Hatchett's special medicine," urged Doctor Palliser, leaning once more over his fretful patient. "It will do you good. It is made up of two ounces of mustard seed, two bitter oranges, one ounce of horseradish, and a half ounce of fennel, all stirred into the best sherry. It is best taken in one draught."

Lord Cecil looked suspicious, but took the proffered glass in a shaky hand, slowly sipping the golden liquid, watching Palliser as he crossed to the white marble fireplace, on the mantle of which rested a parade of exquisitely carved ivory elephants and a graceful Louis XIV ormolu clock inlaid with mother of pearl.

An imperious knock on the heavily panelled bedchamber door announced Aunt Cassandra's arrival. Brushing aside Mrs. Hatchett, she swept to the earl's bedside in a manner that suggested her opinions and authority were not to be trifled with. The housekeeper curtsied to all present and hurriedly departed for her kitchen domain, where her authority was as unquestioned as Lady Cassandra's was in the earl's domestic affairs. Her departure set in motion the tinkling bells of two ornamental Chinese pagodas, originally designed to warn of an impending earthquake and purchased by the fifth earl at a London auction—believed to have been part of Sir Robert Walpole's estate, a distinguished statesman during the reign of George I.

"Now Doctor, what were you giving my brother-in-law to drink?" she inquired, pointing a grey parasol at him, as he remained with his back to the fire, discreetly raising a long black coat to expose a fine set of black satin breeches and tightly laced gaiters.

"Something to revive his failing spirits and bring him good cheer," he responded, avoiding Aunt Cassandra's angry look of stern reproof.

"Tut tut, you mean to cheer him into the next world," she snorted. "I would have given him a glass of his favourite port." Aunt Cassandra tossed her head. The large grey bonnet, decorated with cherries almost as red as her face, shook while she bent over Lord Cecil to plant a kiss on his waxen cheek, quickly removing the half-empty glass to a table inlaid with marquetry.

"Oh, poor dear," said Lady Arabella, sitting up and nervously smoothing out the folds of her green silk dress while dabbing her eyes with a fine lawn handkerchief. "Let me send Bentinck for some port."

"Now, my dear sister," said Lady Cassandra. "You must take courage. It is too late now. There will be troublesome times ahead, and the financial affairs of the Hall will require the closest scrutiny before they pass into my nephew's hands. You are well aware that he is an incurable reprobate, succumbing to temptation at the gaming tables. However, Weybourne Place is but a day's carriage ride away, so I am close at hand to render any assistance."

But Lord Cecil was beyond earthly help. Breathing rapidly, he gave a deep sigh, raising his eyes to the ceiling where legions of painted angels and biblical figures beckoned him up into their eternal embrace.

The chimes of the stable clock would rouse the earl no more.

> Whether old age, with faint but cheerful ray,
> Attends to gild the ev'ning of my day,
> Or Death's black wing already be displayed,
> To wrap me in its universal shade.

Alexander Pope (1688 -1744)

CHAPTER 3:
VISIT OF QUEEN ELIZABETH I

When Queen Elizabeth visited Albatross Hall in 1570, she gave orders that carpets must be on the floor, sweet-smelling rushes strewn about, beds must be free of fleas, and food must be supplied in such prodigious quantities that there would be sufficient for the royal retinue and leftovers distributed to the deserving poor. As a token of her appreciation she gave Lord Ponsonby's eldest daughter a ruby-encrusted gold bracelet, originally a gift from a favourite courtesan, Lady Peake, and to the housekeeper, a brace of pheasants and a dozen hares, still the traditional fare of the Ponsonby family.

Buxom Mrs. Hatchett was also kindly disposed to the ragged urchins, mostly from the village, pleading for table scraps at the kitchen door. Her authority rested in the large wooden ladle hanging on the other side. It not only dispensed soup from an enormous black kettle, but kept Tom, the scullery boy in order. "Now Tom, just you look sharp and fetch the vegetables from Mr. Choke or you'll get a taste of my ladle. As for you, Hetty, it's time you finished scrubbing the table. Master Matthew will soon be here and there's many more relatives a'comin from all parts. Each will have a bedroom and require a meal upon their arrival, so you will fetch the Albatross plates from the hall cabinet, Hetty, and mind you don't break any."

Mrs. Hatchett bustled about the cavernous room, lined with an assortment of gleaming copperware and utensils. Her plain brown serge dress, now tighter at the seams, adorned by a large brooch in the form of a Scottish thistle, securing her checkered shawl, had been worn by her late mother, also in service before her.

Hetty sensed Mrs. Hatchett's watchful eye. She was now even redder in the face than when surreptitiously sampling ale in the brewhouse before carrying the heavy jugs for the servant's midday meal. Giving the table a vigorous scrub, Hetty flicked away the last grain of sand, rubbed her blistered hands on her apron, and tugged at her shabby black wool dress. She well knew when her new mistress was agitated, especially when preparations for a funeral or wedding were in hand. Lady Chadworth, her last employer, had found fault with Hetty before she had died. Following an interview with Hetty, Mrs. Hatchett in a letter to her ladyship had inquired,

Madam,

I beg you to inform me whether Hetty is strictly honest and may be trusted in a house of fine goods; whether she drinks-her nose and face always red in appearance. Perhaps she is guilty of some offense? I understand from Hetty that she works well with her needle and when permitted into the brewhouse, can help with the distilling. It would also be useful to know if she is good-natured and can bear a fault. Also if she is healthy and able to perform tasks which require strength. I entreat you, Madam, not to conceal any of her faults, but to be very honest with me. You can depend on me to keep the strictest secrecy about the contents of your reply. For how many years was Hetty in your service, Lady Chadworth? Lastly, would she be suitable as a domestic servant of the Ponsonby family under my direct supervision? I beg you to do me the favour of an early reply.

Your humble and obedient servant,
Mrs. L. Hatchett
Housekeeper at Albatross Hall

Albatross Hall

Holcraft Manor, October 1784.

Dear Mrs. Hatchett,

Thank you for your kind inquiry of the 11th instant. For the most part of her time spent as my maid, Hetty performed her duties fairly well, but as you suggest, I would advise strict super-vision. She had a propensity to spend much time in idle gossip, and consumed too much ale in the company of other domestics. I once caught her flirting with the coachman, and reprimanded her severely. However she does have her good points, and certainly did good work with her needle and took great care in mending the other servants' clothing, especially replacing the buttons on my coachman's cloak. Occasionally she was required to engage in extra tasks in the kitchen, so I would not hesitate to use her in this capacity. She was in my service for six years, and since her family live in a poor part of the village, I'm sure they would be grateful if you gave her a position at Albatross Hall.

As you can see, Mrs. Hatchett, my recommendation comes with certain reservations. In closing, I trust you are well. I send you my greetings and although I am in poor health, I hope to pay a visit to Lady Ponsonby this year.

Faithfully yours,
Felicity Chadworth

Hetty did show some gratitude for a chance to prove herself worthy of Mrs. Hatchett's confidence. However, she missed Lady Chadworth's boudoir, and the surreptitious occasions spent trying on the treasures of her former employer's jewel box.

At least, Hetty thought, turning to blacken the wood burning kitchen range, she had not been hired at the annual village fair, like many of the workers and agricultural labourers on the estate. It was so demeaning to stand in a group of idle folks seeking work.

"Now then," said Mrs. Hatchett, touching her ruffed white cap and poking back a stray grey hair. "Go and answer Lady Ponsonby's bell and come back at once. No dillydallying around, mind, or wasting your time gossiping with Molly in the scullery." Hetty dropped a curtsey, while the housekeeper prepared a whole lamb for roasting on the huge iron spit supported by an ingenious series of pulleys and chains. At Christmas an ox would provide a memorable feast. Then Mrs. Hatchett ensured that the house servants received some of the festive delicacies. It would be Tom's task to baste the meat as it turned in front of the hot fire. He whistled as he entered the kitchen, carrying a wicker basket laden with vegetables. "Take them to the scullery, Tom, and tell Molly to give them a good wash," said Mrs. Hatchett. "And stop making that noise. Don't you forget that Lord Cecil has just died. Show some respect, boy."

Tom touched his cap, and made a face at Gillies as the gamekeeper passed by for his lunch of bread and cheese and a tankard of ale. "Now young 'un," said Gillies. "I can still teach you how to snare a rabbit and keep the ewes and lambs from straying. I was a good shot in my time too," he continued, seating himself at the table, nodding to Hetty as she returned carrying an empty pitcher and water basin, the vessels of Lady Arabella's ablutions.

Old Gillies had been at Albatross Hall longer than anyone could remember. Even longer than the housekeeper. He had started in service as a rabbit boy at the age of seven, and, although illiterate, had risen to become an expert gun dog trainer before his failing eyesight and poor health caused his early retirement. Now as a self-appointed watchdog, the faithful and eccentric retainer spent the remainder of his days patrolling the great barrel-vaulted hall armed with an antique shot gun (rendered harmless on Lord Cecil's orders), and a pair of handcuffs. Gillies still proudly wore his shepherd's smock. His grizzled, weather-beaten face and stooped body bore testament to the long hours in the park, set in a vale rich in pastureland and well-watered meadows, through which tiny streams coursed past banks shaded and woody. One of the gamekeeper's chief tasks was tending the flock of Jacob sheep which an ancestor, Lord Thomas Ponsonby, had prudently imported from Portugal. (To this day, they still graze the pasture down by the River Avon, a river familiar to the young William Shakespeare as he and his companions sought to poach carp and deer. He was caught by the gamekeeper and taken before Sir Thomas. For his brazen act of felony, he received a whipping, before seeking refuge in London.) It was a long time since Gillies had sheared the sheep of their excellent wool, partly due to the fact that he was barely able to see out of his right eye, almost blinded when a gun he was cleaning accidently discharged. In his prime he had been quite a threat to the poachers who would brutally slaughter the Albatross deer with bows and arrows and crude firearms. Even the hedgehogs were not safe. The village boys had a nasty habit of snaring them and baking them in clay.

The deer could replenish the larder, but Mrs. Hatchett would never allow a baked hedgehog in her kitchen. Flustered from the heat of the revolving spit, she now directed Hetty and Molly to grease several pudding basins, while stirring ingredients for the figgy duff pudding, a favourite of Master Matthew's since his nursery days.

The loud clanging of the doorbell announced the arrival of the new owner of Albatross Hall, Lord Matthew Ponsonby.

CHAPTER 4:
MULBERRY COURT

Mulberry Court was, thought Sarah, her pink muslin dress rustling on the oak floor of the green drawing room, a forbidding place, gloomy, and totally lacking any attractions suited to a girl of her disposition and station.

Eccentric Uncle Charles communicated with his servants only by written notes placed on a silver salver and was rarely seen by his niece, whose sole company was a room filled with glass cases stuffed with ornithological specimens. What had once been an elegant eighteenth century baroque mansion, built on the site of a former monastery destroyed by Henry VIII, was now a faded, decaying museum, frozen in the passage of time.

Sarah bitterly regretted the lack of a companion to liven her solitary days. News from Albatross Hall was infrequent and did not raise expectations that she would be allowed to return home soon. Her only pleasure was riding Chestnut, a gentle mare, in the acres of parkland, always chaperoned by the head groom. On inclement days, the few books in the frescoed library held little interest, being devoted to science and natural history, plentifully illustrated with lithographs of long-extinct animals, relics of a previous ice age. Drawers underneath the bookshelves contained trays of birds' eggs, butterflies and moths, fossils and minerals. Tables were festooned with pungent-smelling dried flowers and herbs, some displayed in large glass cases, thick layers of dust obscuring a faded beauty. Only the iridescence of a splendid blue morpho butterfly held Sarah's curiosity. Cases of stuffed birds seemed to her to represent most of the population of the surrounding countryside. A hideous skeleton of a Nile crocodile, reposing on a mouldering bed of sand, made Sarah shudder. She seated herself at a nearby table and took up her daily journal: a red leather-bound book, secured by a clasp which could only be opened by inserting a small gold key always concealed on her person. Her diary contained her innermost thoughts, secure from prying eyes.

Sunday, May 8th.

My father forbids my marrying Hopkins. Mother did show me some sympathy, tho' she did not express her feelings, only disappointment that I have not yet found a suitable husband. God, what will become of me if I can't marry the man I love? I might as well enter a convent and prepare to take the veil. It cannot be any more disagreeable than being shut up in this wretched place where I am virtually a prisoner.

Tuesday, May 10th.

I am tired of Miss Gaunt and her constant preachings. She only reads her Bible or a book on how to raise a young girl to be mannerly and make a good wife. Perhaps it's because she never married. Anyway, I can never please her. How long will it be before I see my brothers again? I do hope and pray that Henry is not taken prisoner. Dear God, please watch over him. I won't pray for Miss Gaunt. She is such a sour spinster, even though she is Uncle Charles' sister.

Sarah closed her journal and paced the floor. A single taper shone on the nearby round table on which a Bible rested. The wind howled boisterously against the windowpanes, as if to push them from neglected frames by force. A powerful gust put Sarah in a sudden draft as the heavy mahogany door opened. Miss Gaunt entered, dressed in her habitual black bombazine, relieved only by a demure white cap.

"A strict religious education is what the girl needs," decreed Uncle Charles. Miss Gaunt heartily concurred. It was her God-given duty to preside over the rehabilitation of Sir Charles's wayward niece with proper emphasis on piety and direction into the paths of righteousness. Many of the hymns at last Sunday's service were appropriate. Those dwelling on the afterlife according to the gospel of Miss Gertrude Gaunt found special favour. "Awake o sleeper rise from death and Christ shall give you light." For lighter reading, Miss Gaunt favoured the writings of Alexander Pope, praising certain passages to Charles because they imparted a premonition of death.

It was hardly surprising that pinched-nosed, unsmiling Miss Gaunt donned a pair of spectacles and picked up the Bible. She turned at once to the book of Job, most desirable in that it was full of heartfelt lamentations, moral philosophy, and preoccupation with mortality.

"Now Sarah," said that lady, adjusting her spectacles to compensate for her shortsightedness. "We will continue with chapter seven, verses four to ten. I will read them and you will memorize the last two, starting at verse nine."

"'As the cloud is consumed and vanisheth away, so he that goeth down to the grave will come up no more. He shall return no more to his own house." Miss Gaunt stole a glance at Sarah. This last phrase gave her immense satisfaction. "Now," continued Miss Gaunt, repeat the text you learned yesterday, and then recite Psalm twenty-three.

"As my soul liveth, there is not a step between me and death," Sarah repeated. "I will lift up mine eyes …"

A timid knock at the door announced the arrival of Matilda, the housemaid. She smiled and curtsied. "A letter for Miss Sarah," said Matilda. "It is from Albatross Hall."

Miss Gaunt, aware that Sarah was more intent on opening her letter than continuing her religious instruction, dismissed her pupil. "You may go now, Sarah, but be here punctually tomorrow morning."

In the privacy of her chamber, Sarah quickly scanned the closely written sheets.

Albatross Hall, May 12th, 1798.

My dearest child,

It is sad news which occasions the necessity of this letter to you, and I have sent separate letters to your uncle and Miss Gaunt by Bentinck, our new manservant. I have to advise that you prepare yourself at once for a return home. Your father passed away a few hours ago and I know that you will wish to accompany me to the funeral, which will take place shortly after Matthew's return. Whether we can reach Henry in time is doubtful as he is at present on the high seas.

We are going on tolerably well here. The pheasant hunt was excellent and Mrs. Hatchett has a larder well stocked with a hare or two, a side of venison, a lamb, and plenty of cheeses, milk and puddings. We have just received a new shipment of tea and the servant girls all have new calico uniforms. Aunt Cassandra has been most helpful.

My dear, I do hope you have been comfortable at Mulberry Court, taking care to be respectful to your uncle and of course, Miss Gaunt, whom I'm sure will be of great solace to you.

Until we meet,
Your devoted mother, Arabella Ponsonby.

P.S. I have ordered a black dress for you to wear.

The massive wrought-iron gates of Albatross Hall creaked open. Matthew caught a glimpse of the red brick Elizabethan manor house illuminated by the pale sun. Tall octagonal towers were surmounted by cupolas and gilded weathervanes. Dripping ivy crept over the arched stone entrance, the centerpiece of which was an imposing heraldic shield bearing the Ponsonby blue and gold coat of arms, framing a large, web-footed albatross with long wings and hooked beak. In the distance, Matthew noted the heraldic flag surmounting the gate house with its mullioned windows was now flapping at half-mast, in mournful acknowledgment of his father's demise—which caused his son and heir not the slightest regret.

To the west lay the parkland, a tribute to the fourth earl's foresight when he employed the famous landscape architect, Lancelot "Capability" Brown to sweep away the formal terraced gardens with graceful clumps of trees, creating a pleasing vista with meadows and a lake, much enlarged, upon which ducks wallowed in the shallow reeds at the water's edge.

Rumours still persisted in the village that the fourth earl's wife, Lady Georgiana, had drowned herself, unable to come to terms with her husband's infidelity with a housemaid. Before her early and untimely death, Georgiana had strolled the camellia walks and ballustraded terraces. Now the changes envisaged by "Capability" included an artfully concealed ha ha, confining cattle to the meadow beyond. The earl was reported to be delighted with the picturesque effect of the gurgling waterfall which spilled merrily over rocks into the lake, the result of damming part of the River Avon. Village gossips also perpetuated the rumour that the ghost of Lady Georgiana walked abroad whenever a Ponsonby died.

Matthew glanced impatiently through the coach window as it pulled up to the entrance, the coach's iron wheels shedding beads of moisture on the graveled drive. Soon he would be master of all he surveyed, thought Matthew, preparing to dismount and enter his ancestral home. Like Lancelot Brown, he saw great potential for improvement—this time, to his own taste.

"Ah, Master Matthew, nice to see you back sir, but very sad to hear of the squire's passing. I didn't think he would last long after he was took ill." Matthew stepped forward to give the old housekeeper a peck on her now deeply lined face and followed her into the familiar Great Hall. How sombre it looked draped in black hangings. He remembered the marble bust of Queen Elizabeth, still gracing the fireplace, and, now restored to family favour, one of William Shakespeare. Above the Italian fireplace remained the imposing portrait of his Elizabethan ancestors. As a child, Matthew had always wondered why Cornelius Janssen painted the children in miniature adult clothes. There was his illustrious forebear, red-haired Sir Thomas, dressed in grey doublet and hose, with an elaborate white ruff supporting a pointed beard. He appeared to be looking at his lady, her fingers resting on a bowl of cherries offered by a dark-eyed daughter. Sir Thomas had served as one of Queen Elizabeth's justices of the peace, instilling fear in the local populace. He had not, according to legend, hesitated to call on the Star Chamber for redress of his grievances when poachers killed his deer or took carp from the river. His stern, unflinching gaze seemed to follow Matthew into the kitchen, brightened by the reflected light of the fire on orderly rows of gleaming copperware.

"Mrs. Hatchett, how long do you think it will take my impoverished gaggle of relatives to arrive?" inquired Matthew, relishing the meal of roast venison and figgy duff pudding.

"Well," replied the housekeeper, "I heard tell in two or three days, provided there's no more flooding down river."

"Just in time for the funeral," Matthew observed. How foolish they had been to take the Royalist side in the Civil War. Their declining fortunes in support of Charles I condemned them to a life of well-deserved poverty.

CHAPTER 5:
THE JOURNEY HOME ON
H.M.S BELLEROPHON

Lieutenant Henry Ponsonby—second son of Lord and Lady Ponsonby, tall, lean, and muscular, resplendent in his red coat and blue knee breeches—was sailing home in rough seas with his regiment, the 5th of Foot on the British man o' war, H.M.S. Bellerophon. He had fought valiantly with his men in the brutal heat of midsummer near Boston. Since the first skirmishes at Lexington, the rebels had demonstrated that they were no disorganized rabble. The 5th had spent many hours searching out and destroying their stores of food and weapons. King George's men had suffered many casualties. Henry thought he was fortunate to have sustained only a slight musket wound in his left shoulder, his first experience of battle while fighting against skilled, well-disciplined New England militia men.

"They are a set of sly, hypocritical rascals and I despise them," declared his commanding officer, General John Burgoyne. "Why, even closing the Port of Boston after they defied us by throwing tea into the harbour does not seem to have taught the rebels a lesson," said Henry to his companion, Colonel Billop, standing beside him at the rail of the ship. "Mind you, I think the Stamp Act was a false move. Suppose you and I had to place a stamp on all our newspapers and legal documents?"

"Well," replied Billop, "you can be sure that there's nothing so certain as death and taxes, and those foolish colonists, by refusing to pay their share as decreed by Parliament, must now pay instead for the destroyed cargo of tea. I wonder if the colony will survive. Those militiamen gave us such a run for our money. We suffered many more wounded and killed and we put more soldiers into the field. It took us three assaults on Bunker Hill before we could claim victory." He leaned down to rub an ankle still sore from his imprisonment by the rebels in Jersey. They had suspected him of treachery, of being a spy, and had threatened summary justice. The London Chronicle erroneously reported: "The loss of so gallant and noble an officer is much to be lamented."

But reports of the Colonel's death had been premature. At first, life in a tavern in Brunswick, New Jersey, had been fairly comfortable. Even though Billop had been closely guarded, and the angry mob kept at a safe distance, as an officer and a gentleman he had been allowed a pipe and some tolerably good rations. Until his transfer to a jail in Burlington. "Nothing could have been more humiliating," he remembered, "than being manacled to the floor of a damp Yankee prison cell and fed on bread and water. No fighting man could have subsisted long on such a diet. I sent frequent messages to Governor Clinton asking for a prisoner exchange. It took him weeks to arrange for my release. Apparently, there was a plan to kidnap George Washington."

"Did you ever come across Lieutenant Willcox Rand?" asked Henry. "You are still alive. He was also accused of spying and hanged before Burgoyne could intervene. However I hear that quite a few deserters escaped to the province of Canada. They would have been shot if caught. Thankfully we were not ordered to garrison Fort Mackinaw on Lake Michigan, where we could expect harassment from the Indians. I was talking to Major Scarfe as we set sail. He experienced harsh winters in that territory and told me that the bitter winters caused the lake to freeze solid, with huge chunks of ice as big as boulders. The soldiers lived on a frugal diet of beaver, fish, and Indian corn. The boats were sturdy enough to be towed across."

"Why did the Indians call the island Mackinaw?" asked Billop.

"Well, because of its arched, shell-like appearance the land resembles a turtle. I could do with a hot bowl of turtle soup for dinner. Say, did you hear the rumour about the General's elopement?" continued Henry, trying to cheer his friend with a bit of choice regimental gossip.

Billop rubbed his ankle again and shook his head.

"Well it is believed that Burgoyne married Charlotte, daughter of the Earl of Derby, against her father's wishes. After selling his commission he went to France, nearly penniless and in danger of being disinherited by his own family. However, he was said to have made it up with his father-in-law and, later, the earl appointed him a captain in the 11th Dragoons. He is still an excellent horseman, despite his age. Remember he helped the Portuguese to repel a Spanish invasion more than twenty years ago, and it was reported he received a hero's welcome on his return to London. A soldier's soldier, wouldn't you say Billop?"

"I will always look on him as a good general for treating us humanely. Undoubtedly, he is entitled to the nickname, 'gentleman Johnny.' I did consider it my duty as an officer to try and escape. I was in the mood to attempt to bribe the jailer to get me a duplicate key to the arsenal when Governor Clinton ordered my release. So I made my perilous journey back to base on Staten Island last New Year's Eve. This was before orders were given to blockade the city of Charleston. By the way, did you hear any news of Sarah?"

"You mean whether she eloped with Hopkins?" replied Henry, gazing across to where he could dimly see the outline of the Irish coast on the horizon. "I don't think my father would ever consent to the match. He expects higher born folks, those of quality, to marry within their own social class. In any case, Sarah lacks the courage to elope."

He scanned the seas again through his telescope. "There is another ship passing in a westerly direction. I do believe it to be a vessel carrying slaves to the plantations. Poor devils. How difficult it must be for them to be sold into captivity and forced to sail to America or the West Indies in leaky vessels, chained and underfed, sick, and fearful of their fate. We need more men like William Wilberforce to stop this evil trade in human flesh. If I weren't a military man, I would run for Parliament." Henry replaced his telescope in its case. The early-morning fog slowly lifted as the Bellerophon eased her way up the English Channel to the Port of Dover.

CHAPTER 6:
LORD PONSONBY'S FUNERAL

Six black horses bedecked in waving plumes of feathers, their harness bells jingling, pulled a carriage on the side door of which was emblazoned the blue and gold Ponsonby coat of arms. The late, lamented Lord Cecil was taking his final journey along the narrow lane leading through the village to St. Mary's church. This edifice was famed since Saxon times for its flint stone construction and round bell tower. Iron rings attached to the west wall told the story of Oliver Cromwell's troops. To the rings, now flaked with rust, they had tethered their horses in the shade of ancient yews before entering the village to pillage and destroy during the bloody era of the Civil War.

Tradition dictated that whenever a Ponsonby died, the church bells were to be silenced and a falcon released from the Albatross birdhouse the instant the cortège arrived at the lych gate. If the falcon soared above Albatross Hall, the new owner would live a prosperous, healthy life, confident that he would die in his own bed. If the falcon flew over the wide expanse of park, it was a harbinger of evil. At the appointed hour of noon, Gillies released the bird. Matthew looked up (being aware of the legend, which he dismissed as a fool's joke) and watched the falcon soaring above the funeral procession before it halted in front of the venerable Parson Bray, rector of St. Mary's.

The bird flapped in a circle around the tower, changed course, and flew over Albatross Park.

Bray stepped forward, taking Lady Arabella's black-gloved hand, and assisted her to alight from the black velvet curtained coach. "My deepest condolences, my lady. We all mourn the earl's passing. He was such a pillar of the village and the estate," he remarked, brushing an errant fly from his frock coat which barely fastened over his portly body.

Lord Cecil's widow lifted her veil, tearfully acknowledging the rector's greeting, and slowly made her way to the west door. Today's sad occasion reminded her of an earlier loss. It revived the painful memory of a baby cradled in death in her trembling arms as the Ponsonby family climbed Mount Cenis in a swaying coach across the Alps to Italy with Everett's predecessor, engaged to tutor the children in the ancient antiquities of Rome. A year later, another infant had died of smallpox. Lady Ponsonby moved up the aisle, supported by Matthew—a forlorn, pale, but dignified figure, responding with a slight incline of her head as Wick the sexton opened the door of her box pew. The church filled rapidly with Ponsonby relatives, and those friends deemed worthy of seats near the front. Household servants, villagers, and estate workers placed themselves respectfully at the rear.

Magnificent stained-glass windows behind the high altar permitted light to bathe the mourners in a rosy-tinted glow. Muted sunbeams flickered on the heavy bronze coffin draped in the Ponsonby heraldic flag, adorned with a spray of deep red roses—Lord Cecil's favourite flower, an eloquent tribute from his sorrowing wife. Ancient stones, worn hollow by the tread of the faithful over the past centuries, were embedded with handsome bronze plaques showing crusading knights in medieval armour, memorials to earlier Ponsonbys who defended the Holy Land and Christianity against the infidel Moor under Richard the Lionheart in the thirteenth century. Others lay forgotten in their stone-cold tombs, surmounted by excellent carved likenesses of their human form, hands joined in fervent prayer.

Matthew idly leafed through his prayer book, reflecting on the wanton waste of the family fortune, spent on such costly effigies to the departed. Cromwell had the right attitude, he thought, when his soldiers entered St. Mary's on horseback, after wreaking havoc in the village. In a burst of puritanical zeal, they lopped off the heads of numerous saints. The vandals gave no heed whether the carving was of a saint, martyr, or royal personage. Henry IV was relieved of his crown and beard; the virgin Mary suffered a similar fate, with the sacred head of her son left lying at her feet. The decree went out that all idolatrous images be destroyed by axe or broadsword and as many churches as possible were to be desecrated in like manner. The Roundheads were a force to be reckoned with. As for the Royalist prisoners taken after each battle, Matthew thought Cromwell quite justified in exiling them to Virginia before turning his attention to subdue the rebellious Irish.

"I do hope Bray doesn't preach one of his interminable sermons," he whispered to his mother as the Reverend, Bible in hand, mounted the curved stone stairs leading to the richly carved oak pulpit.

"Forasmuch as it hath pleased almighty God to take unto Himself His faithful and devoted servant Cecil, we commend his soul to his Creator, and may he rest in peace."

Lady Ponsonby wept softly. Sarah bowed her head to avoid the stern gaze of Miss Gaunt, seated across the aisle. Bray warmed to his topic. "We brought nothing into this world, and it is certain that we can carry nothing out. The Lord giveth and the Lord taketh away. Blessed be the name of the Lord who is the propitiation for our sins, our blessed redeemer. Blessed be the name of the Lord. No longer will the sorrows and cares of this world trouble a most revered member of this parish."

"The Lord in His wisdom has given to me," thought Matthew, casting a wary sidelong glance at Uncle Charles as the late earl's brother climbed the lectern steps to offer his eulogy.

"The predilections of the late noble earl, my dearly beloved brother, were entirely for the pursuits and pleasures of rural life. Being in possession of an excellent fortune, he could exercise to the fullest extent the old English hospitality and he is to be remembered as a congenial gentleman, a devoted husband, a devoted father to his children, and a kind and generous master to his servants. He leaves a legacy of value and I'm sure he would wish it to remain so—intact for future generations of Ponsonbys as yet unborn. I end my speech by quoting the words of a favourite author of mine, Robert Harris: 'Death knows no measures, no degrees, no differences, but sweeps away all.' This noble earl is gone from us. But he lives in his posterity."

Charles Ponsonby looked directly at his nephew as he spoke these last words, before resuming his seat beside Sarah, sobbing loudly on Aunt Cassandra's shoulder. It was a source of everlasting regret to her that she had been banished from her father's house before he died.

Matthew was relieved to hear the final hymn announced. "The strife is o'er, the battle won." As he saw it, his battle for the estate was about to begin. How long would he have to wait to step into his late father's shoes and become the undisputed master of Albatross Hall?

Old Gillies picked up his shotgun and handcuffs from the sidesmen's table underneath St. Mary's tower as the bell high above, now unmuffled, tolled a solemn farewell dirge. Ignoring Mrs. Hatchett's instructions, the gamekeeper wore his old, shabby hunting cap and hunting boots. Then he assumed his customary position in the church porch, alert for any danger that might befall the family. During his youth, he was told the story of a past sexton of St. Mary's, a man of dishonest intent. In great secrecy, he had pried open the lid of a coffin awaiting burial and removed the gold ring from the still-warm finger of Lady Clare Ponsonby, who had died of unknown cause at the age of thirty-three. The body appeared to move slightly. The terrified sexton took to his heels, never to be seen again.

Gillies, the faithful retainer, ensured no one tampered with Lord Cecil's body. Shouldering his shotgun, he marched back up the centre aisle to stand guard over the coffin. All was now silent. Only the murmuring of bees could be heard through the open window. In the graveyard, the diggers resumed their labours. Nearby stood an old Norman stone font, now in use as a bird-bath, adding its own special charm to the serenity of the scene.

Chapter 7:
The Gordon Riots

Lord Cecil's will is read

"It seems to me," observed Parson Bray, showing a hearty appetite while helping himself to a generous portion of Mrs. Hatchett's succulent lamb, "that the rich never tire of altering their houses, but set up, pull down, and enlarge so that their purses are never shut or their books of account perfect."

Charles Ponsonby raised his glass of wine to his lips and nodded. "Reverend Bray, you are quite right. Remember though that many have demolished their houses entirely to avoid excessive taxation. Some have even replaced windows with bricks, giving the house a one-eyed look. But the rich persist in their frivolous ways. By way of contrast, attend to the little I have spent on Mulberry Court. I don't deny that the place stands in need of repair. You remember that my sister, Miss Gaunt, is very frugal in her habits and dress. After the wages are paid to our servants and household expenses met, she prefers to send money overseas for missionary work." Charles raised his napkin to his lips. "As for the state of our justice system, the treatment of the criminal class is far too lenient. I firmly believe that the old ways of justice laid down by our forefathers were better. Now there is a new movement afoot to give Catholics the vote. Do you recollect the anti-Catholic riots of 1780? Those were six terrible days." Charles placed another log on the crackling fire. "In that year, the mob led by Lord George Gordon attacked the noble members of the Houses of Parliament. Gordon was not in favour of any concessions to the Catholics; but the strangest thing of all was that after being president of the Protestant Association, he converted to Judaism! During the disturbances, some unfortunate lords were pulled from their carriages and severely beaten, windows were broken, doors removed from their hinges. It was impossible to recognize Lord Roseberry. His clothes were torn and his wig shaken of all its powder. It was undoubtedly the greatest civil disorder in our lifetime. Gordon was extremely fortunate to be acquitted of high treason."

Bray nodded in agreement as he eased another apple dumpling onto his plate before replying, "Personally, I favour the ten commandments. Thou shalt not kill, or covet thy neighbour's goods. If I had been one of those judges, I would not have acquitted Gordon and allowed him to spend the rest of his life in Newgate Prison with extra comforts. At the very least, he should have been deported to Botany Bay."

"Such a time of turmoil," responded Charles. "So many of the mob were either shot by the militia or perished in the flames and rubble of burning buildings. Mothers were separated from their daughters, and fathers from their sons. Gordon should have been convicted and sentenced. And as for people like William Cobbett, well we don't need folks like him roaming the countryside, stirring up decent, God-fearing workers against the governing classes."

"Well said," replied Bray. "Reform is an evil if it opposes the will of God. I firmly believe that some men are more capable than others, even though the good book tells us that all men are equal in the sight of God."

The conversation ceased as Bentinck entered, bearing a fine selection of cheeses from the Albatross dairy and a decanter of brandy. A toast was proposed to the new owner of the Hall. Matthew raised his glass and glanced impatiently at his watch. Why waste time talking of the past when there was business to be done?

"You know," continued Charles as Bentinck closed the door, "I fail to understand why Cobbett became such a radical. It seems strange that he ended up in Newgate, charged with seditious libel when he tried to expose financial misdealings in his regiment while serving in Nova Scotia."

Bray replied, "He preached parliamentary reform and I suppose the authorities found his views to be dangerous. Not surprising that he fled to America. A sensible move, I would say." Matthew frowned as once again the door opened and Hetty entered to remove the dishes. The rector seemed to be warming to his favourite subject of politics, law, and order.

Lawyer Feathers awaited the family in the library to discuss the all-important business of the will. Feathers glanced out of the window as the stable clock chimed the hour of two. The mahogany-panelled library was home to a rare and historic collection of books, among them a first edition of Shakespeare's plays edited by Hollinshead. A heavy oak chest bound in iron bands, reputed to contain documents from the Civil War, stood in one corner. On the handsomely carved octagonal table reposed a sixteenth century globe. This early rendition of the then known earth's surface was surrounded by heaps of papers carefully perused by the lawyer, known for his thoroughness in attending to Ponsonby affairs. He adjusted his spectacles and pushed aside a wisp of thinning brown hair as the family entered, seating themselves before him.

Feathers picked up the will and began to read, "This is the Last Will and Testament of Lord Cecil Ponsonby, dated May 20th in the year of our Lord, 1793. All my pictures whatsoever and also all my plate and household goods, linen, and all other furniture of my said mansion known as Albatross Hall are to remain as heirlooms forever in Albatross Hall and no future owner is to permit the removal of them, save for reasons of decay." Lawyer Feathers paused, wiped his spectacles before continuing. "My good and devoted wife, Lady Arabella Ponsonby, is to remain an occupant of this dwelling for the rest of her days. My daughter, Sarah, is to be provided with a suitable dowry. It is understood that this provision will be withdrawn if she marries Hopkins and thereby refuses to accept a suitor of her own rank. My eldest son, Matthew, is to derive his income solely from the agricultural lands and livestock, brewery and dairy, and falconry now forming part and parcel of the Albatross Estate. He is required to maintain the buildings and keep the tenanted farms in good state of repair, nor is he either to neglect the roads and bridges. He is further to apportion one-third of his income to my second son, Henry, when he retires from the active military service of his sovereign, King George III. The servants are to remain at their present posts and are each to be given a small pension on retirement, in addition to provision of a cottage on Albatross lands and a small number of livestock. Distribution of charity to the poor is to be continued annually. To my worthy housekeeper, Mrs. Hatchett, I grant an annuity of three hundred pounds on her retirement. To my loyal gamekeeper, Gillies, I grant a pension of two hundred and fifty pounds and use of the lodge."

Lawyer Feathers cleared his throat and smiled at Lady Ponsonby. "You will be relieved to know that your late husband made provision for the upkeep of his grave. Also that Lord Cecil has directed that five hundred pounds each be given to Parson Bray and Dr. Palliser in token of his appreciation for their excellent services during his lifetime."

Matthew shifted uneasily in his chair. It was a certainty that he could not sell part of his inheritance to defray future gambling debts. The cost of the funeral was six hundred pounds. Who could foretell what other expenses would take their toll on his resources? Even in death, his father had cheated him. Lawyer Feathers took his leave of the family, doubtless glad that his duty had been satisfactorily accomplished.

Later that day, a premature dusk marked a sudden change in the weather. All the flapping, dark-winged inhabitants of the rookery rose in unison as a dense cloud, high above the park. The new squire left Albatross Hall in a foul mood. He paid little heed to the approaching storm as he strode toward the lake, now heaving itself into the rushes, goaded by the rising winds. Where the ducks could usually be found at their nesting sites, large spits of foam oozed among the water irises. All looked utterly desolate and foreboding. Peal after peal of thunder, interspersed with flashes of lightening, raked the lake. Now the rain began to beat the surface, rapidly submerging a small rowboat and forcing Matthew to take shelter beneath a venerable oak. His green cloak was barely protection for a storm like this.

Another brilliant flash illuminated the lake. At the very same moment, a spectral vision appeared, dressed in white robes, its head shrouded in a grey cowl, moaning, and wringing its hands, overcome with grief. Matthew trembled, transfixed by the apparition. He recognized a female shape as the spectre slowly turned toward him, and, raising one arm, beckoned him to follow.

"Who are you? What do you want with me? And why are you here?" he shouted. His voice seemed a whisper on the wind. The ghost made no reply and quickly vanished from his terrified gaze. He recalled the story of Lady Georgiana and her murder. His encounter with her spirit would be kept secret. Soaked and chilled to the bone, Matthew retraced his steps to the Hall. At some opportune moment, he would remove her portrait from the top of the main staircase. His father could not enforce his injunction from the grave.

CHAPTER 8:
WITCHCRAFT

The passing storm in the night caused the Avon to overflow its banks. The old stone packhorse bridge barely escaped being submerged. Much of the winter wheat crop was despoiled. Forlorn and twisted stalks of last year's corn stood testimony to the raging wind and rain. Trees in Albatross park dripped with moisture. From the damp ground arose a dense, clinging mist, obscuring outlines of buildings and fences which lined the King's highway as ghostly sentinels. No stranger to the village could have driven a vehicle with any confidence, as the signposts pointing in its direction were barely visible.

Despite the inclement weather, an early morning visitor to the Hall could be seen in the distance, driving briskly in a light four-wheeled phaeton from the direction of Mulberry Court. Miss Gertrude Gaunt was the sole occupant guiding the dappled grey pony. Occasionally, she glanced at a small parcel of religious tracts lying upon the worn brown-leather seat beside her. Her mission, encouraged by Lady Ponsonby, was as well-planned as that of a battlefield general. She came armed with the sword of the spirit, totally oblivious to the elements which splashed specks of mud into the open sided vehicle. Unshakable in her belief that she must continue to "spread the gospel" amongst the Hall's inhabitants, she came with Sarah as her chief target.

She had little time for Parson Bray's less spiritual approach to the family's need for celestial nourishment. Her mind was "preoccupied," as she invariably put it to those asking questions of a more secular nature, with "higher things." It hardly mattered whether Miss Gertrude turned her attention to the souls of darkest Africa, sorely in need of "saving" or those within her immediate sphere. They needed to hear the "word." Gertrude Gaunt would be the instrument through which they could obtain redemption from their sins by prayer and supplication to the Almighty.

The road curved past the dairy, barely visible to the traveller. Inside, Hetty engaged in her first task of the day, carrying the heavy jugs of milk by means of a wooden yolk suspended from her sturdy shoulders, her nose and face surprisingly red. Her exertions identified her as the Albatross milkmaid. This morning the Albatross cows were cooperative as usual, except Bossie. She knocked over a pail full of milk with a swift kick of a hind leg. In vain, Hetty tried to mop up the liquid flowing into the gutters lining the front of each stall. She knew that Mrs. Hatchett would deduct part of her wage for this mishap, and gave Bossie's tail a sharp pull. She envied Molly her task of pegging out the washing.

Miss Gaunt dismounted, tucked her tracts into a black reticule which contained a handy bottle of smelling salts, and bustled into the Great Hall. Gillies was on duty, patrolling. He had finally been persuaded to consign the coffin of his late master to the care of the gravediggers. "Mornin' ma'am," he said, touching his cap as Miss Gaunt approached, removing her long black cloak to reveal a dress of the same colour.

"Good morning, Gillies. Did you see Miss Sarah pass by to the breakfast room yet?"

Gillies removed his cap and scratched his balding head, placing his rifle on a nearby table. He reserved the antique handcuffs for nighttime use only.

"Can't say as I did, ma'am. I knows that she has spent a good deal of her time in the library of late. But if you specially wants to see her, I will go and find her."

There was no one in the breakfast room. Miss Gaunt took out Lady Ponsonby's letter. She was well prepared for her interview.

Albatross Hall, May 19, 1798.

Dear Miss Gaunt,

This letter is to advise you that Sarah is as restless and unsettled as ever. She mopes around the place like a lost soul. I know not what is to become of her. If you would be so good as to pay me a call in a day or two, perhaps we can talk about her future prospects. I truly believe that she still pines for Hopkins. She shows no interest in her music. The harp remains silent and her embroidery untouched. She takes more pleasure in the library, reading by herself. I am concerned about her health. She is always pale and wan, although the weather does not improve enough for her to take exercise in the park.

Please let me have the benefit of your advice, as both you and Uncle Charles have had more recent dealings with her and might be better acquainted with her state of mind. We all mourn her father's death. However I am desirous that Sarah should find a suitable husband in the near future.

Your devoted friend,
Arabella Ponsonby.

Miss Gaunt replaced the letter, inwardly rejoicing that she could exert further influence on a young mind, and a "lost soul." It was probably too late to make an impression on Lord Matthew who was, in her opinion, an indulgent Ponsonby, unlike his Uncle Charles or Lieutenant Henry. "That young squire is as selfish a man as any of his class—that is, he never does what he does not like and I expect he will spend his whole life in a round of pleasures as suit his taste, yielding to every temptation. I suppose," she continued, as she took leave of Charles Ponsonby at Mulberry Court, "he will betake himself to Bath, ostensibly for the waters, but really to spend his time in wasteful gambling and riotous living. It won't be long before the Albatross income is reduced, and poor Arabella finds herself in dire need."

Miss Gaunt sniffed as she trotted along Albatross Road. A firm believer in life after death, she would be greatly displeased to learn that Sarah's browsing in the library had introduced her to a book entitled, Witchcraft at Albatross Hall, by Roger Mortimer, first Earl of March and titular lord of the Welsh marches. In the 14th Century, he had distinguished himself by making a dramatic escape from the Tower of London, and then fled to exile in Paris, where it was rumoured that he became Queen Isabella's lover. Later, following his return, he was captured near Nottingham, tried by Parliament, and executed. Sarah was fascinated to read that his journeyings around the countryside had brought him to Albatross Village seeking refuge from his pursuers. Heavily disguised, he lived with a family, and to repay them for their hospitality, recorded the following story:

"At that time, superstitions were rife about the power of witches to cast spells, and the family legend told of a marble bust of two infant sons of the second earl—a memorial to their untimely deaths by sorcery and evil influence. In 1334, two maidservants at the Hall, the sisters Margaret and Pippa Flower, daughters of Joan Flower of Albatross Village, after being dismissed from their employment for theft, were charged with having practiced black arts, by the aid of their black cat, Rutterkin, upon the two ill-fated sons, Henry and Francis, so that they became very ill, and despite the best efforts of their devoted nurse, died. In jail, Pippa confessed under threat of torture: 'It was my mother and sister who threatened Lord Ponsonby. My sister Margaret was put out of her laundry service for stealing a piece of her ladyship's linen. Mother asked her to bring home a glove belonging to the earl. She rubbed it on the back of her cat, Rutterkin, and put it in boiling water. Afterwards, she buried the glove in the yard, swearing an oath that Lord Ponsonby wouldn't survive. And neither his lady.' Her mother cursed the earl many times, boiling blood and feathers together, reciting evil incantations and using strange gestures. Mother Flower died in prison. The two daughters were both executed for their crime."

"How sad," thought Sarah, replacing the book on the crowded shelf, "that Mortimer would suffer the same fate." Close by stood an exquisite seventeenth century Dutch cabinet in floral marquetry, and the old oak chest Sarah had noticed while Lawyer Feathers read the will. The large, rusting brass key in the lock aroused Sarah's curiosity and yielded with effort to her touch. Prying open the heavy lid, she discovered an old, faded, moth-ravaged velvet cloak. Peeking out of one corner was a yellowing parchment, dated 6th June, 1653. Sarah had heard from Matthew that Albatross Hall was the scene of heavy fighting during the Civil War. The document offered proof that the family earlier favoured the Roundheads, in the form of a request by Oliver Cromwell. It mentioned an ancestor, Sir Graves Ponsonby, who accepted a summons to serve in the Barebones Parliament, so-named for a leather seller and lay preacher, "Praise God" Barebones.

The document read, "I, Oliver Cromwell, Captain General and Commander in Chief of all the Armies and Forces raised and to be raised within this Commonwealth, do hereby summon and require you, Graves Ponsonby, personally to be and appear at the Council Chamber and hereof you are not to fail." Sarah trembled with excitement. She found a worn Puritan hat, lace cravat, and a pair of riding boots. The strident tones of the breakfast bell interrupted her search. Sarah quickly restored the relics to the trunk and closed the library door.

CHAPTER 9:
THREAT OF INVASION BY
NAPOLEON BONAPARTE

Henry Ponsonby's visit had a serious purpose other than offering heartfelt condolences to his mother and sister. Rumours were spreading throughout England in the early days of the nineteenth century that Napoleon Bonaparte, self-crowned ruler of France and a continuing menace to all surrounding countries, by reputation "Grand Master of European design," threatened to invade England. Henry said to his mother, "My deepest sympathies on father's death. My regiment has just landed in Dover, and my stay here will be brief, as we expect orders to sail for Ireland shortly. Those troublesome rebels are once again asserting their claim to independence ... even Cromwell could not entirely subdue them."

Henry offered Matthew the following advice, "I suggest that if Napoleon is successful in his attempt to invade, you be prepared to organize the local yeomanry. I will assist you to obtain some weapons from the militia to defend Albatross as our ancestors did during the Civil War. It is reported in the London Chronicle that many of our fellow landowners, including the Duke of Northumberland and the Earl of Clarendon, are raising volunteers willing to meet an assault on life or property. At present, they are obliged to drill with pitchforks well-hidden in haystacks." Henry smiled at the company, as he warmed to his theme. "Martello towers built in strategic spots above the coastline will be used as observation points to spy for the enemy, and bonfires lit to warn of the approach of the Napoleonic rabble. I'm sure we can defeat those Frenchmen, as we did the rebels under General Howe against George Washington's troops at the battle of Brandywine Creek when the town of Philadelphia fell into our hands. Well, there you have the latest news."

Henry walked over to the breakfast buffet, laid out on the sideboard he had so much admired as a child. It was an exquisitely carved piece of furniture by a local carpenter, Mr. J.M. Willcox. Adorned with hunting and fishing scenes, the pastoral theme was a delight. Bacchus appeared wearing a crown of grape leaves, surrounded by nymphs offering clusters of the fruit to country girls harvesting grain. Ardent swains tended nearby flocks of sheep and goats.

Hetty entered the room carrying a fresh flask of coffee. Henry filled his plate and sat beside Sarah. "I'm so glad you have returned from exile at Mulberry Court, my dear sister. And Miss Gaunt," he continued, nodding to that affable lady seated opposite, "I trust you are in good health? I often thought about all of you when we took the field against those Yankee rebels. General Burgoyne paid us a high compliment when he said that the Fifth had behaved the best of any of the regiments under his command. Sad though that we lost so many good and brave soldiers. It took us three assaults to take Bunker Hill. Enough of my adventures. Tell me about your doings Sarah. Have you met any eligible young man yet? I can assure you that there are not a few fellow officers who would be glad to meet such a pretty young lady. You look a picture in your pink dress and could turn any man's head with your golden locks and blue eyes."

Sarah blushed deeply and kissed Henry's cheek before replying, "Miss Gaunt and mother are to have a discussion today about my future."

"In that case," replied Henry," we can leave the ladies and take a walk on the terrace. Run and get your shawl and I will see if it has stopped raining." He turned to his brother. "Just imagine Matthew, a French aristocrat, the Marquis de Lafayette, helping Washington and the colonists." Henry continued, "Lafayette has named his son George Washington Lafayette. I read in a Philadelphia newspaper the Marquis's opinion of the town. It was not very flattering. He wrote that it was a dismal place, with a harbour already closed to shipping by ice, and famous only because it is the seat of Congress. He dismisses the inhabitants with the contempt typical of a French noble-man. 'They are a scary kind of people, these doltish Quakers who are good for nothing but to go into a room with great hats on their heads, no matter what the weather, and to wait there in silence for the Holy Spirit to descend, until one of them grows tired of waiting, gets to his feet and talks a great deal of nonsense, with the tears falling from his eyes. So much for the people of Philadelphia, which sooner or later we will take back again.'"

"Well Henry, I see that you had quite an experience serving in America," said Matthew. "I must leave you now to attend to preparations in case of attack here."

Chapter 10:
Mrs. Hatchett makes a list

Mrs. Hatchett was engaged at her pearwood escritoire writing a shopping list for Bentinck to execute in London. It included tea, the finest that could be obtained from Thomas Twining at the Golden Lion, Jordan almonds, spices, coffee beans, starch for Molly, household soap, and good French brandy—supplied for medicinal purposes when occasion demanded, or for the gentlemen after dinner. For the ladies, Bentinck was to purchase port and fine linen. For the servants, he was to bring calico cloth for new uniforms.

Further books devoted to housekeeping contained meticulous records of each servant's arrival and departure from Albatross Hall.

October 19th: Molly arrived to be scullery maid.

November 6th: Tom to be boot boy and general help.

November 14th: Mr. Choke to take post as head gardener and supervise the greenhouses. (Tom to assist Mr. Choke.)

December 2nd: Departure of Hopkins who was dismissed for impropriety with Lady Sarah.

December 4th: Bentinck arrives to take Hopkins's place as manservant to Lord Cecil. (He tells me that he has a very distinguished ancestor.)

March 2nd: Tapper is hired to be coachman. To take the family out in the carriage when required and feed and water the horses.

April 4th: Hetty to be chief maid to Lady Arabella Ponsonby and look after the dairy in addition to her duties in the brew house and kitchen.

I trust Hetty will be a trustworthy, reliable servant, not slothful, but diligent in every task. I shall keep an eye on her. In the past we have dismissed a few servants for exceeding their daily allowance of ale.

There was no entry for Gillies, because he had preceded Mrs. Hatchett's arrival. He could not remember the date of his birth, or even which village he came from, only that he had started in service at the Hall at the age of seven. Gillies related with pride to all comers that he was "the best rabbit boy and in his day had caught many an unwary poacher." A third, slimmer volume recorded the purchase of each piece of china, mostly at local fairs and intended for use in the servant's hall.

Upstairs, when Parson Bray paid his weekly visit to take tea, he was particularly gratified to sip from delicate porcelain cups designed with the blue and gold Ponsonby arms—one of which was now in the hands of Miss Gaunt, comfortably seated in the privacy of Lady Arabella's boudoir. "I have perused your letter carefully once again, Arabella," she began. "You indicated some unease about Sarah's present disposition. However, permit me as a trusted friend to say that I don't agree with your suggestion of sending her to stay with Aunt Cassandra. It will put her at considerable distance from Mulberry Court and I do feel that she needs further guidance before preparing for marriage."

"Perhaps so," replied Lady Ponsonby. "But I am of the opinion that a visit to Weybourne would give Sarah an opportunity to enjoy some fresh air and, later in the summer, some sea bathing."

Miss Gaunt poured herself another cup of tea. "Tut tut! She can get fresh air and exercise here in the park on fine days. On wet days, Tapper can take her for drives in the carriage. My brother and I would be pleased to see her visit at Mulberry Court. You are aware in these troublesome times that we must not think entirely of pleasure, Arabella. We should be vigilant and pray that no harm will come to this nation. We must pray to God for salvation from that undoubted French ogre, Napoleon. May His hand guide and His blessing be ours."

Lady Arabella turned away from her companion and glanced through the window. "I see that Henry and Sarah are walking in the rose garden. If you recollect, he did say at breakfast how attractive and becoming Sarah looked. I agree with his view that she needs to meet young men and women her own age. It would be nice to see her married someday soon. I will have a word with Matthew and see if it would be possible for us to invite some young people from the surrounding country houses to a ball. Sarah needs an opportunity to enjoy the company of another prospective suitor and put Hopkins out of her mind. I strongly suspect that he is not far from her thoughts."

Miss Gaunt took affectionate leave of Lady Arabella. Before returning to Mulberry Court she made certain that printed texts were placed in every room. Sarah was left the following, "O Sarah, watch and pray that you do not enter into temptation."

As was the manner of those times, the news of Napoleon's plan to conquer England was passed by messengers on horseback, travelling at a furious gallop from village to town, from country house to castle.

"Henry," said Sarah, leading him underneath an arch into a garden filled with classical Greek statuary, at the centre of which was a small pond, filled with lily pads providing cover for golden carp, "you have not told us much about your experiences in Jersey and Boston. Did you suffer any injury?"

"Just a trifling musket wound in my left shoulder. But it is healed nicely. My companion, Colonel Billop, suffered more than me. He complained how sore his ankles were from being manacled to the floor of the jail house while we were sailing home. We might meet up again in Europe if Boney gets too ambitious. You must not concern your pretty little head with military matters though." Henry smiled at her as they turned into the path leading to the vegetable garden and kitchen. "It is many months since I saw Mrs. Hatchett."

"Perhaps you haven't forgotten how fond you were of her hare pies," laughed Sarah. Hearing the housekeeper's loud voice through the open door, she paused and they both listened.

"Hetty, finish scrubbing the table and deliver this list to Bentinck. Make haste, we've an extra mouth to feed."

"Could it be mine?" asked Henry, stepping inside and giving Mrs. Hatchett a kiss. "Now see here, Tom," he said, bending low to tweak Tom's ear. "You can earn a Yankee dollar if you shine my boots 'till you can see your face in them. An extra dollar if you brush my uniform well."

"Yes, sir, right away sir," said Tom, completely awed by Henry's red coat, blue knee breeches, white leggings, and long black boots.

"Well I never," said the housekeeper, shaking her head. "I've yet to see Tom move so quickly to do someone else's bidding."

Later that afternoon, just as the westering sun gleamed on the cupolas of Albatross Hall, Lord Matthew Ponsonby mounted the front steps to address the assembly of labourers and tenantry. Gillies led a group of volunteers from the village, his musket on his shoulder, eager to show his master he could still be of service. "Friends, neighbours, and fellow countrymen. You are here gathered upon an occasion which I can only describe as the most solemn and important that has yet occurred. Many of you present will remember my father's funeral. At all costs we must respect his memory, and save our lives and indeed our property from the grasp of that savage barbarian, Napoleon—for to call him a man would degrade humanity. His grasping hand now covets the sceptre of France and desires to have himself crowned emperor."

Matthew cleared his throat. The crowd edged closer. "My brother Henry tells me that a report in the London Chronicle states that Napoleon's character is stained by crimes of such enormity, that at the bare recital of them, the generous mind of an Englishman would recoil with horror. With the blood of thousands of his fellow creatures, having trampled on the liberties of every nation in Europe, he has now directed his evil desires toward the conquest of this free and flourishing land."

Again Matthew paused. He observed Parson Bray and Dr. Palliser standing apart from the crowd and hoped they approved of his speech. It elicited the spontaneous applause of all, acknowledged by a hearty roar of "Three cheers for the master!" With unabashed enthusiasm, the assembly dispersed for the night. The men, to mull over the news in the Albatross Arms. The ladies, to lie uneasily in their beds.

"Who is old Boney?" whispered a small boy to his mother as she tucked him in bed.

"We hope never to find out," she replied, "but if you are a bad boy, Boney might get you." This threat was common enough in many of England's nurseries.

Henry and Matthew drank brandy before a blazing fire after dinner. "That was a very fine speech, Matthew," said Henry.

"Brother, I believe the day of reckoning is upon us."

CHAPTER II:
PARSON BRAY AT THE RECTORY

Before the first cock crowed the following day, the villagers were astir. In fact, some had never slept, keeping an all-night vigil from upper windows, convinced that close observation would bring sight of Napoleon's soldiers marching down the main street. A solitary candle was evidence of sickly children restless in their beds and dreaming visions of some terrifying giant with crooked face, wearing a strange hat and uniform, disturbing to the calm of their nursery. Ah, Boney, what terrors you cause to these innocent lives!

The good, honest folk met in tight clusters at village corners to gossip. Their illiteracy denied them access to morning newspapers. And so it came about that the ordinary business of the day was neglected. Mr. Carver, the butcher, leaned against the door of his shop waiting for customers. The broom seller stood by his cart, searching the horizon for the inhabitants of the great houses. The local sweetshop, no longer popular with children happy to spend a ha'penny on a cone-shaped bag of fruit drops. The plough remained idle. The thatcher did not repair his neighbour's roof. The labourer, hired to cut and trim hedges in the fields, preferred the company of his brethen in the Albatross Arms.

A journeyman entering the village with a sack of tools on his shoulder asked a bystander, "What is the reason for this idleness?" The man removed his pipe, astonished that Boney's threatened invasion was unknown to travellers passing through the village.

"Well," replied Mr. Cob, the baker, strolling over to join villagers chatting outside the Inn, "we are discussing what action we should take if Napoleon invades our peaceful village. Seeing as you are a stranger in these parts, you haven't heard the news?" The journeyman looked puzzled. "We do not know how strong Bonaparte's army will be," continued Mr. Cob, "and whether we will be forced to use our agricultural tools in defense of our liberty. I can use my long paddle and inflict some blows." Here Cob waved his weapon in the air and thrust it within a few inches of the journeyman's nose. "Others have pitchforks and rakes. We have also heard rumours that the Essex marshes are to be drained and a deep channel dug as a deterrent to invasion."

The journeyman touched his cap and silently hoisted his sack before continuing on his way, passing by the red brick rectory and remarking to himself on its rather one-eyed appearance. Some windows were entirely bricked in long before the rector made his abode in a secluded corner near the church. Inside the rectory study, that good gentleman sat in deep contemplation, occasionally glancing through his window overlooking a well-tended, neat garden and then returning to his daily devotions, before taking up his quill to jot down some ideas for next Sunday's sermon. Certain religious books on his shelf were referred to before he prepared to join his wife in the small breakfast parlour with inglenook fireplace.

"My dear," said Bray, greeting her with an affectionate kiss and tucking a large napkin under his ample chin, "I hope I see you well and in good spirits this morning?" Emma patted her husband's hand and together they gave thanks for the bounty spread before them. Mrs. Bray was a lady of kindly expression, noted for her charity and care of the needy in St. Mary's parish. Childless, she had rescued and taken into her household a frail orphan, who, though only six, had been employed minding machinery in a newly built factory in the distant town of Westerham.

"Pray dear, do try one of the newly laid eggs. They are particularly fresh today. Bess fetched them from Brookside Farm. Really, I am very pleased to have her with us. She has grown so well and is eager to please."

"I was quite taken with Lord Matthew's speech last night," said Bray, helping himself to marmalade and toast. "It is reassuring to know that he is at last showing some signs of responsibility as the new squire. He never held his father in high regard during his lifetime, but I do offer him my full support in his determination to protect the Hall and village. It is providential that we are separated from France by a blustery stretch of water."

"I am glad indeed that Matthew is behaving more as he should," replied Emma, pulling her long black shawl closely around her shoulders to keep out the early morning chill.

"I wonder if his change of attitude will continue, or if he will revert to his old selfish ways," said Parson Bray as he sipped his tea. "There is also the matter of Lady Sarah. She is a lovely girl and a good companion to Lady Ponsonby. But I do feel that Miss Gaunt is exerting too strong an influence on her, even though she is no longer at Mulberry Court."

"Perhaps you should pay an early visit to the Hall and use your position as the family rector to have a chat with her," suggested Emma.

"Hah, hah," exclaimed Bray chuckling heartily and wiping stray crumbs from his lip. "Is it your wish that I mount a counter offensive against Gaunt?"

"You read my thoughts perfectly," said his wife.

CHAPTER 12:
SARAH MARRIES
EDWARD DE LAZLO

A few months later, a British admiral was to play an important part in England's deliverance. Like Colonel Billop, he suffered injuries sustained in battle; the loss of one eye at Corsica, and his right arm amputated at Santa Cruz, Tenerife. Thus incapacitated, he continued rendering distinguished service in the royal navy, and was rewarded by the honours heaped on him by King George. Like Aunt Cassandra, he was raised near the salt marshes in Norfolk, one of eight brothers and sisters, children of a devout Anglican clergyman who held the living of Burnham Thorpe. Lord Horatio Nelson achieved renown as a leader of men, able to attack and destroy the French fleet during a victorious engagement at Aboukir Bay on the Nile. During this encounter, he received a head wound which he described as being "tolerable enough for one war."

"With such a reputation for heroism," declared Henry, sampling fruit in the greenhouse, "he will inspire the nation—an ideal person to resist Napoleon. It is not long since the Battle of Copenhagen and if Nelson was able to force the Danes to desist from their position of armed neutrality, I'm sure he has the capability of defeating the French."

"I do hope you're right sir," replied Choke, selecting some ripe peaches and grapes. "We all hopes for peace, but if Boney lands, I'm ready for him along with all the other estate workers." The gardener patted his pruning knife inside his green waistcoat pocket and pulled his wide-brimmed straw hat closely over his head to protect his eyes from the sun's rays darting through the greenhouse windows.

"Tom, take that basket of tomatoes to Mrs. Hatchett and ask her to send Molly for the carnations. They will decorate the Hall, ready for Lady Sarah's wedding festivities." Tom disappeared along the path, whistling cheerfully and dragging an old walking stick through the grasses. He was aware that the housekeeper was in a much better mood than usual today. Thus he might be spared a box on the ear, even though the kitchen was in turmoil as the time of the wedding drew near.

Edward de Lazlo, Sarah's future husband and a favourite at the recent ball, claimed descent from an old, distinguished Norman family. According to Matthew, the de Lazlos had fallen on hard times due to their loyal support of King Charles I and confiscation of their lands by the Roundheads. Edward, a tall, handsome youth, had been educated at Winchester College and later trained as a barrister at the Inns of Court (Gray's Inn). However, his success at the bar was short lived. Now he entertained a yearning for politics, the profession of his late father, Rodney de Lazlo. For her part, Lady Arabella had serious doubts about the prospects of her future son-in-law, and perhaps could rightly be accused of bribery. "Should you marry my daughter," she pronounced, during a second interview with Edward, "I will dispose of certain lands and property settled on me as part of my dowry by my late father, by which acquisition you will discard your rank of poverty and be enabled to live in a genteel manner."

"I thank you most sincerely for your generosity, and will do my utmost to maintain your daughter in the manner to which she has become accustomed," replied Edward, making a low bow. Thus encouraged in his suit, Edward de Lazlo paid court to the fair Sarah Ponsonby.

Parson Bray conducted the service at St. Mary's, and afterwards the wedding procession wound its way, two by two, into the Great Hall. Gillies and Tapper were permitted to watch the celebrations, seated by the door on an oak bench. Here is Tapper's account as he smoked placidly on his pipe.

"All sorts of delicacies were arrayed on the vast dining table. I noticed that the newlyweds had taken their places at the head when the usual ceremony of saluting and wishing of joy passed. Many guests jostled amongst themselves to be the first to offer happy felicitations. After this, they passed the time until supper by visiting all the rooms of the house and then watched preparations for the massive silver bowl of sack posset, the most extraordinary thing I ever did see. So many healths were drunk, so many toasts to the bride and groom, that I was amazed to see that even after one hour's dipping into the sack posset, it did not sink one inch. At a signal from Mrs. Hatchett, all the rest of the servants entered and asked to drink to the good health and happiness of Lady Sarah and Edward. I believe that Hetty came twice to the bowl. The tankards were filled to the brim time and time again and still there appeared to be sufficient left for a small child to drown in. I warrant the bowl held at least two hundred gallons." Tapper took another puff on his pipe. Gillies was quite impressed by the sword borrowed from Henry, with which the splendid cake would be cut by Sarah and Edward. Sarah thought the housekeeper had excelled herself. It was a creation of truly regal proportions with decorations of the most elaborate kind. There were eight beaux and belles mounted on the top, with miniature marzipan servants offering refreshments to the strains of a marzipan violinist. At the base of the gilt-wrapped marvel was a tiny sailing ship, in honour of Henry's return, the name Bellerphon carved on its side.

More toasts followed. Edward made a gracious speech stating, "How happy I am to have gained the hand of such a lovely bride, and to have been so warmly received into the Ponsonby family. My greatest regret is that my widowed mother is unable to be present with us all, being unfit to travel on account of her poor health."

Uncle Charles led the applause and then proposed a toast to the mother of the bride, "Now, raise your glasses, drink to Lady Arabella's good health and let the music begin." Albatross Hall resounded to much merrymaking and dancing until very late that night.

CHAPTER 13:
THE HUNT LORD NELSON DIES

Waken Lords and Ladies gay,
All the jolly chase is here.
With hawk and horse and hunting spear;
Hounds are in their couples yelling,
Hawks are whistling, horns are knelling;
Merrily, merrily mingle they,
Waken Lords and Ladies gay.

Walter Scott

One fine morning, there was such a stir of anticipation from the Albatross kennels. The hounds sensed as if by telepathy that today they would lead the huntsmen, assembled from far and wide. Barking and jumping, eager to chase the scent of the fox, they greeted all comers with such a cacophony of sound that Gillies and Tom, assisted by

Tapper, were obliged to set them free. The stable clock chimed the hour of ten. Matthew awaited his guests, glass in hand, astride his favourite hunter, Roamer.

"Let us drink a toast to my new brother, Edward, and raise our glasses to the most glorious victory of Admiral, Lord Nelson, hero of the Nile, and now victor of the Battle of Trafalgar. We mourn his death at the early age of forty-seven. He has given his life in the service of his country. We pray that when he returns to his beloved land for burial, the nation will do him great honour. Through his bravery and admirable seamanship, thus thwarting Napoleon's ill-advised schemes, we can now all sleep soundly in our beds. God bless you Horatio and all those sailors who fought and died under your command. Indulge me as I quote the following lines by the poet Robert Southey: 'The death of Nelson was felt in England as something more than a public calamity; men started at the intelligence and turned pale as if they had heard the loss of a dear friend.' Some of the ladies were moved to tears. The gentlemen looked solemn.'

"Three cheers for our gallant Admiral, and let us have a good day's sport," said Matthew, before draining his wine glass. "The day is fair and perhaps the fair ladies will join us at lunch. Gillies, are the beaters in position? Parson Bray, a blessing on this day of celebration." Parson Bray's sympathies were entirely with the doomed fox and all hunted creatures. However, mindful of the occasion, he stepped forward with a slight bow to the new squire and Lady Ponsonby and raised his hand to give his customary benediction, asking that no injury befall the riders and that the horses not be lamed while taking fences. This was a signal to the chief huntsman who blew a long blast on his horn. All present cried, "Tallyho!"

The hunt cantered off, the ladies waving. The hounds all frisky and lunging forward in a dense pack on the trail of the fox. Tapper described the colourful scene in a letter to his sister.

Dear Liza,

There was such a braying of dogs and the hunters were pawing the ground in anticipation of a brisk gallop over the Vale of Albatross that you never saw the like of before. My Lady Ponsonby did not need my services today, so here I am instead. Master Matthew was kind enough to offer me a hunter, but I did not ride him because there was not any use risking being hurt just for one day's sport and the possibility of being thrown. I feel safer driving the carriage. A man who goes out in this casual way and hurts himself looks as foolish as an amateur soldier who gets wounded in battle.

Henry rode well despite the musket wound.

So Stokes and I watched with the mob of villagers recently arrived and saw a great deal of galloping about and the hounds conveniently chasing over hills and vales in sight of us all. Then after it was all over and the poor little fox run to ground, Stokes and I betook ourselves to the Albatross Arms.

Goodbye, dear Liza, ever your devoted brother, Tapper.

P.S. Stokes whispered to me that he wouldn't mind being pickled in a cask of brandy as Nelson had been for his final journey. I told him that this would be highly unlikely unless he was willing to give up being the village shoemaker and go into the navy. What a terrible loss to Mrs. Hamilton. I understand that she now has a lock of her hero's hair.

There was a certain placid rhythm to life at Albatross Hall which suited most of the inhabitants. The exception was Edward, who missed London life, and confided in his diary his misgivings on his position in the household.
Today, August 15th, I again detected a certain hostility in Lady Arabella's attitude. Even worse, that our affairs are discussed by the servants whispering together behind closed doors. I am sure that, after doing her bidding, they stand with ears pressed to the keyhole. It is most humiliating to note the obvious dislike my mother in law has for me. At first, she welcomed me, but now informs me that I obtained a promise of land from her by fraudulent means. For my part, I could accuse her of bribery as she never explains her

accusation and did offer encouragement when I was courting Sarah. Yet she tells me to my face that she never yet saw a gentleman in her life who would give her less cause of offense than I.

August 17th. It is a fact that my life here has grown unbearable. For the sake of my wife and our unborn child, I have every intention of returning to live with my mother at Tixhall. I have endured with patience many slights and hard usage. Her ladyship never asks me to accompany her on outings in the carriage to see her sister at Weybourn or Mulberry Court. My place at table is always set at the lower end. After supper, she never invites me to play cards, but only listens to Sarah play and sing with such intent expression on her face. After the morning service, she sweeps by me to her carriage, her head held high. My frank discussion afterwards with Parson Bray did not enable me to come to any other conclusion but that I must leave. He did suggest that I might enter the church, being still only in my twenties, but I declined his offer.

August 20th. Matthew confided that he has plans to go to Bath, attracted to the gaming tables. So it appears that Lady Arabella will be deprived of his company and that of Henry, now returned to his regiment. This is such a peaceful place, and yet there is no future here. Yesterday another idea occurred to me that I might stand for member of Parliament.'

The hay making started in early September and ripening blackberries festooned the hedgerows. Some of the estate workers were out in the fields filling their baskets with wild mushrooms. Sarah returned from a visit to Mulberry Court with her mother in the carriage, bowling along at a brisk pace. Tapper gave the team a flick with his whip. He knew that when home-ward bound, the animals increased their speed. Besides, Mrs. Hatchett would be ready with his tea.

Sarah rested her swollen feet on the cushions and sighed. "I must tell you, mother, that Edward is very unhappy in his present way of living and would like to return to London and try for a seat in Parliament. He is quite taken with the fact that Charles Fox became a member at nineteen. Edward is impressed with Fox's leadership of the Whig party and his strong support of the French revolution. My husband complains that you no longer care for him." Sarah dabbed her eyes, now quite agitated. "It grieves me so to think that before we were married you implied he was poverty stricken. Could it be really true that you object to his family as not sufficiently wealthy and resent the portion of land you settled on him to provide for our future home? Now he spends his days accompanying Matthew around the estate with the bailiff and takes pleasure in meeting the tenant farmers. Matthew admonishes them to keep their roofs and fences in good repair, despite the fact that it is really his responsibility. However Edward surprised me by recounting that my brother told Mrs.Grogg at Bluebell Farm that he would pay for the education of her child when her husband died of smallpox. It is to my brother's credit that he has taken a fatherly interest in young Billy Grogg. Only last week he sent Dr. Palliser to see Billy when he injured himself with a pitchfork, after finding it hidden in a haystack."

"As far as Matthew is concerned," responded Lady Arabella, "I am happy there is something of your father's character in him. I believe he is a changed man, being neither foolish nor self-indulgent, as in his early youth. Now that he has taken on the responsibility of Lord of the Manor, I am pleased to learn that he is devoting time and labour to the interest and welfare of our workers …"

Sarah replied, "Let us be thankful that he seems to have turned over a new leaf. It will be to everyone's advantage if he finds a bride to satisfy, as I have been fortunate enough to find Edward." Sarah leaned toward her mother, placing a gentle hand on her arm. Her mother had visibly aged since Lord Cecil's death. Perhaps the arrival of a new family member strained her emotions, causing jealousy. "Remember, Mama, that you are to have the joy of becoming a grandmother. When Edward and I go to live at Tixhall, you must visit whenever you like. Then you will have the pleasure of becoming acquainted with Mrs. De Lazlo."

The carriage was met by Bentinck who handed his mistress two letters. One announced Aunt Cassandra's intention to visit within the next few weeks. The second, that an old family friend, Sir Walter Scott, accepted with profound pleasure Lady Ponsonby's gracious invitation to renew their acquaintance at a future date mutually convenient to them both.

CHAPTER 14:
MATTHEW GOES TO BATH

Introduces Mrs. Fowey and Jane Dean

Matthew considered the long journey by public stagecoach to Bath tedious, frequently delayed, as it was, by the necessity of changing the horses at regular intervals at hostelries run by gouging landlords, assisted by slovenly, sly ostlers who habitually substituted poor quality hay for good quality oats, always at the expense of the unwary traveller. He found the incessant chatter of a female passenger, continually addressing her travelling companion with complaints of numerous unspecified ailments, very tiresome. Apparently, they were the cause of Jane Dean seeking the benefits of the spa waters known since the times of Emperor Claudius.

"Likewise, Mrs. Fowey," responded a voice coming from an equally shabbily dressed woman. "Me dear, you and me wos allus afflicted wi the gout and sichlike and mebbe we'll return 'ome more cheerful and in better 'ealth. We might even take a turn at tables if our money don't run out fust. Bound to be cheap logins'. This rattlin' coach lurches o'er the rough pike that it don't do mi poor 'ole heart any good. Sure if it ain't a beatin' faster to the beat of the hosses hooves. As for me poor ead, it aches so it seems fit to burstin'."

"Well," said Mrs. Fowey, "you look so bundled up, Jane, that I'm sure I don't know as how you can hear your ticker a beatin' under all them layers of clothin'. Much less to get out and walk when we reach Dorkin'. What happened to Joe?"

Jane Dean, not without breathless exertion, extracted one withered arm from a dirty cloak and patted a rheumy eye. "Why bless my soul if I didn't up and bury Joe only last week, Mrs. Fowey. Gamekeeper thought him a poachin'. Took him out of one of those terrible traps wi' sharp teeth as he'd rigged up to snare a rabbit. Caught Joe's leg in a grip like a vice, it did. Gamekeeper said he'd niver seed such a bad, bleedin' wound. As you know, Mrs. Fowey, our Joe would never take what didn't belong 'im. Died o'. poisonin' two days later. Even the surgin couldn't save 'im." Jane lowered her voice to a confidential whisper. "You should have seed how many leeches he charged me for. Why they wos a'crawlin' all over his putrid body. He shall have a tombstone in his memory. On it will be these lines I composed myself:

Here lies poor Joe Dean,
Died of a wound which wouldn't heal.
His name will live for evermore,
In stories told by gamekeepers of yore.
No longer will he holler by the back door."

Jane Dean disappeared into her cloak, overcome with grief at the death of her husband.

"For shame, for shame," cried Mrs. Fowey, quite moved by her companion's gory tale. Matthew couldn't think of a finer way for a trespasser to meet his end. He wondered how much longer he might endure the endless prattle between the two old crones, and wished that he could exchange places with Bentinck, perched up beside the coachman on his box. The post horn sounded a long, deep note. The coachman called "DORKING, DORKING. All be so kind as to dismount while the horses are changed. Please be ready to leave in half an hour. Next stop: the ancient city of Bath."

"By the by, Mrs. Fowey," asked Jane, as they hobbled out of the carriage and into the Shoemaker's Arms, "seein' as you're a widder too, what happened to Mr. Fowey?"

"I'll tell you on the way to Bath," replied Mrs. Fowey, regaling herself before the inn fire with a steaming tankard of rum and water, sharing half of its contents with her friend, and accompanying it with liberal helpings of pasty from Jane's capacious food basket.

"Tallyho," cried the coachman, remounting his box next to Matthew. With a crack of his long whip, the new team of four plunged westward in the direction of Andover and Bath.

The Dolphin Hotel, in the venerable city of Bath, was conveniently located close to the King and Queens Baths and the ancient Abbey. It offered comfortable accommodation with a suite of well-furnished, genteel rooms, was famed for its fine fare, and was but a short walk from the Pump Room. Gatherings in the Assembly Rooms or Pump Room with those of similar rank, deportment, and good breeding were frequent; the latest fashions of the day added a certain elegance to such occasions.

Fortunes were won with astonishing speed at the gaming tables. They could just as quickly be lost—bringing the reckless to ruin, prey to unscrupulous lenders who lounged about the place, concealed in the shadows of tall pillars. Yet they were constantly ready to move forward with bundles of cash, proffered at exorbitant rates of interest commensurate with their victim's folly. Thus the players of whist or Faro could be rich one day, liberal to friends and strangers alike, and fall into bankruptcy the next. Even the threat of admittance to the debtors' prison had no deterrent effect.

Some travellers considered Bath to be a sink of profligacy. Nevertheless, they told friends and acquaintances they had gone to the old Roman town to "take the cure" in the hot springs bubbling beneath the Pump Room. The less fastidious could drink from a fountain set in an alcove on the floor above, where a thriving family business was run, conducted by the dispensers, who were kept busy refilling glasses of various sizes with sparkling hot water to the prescribed "one pint per day." The baths were reported to have healing qualities for those afflicted with gout, consumption, and diverse diseases of the flesh. Ladies attended by reluctant maids held their long dresses at waist height. One unfortunate attendant lost her petticoat while assisting her heavy mistress to the steps. A gentleman described his fellow bathers as either "sick, lame or blind." They had running, oozing open sores. He wondered if this sulfurous water "putrified with the stench of decaying bodies would be suitable to drink." Following this perceptive analysis, he only took claret for refreshment. Others agreed that the place was odorous and found the smell from mud, exposed by the river at low tide, most unpleasant.

Still other critics concerned themselves with the city's source of drinking water, said to come from the hills above, into which people were reputed to cast dead dogs and cats. Although a fashionable resort, Bath was in decline when Matthew and Bentinck arrived. It still remained a place of pilgrimage for those willing to hazard the journey and the perils of highwaymen. Once in town, visitors would transfer to red sedans with double handles born by chairmen, or be driven in phaetons and carriages, jostled by the hawkers and pedestrians crowding the streets, flowing in a continuous human tide before Bath Abbey. The marketplace and greengrocer's shops offered, to those who could afford them, all manner of delicious fruits: French plums, tamarinds, almonds, and raisins.

The morning following his arrival at the Dolphin, Matthew took his ease after a leisurely breakfast of cold meats, hot rolls, and a fine selection of fruits procured by Bentinck. The adjoining bedroom boasted an antique four-poster bed, hung with red silk. Next to it and the commode, stood an ample dresser supporting a heavy jug of water, placed in a large bowl. The windows afforded a fine view of Milsom Street below and Beechen Cliff in the distance.

"Bentinck," said Matthew, idly flicking crumbs off the oak dining table, "I have been perusing the Bath Standard and I am informed that the waters might be unhealthy. Therefore, I intend to stroll around the city and inspect the very fine architecture. I wish you to deliver a message to Sir Miles Standish at thirteen Laura Place. Give my best regards to him as an old friend. If he is free this evening, we will play cards in the Assembly Room before the dancing begins. I do not care for minuets or cotillions, but look forward to being entertained by music from the gallery and the company of ladies and gentlemen of like disposition."

Milsom Street was congested with vendors crying their wares, and vehicles of many kinds carrying passengers either sightseeing or preparing to take the waters. Shoppers crowded the pavements, and stray dogs did the rounds of the local butchers. Heavy rain fell. Matthew sought shelter in the nearest coffee house, full of patrons deep in conversation discussing the previous day's duel. "Perhaps it is as well that no ladies are present," thought Matthew, placing a wet cloak and hat by the door before ordering coffee.

"It was such a pity to see two old university friends from Oxford in combat." The speaker, dressed in long, black robes and periwig, was the noted barrister, Sir Thomas Erskine famous for his vigorous defense of personal liberties, endorsement of parliamentary reform and later distinction as Queen Caroline's lawyer at her trial in 1820 by Parliament.

"You're right, Guv. But mercifully neither party was killed. After putting up their pistols, they shook hands and left the field of battle with their arms around each other's shoulders. The dispute was about a promised church living. I hear tell that the young curate obtained a living at sixteen hundred pounds a year."

Old Alfy, well known in Bath for his frequent visits to numerous watering holes, appeared well satisfied with his speech in front of Sir Thomas and the newcomer. "I sees that you are a stranger in these parts," he remarked, reaching for his pipe out of a shabby brown waistcoat pocket.

"I think it is high time we outlawed duelling, such a barbarous sport, as a means of settling disputes. A police force is required to maintain law and order," said Matthew, bowing to the nobleman.

"I heartily agree," replied Sir Thomas. "I have just come from the middle of the country. The Morning Herald gave an account of the activities of a certain Mr. Lud. He destroyed some machinery. Other misguided factory workers in Lancashire and South Yorkshire followed his example. The mill owners are rightly incensed. The rioters smash every piece they can lay their hands on when the employers won't give into their demands. This news will give the government an excuse to use repressive measures," concluded the lawyer, shaking his head.

"Although, I concede the labourers feel threatened that the new-fangled machinery will take away their jobs," said Matthew. Problems of industrial unrest were of no interest to him. Of greater importance was the imminent threat of Napoleon's invasion. Matthew removed his outer garments from the door hook and bowed to the company. "I beg you will excuse me, now that the rain has ceased. Perhaps I will have the pleasure of renewing your acquaintance later." As he walked briskly by the Upper Assembly Rooms, designed by John Wood the younger, Matthew scarcely avoided being knocked down by a litter bearing a beautiful lady whose face and figure seemed to strike a chord in his memory. Charlotte Greville, wearing a large pink ostrich-plumed hat and silk dress, passed him by, going in the direction of Pulteney Bridge and across it into Sydney Gardens.

CHAPTER 15:
THE ADVENTURES OF
MRS. FOWEY AND JANE DEAN

"Do you really mean to tell me," said Mrs. Fowey, clutching Jane's arm tightly as the two companions emerged from the hot waters of the old Cross Bath, "that there is any truth to the story you hee'rd last night in the George and Dragon 'bout that ancient pig keeper?"

"Mebbe and mebbe not. All I knows is what I hee'rd wi me own ears from some strangers a talkin' near the fireplace 'bout some pigs as 'ad a sort of skin disease. It turned out that arter the pigs left the hot muddy water near the Avon where they'd been a wallowin' that they came out clean as a whistle, cured."

"Pooh, pooh, Jane," said Mrs. Fowey, wringing out the hem of her skirt and tying her bonnet strings, "it was probably some fairytale passed through ginerations o' fools. Mebbe we should take a good look at your skin when we've got these wet clothes off and hung out to dry. P'r'aps you've got spots as needs gettin' rid of."

"Go on wi' yer. I've had the weazles and the cow pox too when I wos a young un, but I know what we'll both be a gittin' of if we don't hurry back to our lodgins: our death o' cold."

"Er gi' me yer hand and we'll ride in a carriage to Cheap Street. Good job our rooms is cheap too," chuckled Mrs. Fowey, hailing a passing conveyance drawn by two horses and pulling Jane in after her. As the carriage departed at a brisk trot, Mrs. Fowey jerked her head out of the window.

"Well, bless my soul, Jane. There's that snooty gent who refused to gi' us the pleasure of his company on the last leg of our journey. Sat up on the box next to coachman, he did."

"What did the coachman say 'is name wos?" asked Jane looking at her friend's finger pointing at Matthew walking on the opposite side of Abbey Lane.

"I believe it wos Lord somebody or other, like Peabody," said Mrs. Fowey, nodding her head.

"Well who iver it wos, we don't care for the likes of 'im. Anyway, his servant seemed a much better sort o' chap. 'Ad a fancy sort o' name too—reckon it wos Bedlink."

Chattering gaily about the subject of their conversation, Mrs. Fowey and Jane Dean stopped the carriage at the house of their amiable landlady, Mrs. Clegg, a very buxom individual, vigorously engaged in scrubbing the front steps. Later that same evening, Matthew returned to the Assembly Rooms to join his friend Sir Miles Standish. A game of Faro, favourite of high society, attracted a large crowd of devotees willing to place bets on the dealer turning up a certain combination of cards. As one player groused, the odds in favour of the dealer were almost as great as in roulette. Such was the enthusiasm of some ladies, they would recklessly throw rings and other valuable trinkets on the table, having disposed of ready cash in a desperate move to offset mounting losses. Or they would indulge in the illegal practice of charging Faro dealers fifty guineas to set up tables in their homes. This activity at the gaming tables did not go unnoticed by less-respectable characters, artfully concealed in doorways and behind the large pillars surrounding the Assembly Room.

"Now, my friend," said Sir Miles, fashionably attired in brown jacket ornamented with pearl buttons, yellow lace cravat, and velvet breeches, "for the sake of our old friendship, do me the honour of placing your bet and see if good fortune smiles on us tonight."

Matthew rivalled his friend in sartorial splendour, sporting a fine wool coat, single-breasted white waistcoat, sage kerseymere breeches, and Parisian silk stockings. He added his wager to the growing piles of coins in front of each player. The dealer turned up some cards. Spectators and participants alike craned forward. Matthew and Sir Miles lost their bets. A second round brought the same result. One of the ladies present, dressed in white and fanning herself with a delicate lace and ivory fan, placed her bet on the table. Matthew watched, mesmerized by a slender velvet-gloved hand which suddenly appeared, scooping up a handful of guineas to applause from the onlookers. He started suddenly from his chair, turning pale.

"You look as if you have seen the ghost of Lady Georgiana or the shadow of that black falcon you were telling me about earlier at dinner, "said Sir Miles, laying a hand on Matthew's arm.

"I'm sure I saw that lady a few years ago in Rome. I recognized her again just yesterday, carried in a sedan. Perchance you know her?"

"Her name is Charlotte Greville," replied Sir Miles. "She lives across the River Avon in a place called Bathwick and frequently comes here to play. I hear she has a reputation as a widow of great wealth, with a house full of servants, and patronizes the finest London dressmakers. I believe that she travels abroad regularly, finding English winters too cold and damp. Let me introduce you to her."

Sir Miles took Lady Charlotte by the hand. "Lady Charlotte Greville, it is my pleasure to introduce you to Lord Matthew Ponsonby of Albatross Hall. My friend tells me that you met in Rome while departing from the studios of Pompeo Batoni."

"Your most humble and obedient servant," said Matthew, kissing Charlotte's extended hand and making a low bow.

"How strange it is that we should meet again, so many years after our first encounter in Rome," said Charlotte softly, blushing and curtsying in return.

"Perhaps you would do us the honour of joining us at our table?" Sir Miles carefully placed a chair next to Matthew. "We might share some of your good fortune and recoup some of our losses. Tonight we have not made a single guinea between us. My friend expects to stay in Bath only a few more days."

Matthew looked at his new companion with undisguised admiration as the Faro dealer plied his trade once more. The room became crowded with new-comers. Elderly visitors sat down to whist and idle gossip with acquaintances, former friends, members of the nobility (especially), and parliamentarians representing every rotten borough in the county. It was a disgrace, some said, that some of the boroughs numbered a handful of eligible voters—none of them from the working classes.

Mrs. Winkler confided in her neighbour that she had never heard the likes of the rumour about Lord Knatchbull and his adultery with a Mrs. Siddons. "Quite intolerable that a God-fearing, highly respected family man and father of ten should take up with an actress of doubtful reputation. I really don't know what England is coming to." The master of ceremonies announced that dancing would commence shortly at the far end of the room.

The strains of music from a string ensemble drowned out Mrs. Winkler's further observations, as dancers twirled around the floor, executing the complex steps of a cotillion while frequently changing partners. Matthew noticed couples sitting on low banquettes watching the performance, whispering behind discreetly placed fans. Some of the spinsters were highly rouged with black spots on each cheek. They looked so artificial compared with Charlotte's natural beauty.

"You have a golden touch. I think you must be an ancestor of King Midas," laughed Matthew, as again Charlotte removed a small heap of guineas, depositing them in a black velvet reticule.

"My late husband came here often when he was still able to walk. To be truthful, he preferred Brighton, deeming it to be a much more fashionable place. I believe he was influenced by an odd desire to join the Prince of Wales's set. Since his death, I have continued to make my home here in Sydney Gardens across the River Avon. I prefer to spend my evenings here at the Assembly Rooms, away from my talkative servants and close neighbours."

The music finished, and the company present drifted away in groups. Charlotte rose and wrapped a fine Honiton lace shawl around her slight figure.

"If you will permit me," said Matthew, taking Charlotte by the hand, "we could become better acquainted by taking a stroll together at a time suited to your convenience, perhaps tomorrow morning?"

Charlotte smiled as Matthew handed her in a waiting sedan. "Here is my address," she said, giving Matthew a white card fragrant with the perfume of Devon violets. "I will expect you before noon."

CHAPTER 16:
ROMANCE

Matthew touched the breast pocket of his coat, aware of the untimely letter from his mother and stole a glance at Charlotte walking at his side. She looked pretty in her flowing white dress, covered with green velvet mantle, shielding her face from the sun with a cambric muslin bonnet and matching green parasol.

The narrow path to the top of Beechen Cliff, lined with oak, lime, and beech, was secluded enough for the lovers to engage in undisturbed conversation. Matthew listened attentively as Charlotte described her husband's tragic death in a fall from his horse, Victor, at the age of twenty-nine. Her marriage at eighteen was encouraged and arranged by her parents, who approved of the Honorable Rupert Greville: "He is a graduate of Winchester school and Oxford, mannerly, courteous, and decidedly handsome. Many a young girl of noble birth with the right connections would be happy to take Rupert Greville in marriage. You have an obligation, Charlotte, to respect our wishes in the matter. Remember too, that some relatives have high expectations, being courtiers to King George." The marriage contract was signed with due ceremony. The wedding gifts and dowry were sufficiently lavish to impress all visitors to Charlotte's family estate.

"As you can see, I no longer wear mourning clothes for Rupert. My attire at the Assembly Rooms made clear my decision to put away the sadness of the past and return to the social scene, as my circle of acquaintance has urged me to do."

"A wise decision too," replied Matthew, patting her hand in approval. Sitting on a wooden bench which afforded glorious views of the Avon valley far below, they discussed the future and how fate had drawn them to this idyllic spot. Sunlight and shadow coursed the manicured fields. In the distance, miniature sheep and cattle meandered close to the riverbank. Matthew felt a growing passion for this young widow, the simplicity of her manners, and the elegance of her dress. However, he was not certain of Lady Arabella's reaction to Charlotte as his wife, the future mistress of Albatross Hall. Would she oppose the match, as his late father had in the case of Sarah and Hopkins?

Faintly on the breeze, they heard the chimes of Bath Abbey clock striking four. Arm in arm, they retraced their steps, parting at Beechen View House where, with a low bow and wave of the hand, Matthew bid Charlotte adieu, and took a chaise to the Dolphin.

Bentinck heaped more logs on the hearth. A cheerful blaze crackled up the chimney as his master entered the room, removing muddy boots and the letter from his coat pocket.

Albatross Hall, Thursday

My dear son,

For your sake and mine, I pray you do not spend many more days in Bath. Our reserves are dwindling, despite the income from our tenants (although some are sadly in arrears) and the crops from our fields. We have been able to scrape up enough money to purchase new laying hens and will send Hetty to sell surplus eggs in the village. A few of our older milkers have gone to the market. Three fetched the price of forty-five guineas. However, Gillies hired extra sheep shearers, and our new man, Jed, is proving to be most reliable. Mrs. Hatchett is very pleased as he is quick and thorough in his duties, and has taken Hetty under his supervision. This is a great blessing. But Jed informs me that she is still spending too much time in the brewery. You will be glad to know that Tom is a good rabbit boy.

Aunt Cassandra writes to say that she still intends to pay us a visit. She is afflicted with the rheumatics and relies heavily on a walking stick, supported by her maid. Sarah is well and sends her love. She complains of getting fatter by the day. It will be some months before her confinement, however. Edward has made great friends with Mr. Fox, delighted to have been chosen to run in a by-election at Hammersmith. There is not much to report from Henry.

Miss Gaunt and Charles were here again the other day. She asks me to warn you that you stand as much chance of being robbed at the gaming tables as on the highway. The rioters are continuing to destroy factory machinery in the district. These disturbances make us all very uneasy. Mrs. Hatchett says that if they come to Albatross, she will be ready with her ladle! She mentioned that she found the portrait of Lady Georgiana missing from its place on the staircase. You must have replaced it with the one of yourself by Batoni. She tells me that further monies are required to keep the larder well stocked, not only for your homecoming, but also for invited guests. I hear rumours that the Prince of Wales intends to be in the county on his return journey from Brighton. The newspapers are full of the story that he has defied his father, and report the king greatly displeased, since gossip about his liaison with Maria Fitzherbert leaked out. The conduct of the prince's younger brother, the Duke of Clarence, is deplorable.

Your behaviour as the new squire should be above reproach. Forgive the ramblings of an old woman, but you must take care of yourself. Be observant of suspicious strangers.

Blessings and love,
your devoted mother.

Matthew laid his mother's unwelcome letter on the dining table and turned his attention to the cold repast laid out by Bentinck. First, he was obliged to return home for his father's funeral. Now, when he intended to return to the gaming tables to recoup his losses and pay court to Lady Charlotte, he would be obliged to give Bentinck instructions to go to the booking offices of the Bristol Flyer the next morning.

On entering the dismal premises of the Southern Stagecoach Company, situated on Claverton Road, Bentinck was immediately accosted by two sorrowful creatures. He narrowly avoided colliding with one shabbily dressed individual, who, much to his surprise, showed immediate recognition.

"Ah, deary me, deary me," exclaimed Mrs. Fowey, sidling up to Bentinck with outstretched palm and leering into his face. "Lovey, bless yer 'eart. I believes you to be a dear honest gent, with some charitable feelin's for the poor. Seein' as yer master is not with yer, and this bein' jus between you an us, could you find it in yer dear kind 'eart to spare us wornded out wimen some coins to get us back 'ome to London? Mebbe a little extra for some food and drink too?"

Jane Dean, acting on cue, wept copiously on Bentinck's left side while Mrs. Fowey gripped his right arm as if her life depended on it. She repeated her tale of woe in a wheedling voice, managing to give Jane a broad wink behind Bentinck's back. He held all beggars in contempt. Wishing to be rid of two old hags and the sooner the better, he handed over a couple of guineas. "Now be off with you! Take my advice, don't drink any more gin or I'll consider my money wasted."

"Thankee kind sir, much obliged to 'ee. God bless you for taking pity on us. My 'ole man in 'eaven sends 'is blessins too." Jane quickly dried her tears as the women returned to the booking office. After they transacted their business, Mrs. Fowey and Jane Dean could be seen an hour later by passersby laughing merrily in the window of the Pig and Whistle, drinking steaming mugs of porter.

"So when do you expect Matthew to return home, Arabella?" asked Miss Gaunt, arranging her weekly pile of newly printed tracts to pass out in the village on her way back to Mulberry Court.

"I have advised him to come home at the earliest moment," she replied from her comfortable chair by the fireside. On a table nearby lay an unfinished baby jacket for her first grandchild. The tea tray held a generous portion of Mrs. Hatchett's Dundee cake, to which Miss Gaunt was exceedingly partial. She carefully removed the last morsel from her plate and sipped her tea.

"I will pray for Matthew's safe return, but only on the condition that he has not fallen into the way of temptation by gambling or in dalliance with undesirables."

"Please allow me to offer you another piece," suggested Lady Arabella. She knew that once Gertrude had embarked on a religious "theme" it was prudent to change the subject.

"I reminded him of his responsibilities to us, so I have confidence that he will heed my wishes. I did tell him that the Prince of Wales will be in this part of the country. It is our duty to entertain him and his entourage, should he wish to do us the honour of coming to Albatross Hall. We might arrange a pheasant shoot for him, if Gillies can be persuaded to set up some covers and organize a party of beaters to drive the birds forward to the hunting party."

"If I were in your position, Arabella, I would prefer to be with Sarah at Tixhall than act as hostess to such a dissolute man. I hear that he is a constant worry to his father. They have a mutual loathing of each other, even if the prince marries a suitable foreign princess and she produces a male child." I leave to the reader's imagination Miss Gaunt's reaction had she known of the prince's secret marriage in 1785 to a Catholic widow, Maria Fitzherbert, and that by way of "persuasion" he threatened to run himself through with a dagger if she refused him. Nevertheless, the ceremony took place against the advice of Charles Fox. The marriage was illegal and therefore excluded young George from the succession. Miss Gaunt shook her head in despair. So many tongues wagged freely about the prince's morals, his fondness for playing cards and the unheard of extravagance of his new residence in Brighton, built by Henry Holland in 1784.

"I really don't know what account he will give of himself to his Creator on the awful day of judgment," sniffed Gertrude, preparing to leave. "Just supposing he had become regent in 1788 during the illness of his father. Mercifully, he recovered and I attended the service of thanksgiving in St. Paul's. I pray there are no further signs of mental illness to confine him to the palace."

"My lady, the master and Bentinck have arrived," said Jed, opening the door. "They will be with you shortly, but they are somewhat disheveled, sustaining a few minor injuries when the Bristol Flyer overturned, throwing all of its passengers onto a desolate stretch of highway shortly before London. They beg your leave while they change their garments. I am sure your Ladyship will understand." Lady Ponsonby rose, greatly agitated, but Jed reminded her that since only one passenger had been killed, she must calm herself. "At least, madam, you have the satisfaction of knowing Matthew is safe and does not require the services of Dr. Palliser."

As Matthew told his story over dinner that evening, he explained that the coach, with every seat occupied and laden with various baskets, boxes, and bundles, had had the misfortune to lurch into a very deep, hidden rut in heavy rain and fog. The horses had bolted the scene in terror, perhaps terrified as much by their sudden release from the traces as by Mrs. Fowey's incessant shrieking. The women had fainted, the men had shouted for help, but to no avail. All was pitch darkness, the coachman having accidentally extinguished his one remaining lamp. It was not until the first streaks of dawn, that a wheel had been discovered, lying beneath a hedgerow. Another wheel, loosened from its axle, had rolled over poor Jane Dean, pinning her to the ground where she lay motionless. "Dead, dead as the door knocker on mi front door," Mrs. Fowey had announced, kneeling beside the body, rocking herself to and fro. "By the way, the stagecoach was a total loss," continued Matthew, "but we were fortunate to be picked up by a passing wagon going in our direction. The sacks of corn the carter was carrying allowed us some comfort."

"I am so thankful that you are safe," said Lady Ponsonby. "Now is the time for you to take over the running of Albatross and look for a suitable bride to assist in the supervision of the domestic staff. I feel my advancing years, my son."

"Talking of a future wife," said Matthew, seizing a good opportunity to broach the subject of his intentions, "I think I can tell you that I have found the perfect girl. She is just twenty-seven, very beautiful, has exquisite manners, is wealthy and emerging from a period of mourning for her late husband."

"Do you mean to tell me that she is a widow?" asked his mother, greatly astonished. "Has she any children? And what pray of her family background?"

"I'm sure mother that if you allow me to present Lady Charlotte, you will gain a favourable impression."

"That remains to be seen, Matthew. I wish your father were still alive. Granted, I may come to like her in due course and accept her as my daughter-in-law. But then again, I might not. You did not have the consideration to write me of your intentions from Bath, but have chosen a very difficult moment to give me this news. For now, I consider the subject closed." Lady Ponsonby took a candle from the sideboard and left Matthew deep in thought as he gazed through the dining room window, glass of brandy in hand.

CHAPTER 17:
THE PENINSULA WARS AND
THE BATTLE OF WATERLOO

Wickham Manor, West Yorkshire.

To Lieutenant Henry Ponsonby,

Duke of Wellington's 4th Cavalry Division,

Torres Vedras, Portugal.

My dear brother officer Henry,

I acknowledge with great satisfaction the letter written while you were in Ireland. I would have replied sooner, but since we parted, my health has not improved and I believe (although my doctor does not confirm this) that consumption will see me off in a matter of weeks. My ankles are causing me some discomfort, both being swollen, my stomach is never calm, even though my diet is much improved over the foul bread and water offered me in that abominable Yankee prison. I also have difficulty breathing. But, dear fellow, enough of my woes.

I read that you have joined Wellington's forces in the Peninsula campaign. So now you have the task of ridding Europe of that monster, Napoleon. He seems quite determined to put a stranglehold on our trade routes. To give him his due, though, he is undoubtedly a brilliant tactician and leader of men. Let me know how everything goes with you and what the prospects are of an English victory. The London papers say that some Portuguese peasants are serving in the capacity of spies. God help them if they are captured by Marshall Massena.

Did you hear about the royal military canal in Sussex? The Yorkshire Advocate is full of praise for Colonel John Brown. He has designed an artificial barrier twenty feet wide, seven deep, and twenty-three miles long, stretching from Seaford in Sussex to Aldeburgh in Suffolk. Elm trees are planted on either bank to shield the defenders and there are guardhouses at every bridge, manned by local yeomanry.

William Cobbett salutes the waterway: "Here is a canal ... to keep out the French, the armies kept back by a canal ordered by Pitt." Well, I suppose the whole scheme will be redundant as it appears Boney has other plans. I heartily wish you a safe return.

Goodbye,
your friend, Billop.

P.S. If you do not hear from me again, you can expect the worst. I forgot to inquire about your mother's health. Please remember me to her and write when there is a lull in the fighting. Take care to avoid being wounded. A dead hero cannot speak from the grave.

After his Irish experiences, Henry was not fully in agreement with his new commander in chief that "there was not a man in the army who does not wish to return to Portugal." Such confidence, unjustified since Wellington suffered a defeat in Spain. As Henry put it to his new comrade, Captain

Moreton, "Taken as a whole, I have a strong feeling that I would rather be back in North America than fighting the French here. Some of our foot soldiers are decimated by hunger and fever, despite Wellington's best efforts to keep the baggage trains coming. together with the usual assortment of rag tag camp followers. The muddy roads make it hard to pull our heavy cannon. I hear rumours circulated by the French that Canada is a country inhabited by bears, beaver, and barbarians, covered eight months of the year by snow."

"Well it was a good thing that the French were too late to go to the assistance of the Irish when they landed at Killala. It is like a fire—you put it out in one place and then receive orders to squash a rebellion in another. Remember that we had quite an advantage, with around seventy-six thousand troops to less than fifty thousand mustered by the so called 'United Irishmen.' How fortunate that General Lake stormed Vinegar Hill near Wexford and routed them," replied Moreton. Several notes played on a bugle summoned the combatants to their posts.

"Mark my words, Moreton, if we do not succeed here and finish the business, Napoleon will be puffed up with his victories. It will take the combined efforts of our armies to hold him at bay. His men are given to plunder, although I must admit that our own countrymen are not above stealing. Take William Bankes, for example. He stole a Raphael from the Escorial near Madrid and later purchased a donkey to get him and the painting to the coast."

"Never mind the sea—I think eventually Boney is going east to Moscow."

"The Russians will hardly embrace him when he arrives at the gates," said Henry, adjusting his sword in his belt and mounting his charger. "Bear in mind that Napoleon has controlled all of western Europe, from Seville to Warsaw and from Naples to the Baltic. There seems no limit to his ambition. After the Battle of Austerlitz, when he defeated the Austrian and Russian forces under Kutusov, he has shown an uncanny ability to keep his troops loyal. Only a born leader with determination could inspire his men to make the tortuous ascent of the Alps."

Moreton contemplated the outcome of battle. "I take comfort in the fact that Napoleon will find it difficult to take Lisbon. Wellington showed his true genius when he organized the defense of the town with two mutually supporting batteries. The deep lines of Torres Vedras run for thirty miles through the hills between the River Tagus and the sea. Those Portuguese labourers did a good job."

"I certainly take my hat off to the peasants. However, I fear that their clothing leaves them too well exposed to musket fire and bayonet. Their bare legs, breeches, and short brown cloaks don't give them the appearance of real soldiers," said Henry. "They carry ancient blunderbusses and, like my brother's farm labourers, defend themselves with pruning knives and staves."

Wellington prudently made his headquarters inside the convent of Bussaco, not far from the road to Coimbra. All along the Bussaco high ridge, he placed sixty cannon and fifty-one thousand of his men for a distance of ten miles. It was September 27th, 1810 and the eve of a crucial battle. Several infantry were feeling some discomfort. As Sergeant Grimble said to his friend, Raffles, as both men lay deep in heather on the crest of the mountain, "What do you think of those Frenchies on the other side? They have been granted permission to have fires outside their bivouacs. We are obliged to eat a cold supper as fires are forbidden."

"If we gain the upper hand because of our invisible position, it will be worth it," replied Raffles, turning over to relieve his aching limbs. Raffles could not know how prophetic his words would prove. The next morning, a fog obliterated Wellington's view of the French corp and his own riflemen. Skirmishers on both sides went into action. Deafening sounds of cannon and musketry echoed across the valley below.

Napoleon's general, Massena, attacked, sending in Reynier's corp, but they were repulsed by Portuguese artillery. Wearing only a greatcoat and cocked hat, Wellington surveyed the carnage below. He ordered two six-pounders into action. They had the desired effect of devastating the French flank with grapeshot and cannister. Colonel Alexander of the Irish Connaught Rangers inspired his men. "When I bring you face to face with those rascals, drive them down the hill, and push home the muzzle." The ferocity of the Connaught's onslaught caused the enemy to fall back, catching those in the rear. The panicked men rushed headlong down the side of the ridge, tumbling over loose boulders slippery with blood.

"We must keep them at the bottom and win the day," shouted Henry, as he led a cavalry charge back up the mountain, supported by withering artillery fire. Turning briefly in his saddle, he caught a further glimpse of the enemy tumbling and gaining momentum, falling in unbroken descent—mangled bodies, equipment and drums all a mass of confusion.

"Don't be too confident of victory," warned Moreton, as he cantered up the trail after Henry. "The French won't give up without a desperate struggle. There they go again under General Maximillian Foy in a second attempt to gain the top." Piteous cries from the wounded and dying rent the still air as the early morning fog gave way to clear skies.

Wellington ordered Leith's division to join the battle, now raging over the slopes. Through his scouts and spies he kept abreast of the latest developments. If more intelligence was required before another action, he always responded, "I will get up upon my horse and take a look." Henry was appointed aide de camp to the commander for his gallantry in leading a successful charge onto the ridge. During a brief lull, General Hill's second division marched undetected to a southern point on the ridge, under cover of dense forest. They gave a very good account of themselves, aiming their weapons at the French army, which appeared, to one Captain Sherer, as an enormous, tightly wedged, dusty cloud of moving men and bayonets, glinting in the noonday sun. After the battle, Massena expressed amazement at the solidity and solemnity of the British line of red coats which appeared as a great red wall, implacable and undeterred by his advancing soldiers. Within a mere one hundred metres, the red coats launched intense firepower, decimating the French line.

"Wellington holds Massena in high regard, though," said Henry. "I overheard him say to Captain Ridley that so far as his experience went, Massena was one of the best of the French commanders."

Moreton replied "There will be a review of the whole day's performance. The Portuguese acquitted themselves very well. They lost almost the same number of brave soldiers as ourselves, but Massena's losses were significantly higher."

The road to Coimbra was jammed with battle-weary troops, the English followed by the French. Both sides terrified the good citizens of the town by looting and pillaging. As a remembrance of his stay at the convent of Bussaco, Wellington planted an olive tree in the grounds. It still bears fruit today. The armies would meet again on the battlefield of Waterloo.

CHAPTER 18:
MRS. HATCHETT PREPARES
FOR THE PRINCE OF WALES

Mrs. Hatchett was unusually flustered because of the Prince of Wales's acceptance of Matthew Ponsonby's kindly, but ill-timed invitation to visit Albatross Hall a few weeks after his return from Bath. The housekeeper was required to show exceeding ingenuity in the preparation of an elaborate feast for a man with a reputation as a connoisseur of fine wines and exquisitely prepared food. Another problem was her budget, only slightly increased on Matthew's instructions—partly due to his gambling away a portion of the family fortune and poor returns on the corn harvest. Extra domestic help was to be engaged from among the village girls, following a satisfactory interview with Mrs. Hatchett.

The housekeeper was resolute in her opinion that selected items must be "in season." Lady Ponsonby and Matthew, both ardent to show Albatross hospitality at its best, collaborated on the planning of the feast, to be "fit for a king, or at least one in waiting." Matthew favoured cream of turtle soup, fresh Albatross trout, followed by whole spit roast leg of lamb. Lady Arabella suggested raspberry soufflé, assorted fruit jellies, cakes, puff pastries, and local cheeses.

"Perhaps a fine Stilton from Rowan Grange Farm?"

The grand finale: an elaborate cake with the Prince of Wales's motto, "Ich Dien" neatly inscribed and complimented with three feathers to be ordered from the village baker by Jed.

"But begging your Ladyship's pardon, it will take days for all the preparations to be completed," remonstrated Mrs. Hatchett. "Especially so if the local gentry are invited."

Totally unmoved by her comments, Lady Arabella made it clear her wishes should be adhered to. As she pointed out, it was unlikely that Miss Gaunt and Charles would come. Aunt Cassandra's presence was doubtful. Henry remained in Europe. News from the front was slow to reach home.

Mrs. Hatchett, feeling much out of sorts, found it necessary to draw up a timetable to accommodate the prince's return from Brighton. Before retiring for the night in her small bedroom, she reflected that housekeepers could easily be replaced. However, remembering the will of the late squire, she could live quite comfortably on the annuity of three hundred pounds. Hetty and Molly felt her to be decidedly out of temper when, two days prior to his royal highness's arrival, the icing glass required to set the jellies was not behaving as it should. The carefully moulded creations made out of freshly squeezed fruit threatened to collapse. The cream turned sour. The fresh asparagus to accompany the lamb was not yet ready. "Mr. Choke, I trust you will be able to obtain some good cauliflowers instead," said Mrs. Hatchett, as he entered the kitchen for his usual lunch of bread and cheese.

She took up her command post at the table, inspecting the trays of hare pies Hetty had just removed from the oven, while Tom maintained his customary vigil over the lamb, sizzling on the spit. Meanwhile, in the scullery, Molly and one of the village girls cleaned the trout, taken on the previous day from the lake.

The inns and public houses down in the village, in particular the Albatross Arms, were crowded with locals. It was a rare occasion to be honoured with a royal visit. The discussion centered on the prominent role they would play, providing an escort for the procession when it reached the packhorse bridge. Not since the possible invasion of "old Boney" had there been such excitement. The general gossip embraced rumours of the prince's secret marriage to Maria Fitzherbert. Naturally the villagers were curious to know if she would accompany the heir to the throne.

92

Mr. Cob finished his masterpiece and pronounced it exceedingly appropriate that the Prince of Wales's motto "Ich Dien" or "I serve" had been ordered to be placed on the top of the cake. "Ha ha, I doubt if Prinny will see the irony—he who serves always serves the lady." Most of the patrons of the inn joined in the general merriment.

Then Stokes stepped forward and gave an amusing imitation of a large sea creature, bobbing up and down and waving his arms, while spewing ale through his open mouth. "Now," he said looking around at his audience, "who do you think I am?"

"Why the Prince of Whales," they chorused.

Mr. Morgan, the village mayor, admonished the villagers for their levity and told the shoemaker how foolish he looked. Such blasphemy would have bought punishment in the village stock,s to be pelted with rotten fruit, during Queen Anne's reign. He suggested the village band rehearse "God Save The King" as part of the welcoming ceremony and that some English country airs might conclude the brief programme.

"What do you suggest, guv?" asked the band leader. "Would you like 'The Lincolnshire Poacher,' or how about 'The Shropshire Lad'?" Ladkin stroked his beard. "I think we all know, 'Heigh ho, come to the fair, your worship!'"

"Go on with you, you rascal. I almost took you to be the village idiot," replied the mayor, scandalized by this assault on his dignity. "Let us remember that, whatever we think of the prince's morals or girth, we are to treat him with respect as our future sovereign."

Crestfallen by the mayor's remarks, the villagers, led by the band leader, dispersed; some to rehearse, while those with business at the hall loaded up waiting carts with provisions and wines.

In the countryside, the gentry were making plans of a different kind. How they would vie with each other in the fashions selected. How well turned out their equipages would be. Whether to wear the family coronets or leave them in the bank for safekeeping, being in some instances only too familiar with highway robbery. The coveted invitations delivered by Tapper were prominently displayed on each entrance hall table, whether inside a great house or manor farm, so that visitors could not possibly be unaware of the importance of the owner's status in society.

No expense was spared on lavish corsages and wreaths for the hair of the young ladies, nor effort by their personal maids to crimp and curl with papers and tongs. Many were the boot boys who polished and spat on their master's boots until they could see the reflection of their faces in the shiny leather. After all, lowly task though it might be, being a house servant was better than working for the chimney sweep and getting stuck up one of the enormous chimneys that sprouted from each country place, forced to wear grimy sooty clothes which, like the wearer's skin, would never come entirely clean.

Parson Bray scrutinized his invitation while seated in his study. He had just finished the last chapter of Pilgrim's Progress by John Bunyan, and thought a theme based on the Slough of Despond might be included in a future sermon. He drew particular inspiration from the devotional writings of Bunyan penned during the twelve years he spent in prison. Next Sunday's sermon, now forgotten, was tucked away in a drawer underneath his oak desk. As his door was ajar, Emma looked in. Her face beamed with pleasure.

"My dear, please allow me time to get your best suit pressed. The invitation will give me the opportunity to wear my long green muslin with satin sash. I will also wear the beautiful emerald necklace my mother left me and I think my cream bonnet with osprey feathers will provide the finishing touch."

"I know you will look at your best, Emma, and I shall be proud to escort my dear wife to the Hall. Now, you will please excuse me, I must go and visit Mrs. Grogg. She hasn't been at all well since becoming a widow. I intend to take a small plaything to young Billy. I know he likes carving and I have stored in the attic a little wooden wagon. He is a good boy at Sunday school and brings his picture book full of biblical stories. It is one of his treasures, and he always wants to hear again and again the story of Noah's ark."

"Such a dear, sweet boy," replied Mrs. Bray. "It has taken him quite a while to recover from his injuries. He could have lost an eye with that pitchfork. He is becoming very useful to his mother. I must give Bess her instructions. As you said earlier, it would be a good experience for her to go up to the Hall and help Mrs. Hatchett with her work. I know Bess has a liking for Molly."

Bess always enjoyed her walk through the bluebell woods to Rowan Grange Farm. She took particular delight in its rich ornamentation and carved finials in the shape of animals. There was a smocked shepherd with a lamb tucked under his arm, a dog following placidly behind, and two sheep, all standing in procession along the triangular shape of the roof. "Altogether a scene of peace and tranquility," thought Bess, as she made her way along the granite boundary walls to the side door of the Grange, lime-washed to protect the flint and red brick building from rain and snow. The whole place exuded comfort and was one of the most prosperous farms in all of the surrounding countryside. Of course, prosperity depended to a large extent on the vagaries of the English climate and the fertility of the soil. Some farms were poorly managed, ill kept and their crops not rotated. Others were fine examples of English style and purpose.

"Our farmers round, well pleased with constant gain, like other farmers flourish and complain," wrote the Reverend George Crabbe, who lived in the county of Suffolk. Like Dr. Palliser, he trained in medicine before taking holy orders. Later he found his true vocation as a poet, and wrote the epic story of Peter Grimes, a sadistic fisherman.

Bess stepped timidly up to the door of Rowan Grange and inquired if a supply of the farmhouse's best Stilton could be procured as her mistress, Mrs. Emma Bray, intended to present it as a gift to Mrs. Hatchett. The basket being heavy with the choicest of cheeses, Bess trotted back in the direction of the rectory as quickly as she could. Before she reached the woods, she caught a glimpse of Lord Matthew on the other side of the boundary wall, seated high on his horse and whistling the sonnet that "there was a lover and his lass with a hey and a ho and a hey nonny no, that by the boundary wall did pass in spring time." This tune was meant to attract Bess's attention. There was no other female present. Matthew doffed his low-brimmed black hat and dismounted.

"Where are you going to on this fine, sunny morning, my pretty maid?"

Bess felt her body tremble as she curtsied. "Sir, I am on an errand for my mistress and my basket holds prime cheeses. I am expected back shortly at the vicarage and have no time to chat with you."

"Hoity toity! In that case," replied Matthew, "do me the favour of a little kiss. You need not be afraid," he said, reaching to take Bess in his arms.

Bess, thoroughly alarmed at the impropriety of the squire's advances, eluded his grasp and fled. The cheeses bounced out of the basket, rolling into the roadside ditch, home to a large patch of nettles. In rescuing her prizes, Bess received stings on both arms. If Mrs. Bray saw her blisters, she would ask probing questions. This unfortunate encounter must therefore remain a secret.

Unperturbed by his rejection by a mere country wench well below his station, the squire cantered home, heedless of Bess's plight, and thought of his invitation to Lady Charlotte Greville. This was his secret. A surprise for his mother. He would instruct Bentinck to lay a place for her in the banqueting hall. If she didn't come, he could spin the tale that the empty seat was for the "unseen" guest.

CHAPTER 19:
ALBATROSS HALL, 1810

Albatross Hall, 1810

My dearest Charlotte,

I think of you every day and trust that time and distance will not separate us for too long. As you will have already noted, enclosed with this letter is an invitation to the dinner to be held at Albatross Hall in honour of the Prince of Wales next week. I am most desirous of your company, if you would do me the honour of attending. It will be an excellent opportunity for you to be introduced to society, domestic staff, and, in due time, the farm tenants. Most importantly, I will have the pleasure of introducing you to my mother. She is showing signs of her age, and although prone to deafness, has shown great interest in the arrangements. Furthermore, she has reminded us that this will be the first visit of royalty since the time of Queen Elizabeth's visit. You will meet Aunt Cassandra, mother's sister. She is a forthright person and expresses her opinions freely. I believe that her rheumatics are an irritation, as she is forced to use a cane. Much to our surprise she has changed her mind and will make the journey from Norfolk.

It is unlikely that you will see my sister, Sarah, as things are not going very well with her. The doctor has advised her to rest as much as possible before the baby's arrival.

My own love, please write by the next post and tell me the expected time of your visit.

Your very affectionate Matthew.

Albatross Village was transformed by colourful bunting, suspended in every possible space. It fluttered between flagpoles and hung from thatched cottage roofs, dived across fences and railings and even hedgerows, whose scarlet hawthorn berries were almost invisible. The Union Jack flew proudly from the tower of St. Mary's Church. The packhorse bridge was festive with pennants of various hues arranged over its grey stone parapet, covering the mottled green and brown lichen. Children, happy to be released from school for the day, scampered along the crowded streets, getting in everyone's way. Harried parents hurried them along, jostling other village folk as they sought the best position from which they would have an uninterrupted view of the prince's procession.

The band, resplendent in grey uniforms and red caps, sporting jaunty cockades of white feathers, assembled on the bank, ready with a fanfare and martial airs, ending with a solemn rendition of "God Save the King."

Preparations at the Hall needed last minute attention. Molly was heating flat irons to primp up linens and the delicate lace on the sleeves of Lady Arabella's new blue gown. She was no longer in mourning for her late husband. Bentinck was proud of his new footman's uniform. The loose buttons required Hetty's deft needle. Molly, assisted by Bess who prayed not to catch sight of the master, arranged the splendid dinner service, embossed with the Albatross coat of arms, on the mahogany dining table. Each of the twenty guests would be seated on handsome Chippendale chairs with lyre-shaped backs upholstered in rich crimson velvet. Arranged down the centre were three silver epergne, polished by Jed, holding arrangements of pink and white roses, picked earlier that morning by Mr. Choke. Nestling in the centre of the white damask tablecloth stood an elaborate candelabra, exquisitely carved by a master silversmith, featuring four gilt albatross, one at each corner. Each place card was inscribed with the name of a guest. It was Matthew's intention to ensure the seating arrangements adhered to a strict order of precedence. He could be observed high in the minstrel's gallery at the end of the Great Hall, giving instructions to the minstrels invited to play soft music during the meal. Their selections must include "Greensleeves" and love songs for Lady Charlotte's pleasure and his illustrious guest. The stern gaze of Sir Thomas Ponsonby, the dominant figure in the painting on the opposite wall, caught Matthew's eye. It reminded him of Queen Elizabeth's visit to Albatross more than a century ago. This occasion would also be memorable—his reputation as a fine host in the county assured. Few county families could boast such an eminent figure as a guest, especially one destined for the throne of England.

The sound of jingling harness bells approaching, mingled with a peal of bells from St. Mary's Church, a mile away across the park. Down by the bridge, the rumble of carriage wheels dictated progress of the royal procession.

"Now Joey, count the carriages of them fine folks as they drive in front of us," whispered Mrs. Cob to her youngest lad. "See as you keep clear of the horses' hooves and don't let go of your flag."

"Who is that fat gen'lman a wavin' and bowing at us. I niver seed the likes of him before. Why mam, he fills the carriage and there ain't no room for another."

"Hush Joey, he is the Prince of Wales and some day he will be king. You mustn't talk like that," she replied, curtsying as the prince acknowledged the hoarse cheering and loud huzzahs of the villagers, all wearing their best attire.

Not far away, young Billy Grogg, fully recovered from his pitchfork wound, was idly churning the water underneath the bridge in a vain attempt to catch small "nippers" with a net and his wagon, lodged in chickweed. The fast-flowing current concealed slippery stones. Billy lost his balance, emerging with wet clothes but no wagon, quite oblivious to his mother's frantic cries.

The villagers pressed forward and took their places at the rear of the procession. They desired to unhitch the horses and draw the prince's carriage to the Hall as a mark of respect. Lord Ponsonby gave strict orders that this loyal gesture might prove injurious, and thus forbidden. Mr. Morgan stepped out in front of the market cross in the middle of the village square to offer an address of welcome as the prince alighted from his carriage.

"Sire, we welcome you, with hearts full of gratitude, to our humble village. On behalf of everyone present, we bring you our loyal greetings." The mayor paused and cleared his throat while Mrs. Grogg found her disheveled son, boxing him soundly on his ear. "We are deeply honoured that you have graciously consented to visit on your return journey to London and wish you to know of our respect and affection for your father, King George. May His Majesty continue to make a complete recovery from his illness. I remember well the solemn service of thanksgiving in St. Paul's Cathedral some years ago." The prince frowned. An opportunity to take over as regent was denied when the king's doctors, after much deliberation, gave assurances of his father's eventual recovery. In his opinion, they were only one step ahead of quackery. "We also offer our devotion to your esteemed mother, Queen Charlotte, and assure both yourself and Her Majesty of our obedience as faithful servants of the crown. Your Royal Highness, I would like, with your kind permission, to present you with a framed copy of this address."

The prince bowed stiffly, gesturing to a courtier to accept the document from Mr. Morgan's hands. The brief ceremony was now over. It would remain in the memory of all those present to be told and retold to future generations. But to the villagers' disappointment, "that woman," Maria Fitzherbert, was nowhere to be seen.

"You know," said Stokes to Tapper, standing close by, "there's still a chance that she might show up at the Hall later."

"Not if Miss Gaunt is there. I heard her describing Maria Fitzherbert to Mrs. Hatchett as a true jezebel, a bold woman, not fit company for right minded folks, especially since she is a Roman Catholic. I should like to see Lord Ponsonby marry, though. A good wife to help him manage affairs and allow my mistress some relief from her duties."

"Well who knows what time and the future may hold," said Stokes as they parted.

In the early afternoon, Bentinck scrutinized the guest list with utmost care. Two places were to be left vacant as a precaution against the appearance of Miss Gaunt and Uncle Charles. A third place was set aside for a mystery guest.

A loud trumpet fanfare heralded the arrival of the prince and his party, with Lady Arabella and Matthew in close attendance at the head of the great hall staircase.

Each guest was formally presented as Bentinck announced their arrival. Aunt Cassandra made a dignified approach, curtsying to his royal highness, nearly tripping over her walking stick. It caught fast in the long red velvet train she wore, causing her great loss of composure. Some tittering and muffled giggles from Molly and Felicity, stationed near the door, waiting to assist with service at the table, suggested that Aunt Cassandra's attire was more suited to a coronation—if perchance there was a page to bear the train. To complete the intended regal impression, it only needed an ermine border.

"Mr. and Mrs. Pendleton from Blackstock Manor." (Interesting new neighbours to be cultivated, thought Matthew, owing to their reputed wealth and undoubted gentility.)

"Parson and Mrs. Bray from St. Mary's Rectory. Dr. and Mrs. Roderick Palliser. Mr. Archibald Feathers. Sir Harry Bourton. Sir Frederick and Lady Gresham from Fairlie Place. Mr. and Mrs. Horace Travers. The Honourable Cynthia Preston. Lady Charlotte Greville."

At this last announcement, Lady Ponsonby looked visibly agitated, surveying the newcomer through her lorgnette with a haughty expression. Charlotte was not welcome at Albatross Hall.

"Matthew, pray tell me if that is the woman you hinted at on your return from Bath? I do not approve of strangers entering my house without my foreknowledge."

Since his father's death, Matthew noticed his mother had adopted an uncharacteristic assertive manner. Could it be that, in spite of her desire for Matthew to marry and produce a grandson, she looked upon a future bride as a potential rival to her position as the dowager first lady of Albatross Hall? Whether influenced by Miss Gaunt or Aunt Cassandra, it was hard to say.

"Yes mother, Lady Greville has made the long journey from Bath with her maid servant. I would like to introduce you to her before we all go into dinner."

Charlotte, blushing and trembling slightly, allowed herself to be presented to Lady Arabella, offering her hand, as she made a deep curtsy.

"I have heard little about you from my son. I trust you have no serious intentions of becoming his wife as I understand you are a widow, and thus married before. Those who aspire to be Ponsonbys must behave in a certain manner and bear an irreproachable pedigree." Lady Arabella spoke coldly as she replaced the lorgnette in its handle and turned back to her sister. "My dear Cassandra, we are all so glad that you could come. You will be sorry to learn that Sarah and her husband are unable to make the journey from London. Sarah is quite unwell. If Dr. Palliser agrees, I will visit her shortly. By the way, what do you think of Matthew's guest? I regret she is a widow, but apparently childless."

"It is too early to venture an opinion. She is very pretty and that beautiful blue silk dress suits her admirably. Do not judge her too quickly, Arabella. If Matthew is in love with her, you may consider her as a prospective daughter-in-law. As far as Sarah is concerned, especially now that her confinement is approaching, I think the change of air and her company will do you good. Edward is in attendance in Parliament much of the time, delivering many well-received speeches. He espouses reform of the current penal system, and also universal suffrage. 'One man, one vote.' That sort of thing. I understand from his recent letter that he is now secretary for colonial affairs under Viscount Castlereagh. Sarah Siddons is performing one of her Shakespearean roles as Lady Macbeth to great acclaim on Drury Lane. I believe that Mrs.de Lazlo's house is a short carriage ride away from the theatre. The gentlemen are about to escort us in to dinner. Please ring for Hetty and ask her to assist me with my train."

CHAPTER 20:
THE BANQUET IN HONOUR
OF THE PRINCE OF WALES

Parson Bray took his time in delivering the grace, savouring every moment of this opportunity to display his oratorical skills in the presence of such distinguished company. He praised God for the ample bounty set on the table and piously opined that "we must not forget the poor who are ever with us, in dire need of our generosity and assistance."

Toasts were proposed by Matthew, arrayed in the same finery worn for his Batoni portrait and adjusted by Hetty to accommodate his increasing girth, although it must be said that he could not quite match the corpulence of the prince, with the blue ribbon of the garter pressing tight across his be-medalled chest.

The company raised their glasses in honour of King George, Queen Charlotte and all the members of the royal family, now a numerous brood, rivaled only by the prince's younger brother. He scandalized his father by setting up house with a famous actress, Mrs. Jordan, siring ten children, then pensioning her off when his wandering eye beheld another favourite. Gossip circulated in court circles that King George suggested Mrs. Jordan be paid off with the sum of five hundred pounds. This offer met with a sharp rebuke from the actress, "No money returned after the rise of the curtain."

The Prince rose and offered his gracious thanks to Lord and Lady Ponsonby. "Madam," he said, as Bentinck served a bowl of steaming turtle soup from an enormous tureen, "I do not know how you have accomplished such a splendid menu without the aid of many extra hands." Lady Arabella bowed her head in acknowledgment of the Prince's flattery. It had been quite a problem to find servants competent to work in the kitchen and serve at table. Many of the young girls left the village to find higher paying employment in cotton mills in the industrial north. In truth, she found it difficult to accept the social changes now sweeping the land, very concerned with the plight of soldiers returning from the Peninsula Wars with no prospect of employment to occupy them. Gertrude Gaunt wondered how the starving would be deterred from criminal activity in the major towns. Henry remained in Europe as a precaution against Napoleon's further hostile intentions.

"Your Highness, my faithful housekeeper, Mrs. Hatchett, was obliged to conduct several interviews before our needs could be met. We were fortunate enough to have Parson Bray's adopted daughter, Bess, to assist Molly. Bess was a sickly, frail orphan of six when Mrs. Bray took her away from her factory workplace. Just imagine all those hours spent in picking cotton out of idle machinery. But I'm sure your Highness is aware of the working conditions of the poor. In our humble abode, we do what we can to entertain your Royal Highness. As far as the meal is concerned, Mrs. Hatchett stipulated that only the freshest of seasonal fruits and vegetables, fish, and meat be served."

"Take my word for it, Lady Arabella, my chef at Carlton House cannot prepare hare pies quite as tasty, nor lamb so succulent. The cheese from Rowan Grange is superb."

The raspberry soufflé, a delicate, light confection, gave great satisfaction. The cake was a complete triumph. The prince praised its glorious, artistic design, stipulating that small painted miniatures of himself wearing a gaudy military uniform, designed by his own hand, be given as tokens of his esteem to Mrs. Hatchett, Molly, and Mr. Choke. The latter gallantly offered his gift to Bess Bray. The young lady always had a cheery word for him when she passed him by in the garden.

Wine flowed freely, and the buzz of conversation increased as each empty glass was refilled. Lady Violet Gresham, seated on Lady Charlotte's, left remarked to no one in particular how the Great Hall was just as she remembered it since her débutante days, when she paid a visit with her parents before presentation at Court in the early part of King George's reign. It was surprising how the hammer beam roof had defied the predations of wood worms. She noted the pietra dura table from Italy moved to one side, placed in a temporary position underneath the portrait gallery. The marble busts of the bard, William Shakespeare, and Queen Elizabeth I still maintained their vigil from the fireplace mantle. Several interesting Mortlake tapestries arrayed on the paneled wall were the only new additions she could see, although she found their depiction of ancient battles not to her liking. Of more appeal was the richly embroidered scene illuminating the crowning of the first holy Roman emperor, Charlemagne. The bejewelled gold headpiece inset with emeralds and other precious gems was very striking.

"How sad it is that the king's health is so precarious," said Aunt Cassandra, interrupting Lady Violet's reverie. "I suppose he never recovered from the loss of the colonies. Nevertheless, he is devoted to his wife, and strictly adheres to his coronation oath to uphold the Protestant faith. I am not in the least surprised to hear that his son's immoral behaviour is repugnant to him. Small wonder that the prince has left that woman, Maria Fitzherbert, behind in Brighton." Aunt Cassandra lowered her voice, "See, Mrs. Gresham, how he stares at Charlotte Greville. He can hardly keep his lustful eyes from her bosom. I suppose he wouldn't mind making her his next conquest. The only deterrent is that he is wedded to the Protestant princess, Caroline."

"Eh eh, what's that you say, Cassandra," inquired Sir Harry Bourton, cupping a hand over his "good" ear. Like the ageing sovereign, Sir Harry was partially deaf.

"I feel that he was very saddened by the loss of our American colonies," repeated Cassandra. "A pity too that he quarelled frequently with Prime Minister Pitt. Let me see, I believe it was in 1806 when Pitt died. The king blamed his predecessor, Lord North, for the loss of our possessions in North America, fueled by North's retention of the hated tax on tea, which as you know culminated in the Boston Tea Party. I have always been a confirmed tea drinker myself. It seems a terrible waste dumping such precious cargo into the harbour."

"Quite right," replied Sir Harry. "I hear tell there is still plenty of smuggling going on along your Norfolk coast. Tea is still one of the contraband items as well as tobacco and brandy. Don't suppose the cellars here contain any smuggled spirits do you, Cassandra?" Harry gave her a playful nudge. It was apparent that the old rogue still fancied himself with the ladies.

"No, I do not," she replied, laughing. "But I must tell you an amusing story of a country parson, Mr. James Woodforde. Well, he passed away in 1803, not long before Pitt. He didn't live far away from me, having arrived in the neighbourhood after leaving Somerset where he held the position of curate. Later he became Rector of Longueville near Norwich. He had a keen interest in food, played whist and went fishing, when his duties in the church allowed. One night, while preparing for bed, he heard a whistle by a smuggler named Andrews under the parlour window. It is said that from that time on, Woodforde himself engaged in illicit enterprises at low tide, using a spy glass to watch for incoming boats moving noiselessly in the shadows. Perhaps there was something in his character which led him to associate with disreputable scallywags. Anyway, I have read some of his diaries and find his account of how a certain Mr. Reeve injured his gum while trying to pull a tooth very amusing."

"What's that you say. Did Reeve pull off Woodforde's ear by mistake?" asked Sir Harry, giving Cassandra another poke.

"No, no, not at all. I believe that Mr. Reeve was short sighted and in dire need of spectacles. For your information, Reeve did not remove the gentleman's ear, only his tooth." The audience laughed heartily at Aunt Cassandra's anecdote and teased that the good lady herself should deal in contraband, being so close to the coastal marshes.

Lady Charlotte had heard similar tales on her journeys to Bristol, and thought seafarers and highwaymen were subjects of little interest, not worth discussing. She made no effort to join in the conversation, fully aware that she was the object of attention by the guest of honour and Lady Arabella, who would discreetly raise her lorgnette in Charlotte's direction when not addressing her dinner partners.

"As I was saying to you, Lady Cynthia," remarked Charlotte, attempting conversation with the lady on her left, exquisitely attired in a lemon silk and lace crinoline and wearing a large green "Gainsborough" picture hat, "I find the London dressmakers expensive, but my blue silk quite irresistable. My headress of white feathers is, so I'm told, the latest style. Pray tell me if you go to London yourself for the new fashions or buy them elsewhere?"

"Indeed, I always go to Paris and can assure you that the clothes there are decidedly more elegant. There are a few French designers I especially favour with my patronage. As you observe, my gown is of the finest oriental silk that money can buy," replied Cynthia, patting her swan-like neck encircled by a family heirloom of diamonds and emeralds.

"I trust the English Channel is not excessively rough when you make your next trip," said Charlotte, piqued by Lady Cynthia's patronizing tone. "I always spend my winters abroad, and much prefer the antiquities of Rome to Paris. Paris is so dirty. Do be careful with your necklace. There are a number of highwaymen lying in wait, not in the least deterred by those felons convicted and swinging from gibbets. However, I will concede that you are a lady of pleasing discernment in the matter of fashion." Charlotte glanced at the head of the table. Matthew and the prince were deep in conversation about their recent travels.

"My dear Ponsonby, I must tell you how simply delightful Brighton has become. I find the new-fangled bathing machines along the water's edge excellent when towed into the waves. There is the added benefit of refreshing sea breezes. At night, we play cards and listen to light entertainment. I can forget the stuffy ways at Court and enjoy the company of the woman I love. A most gratifying life, although my father does not approve. He made it clear that to cover my expenses, he expected me to marry a Protestant princess and produce an heir. And thus I obliged him by marrying Princess Caroline of Brunswick. We are both devoted to our daughter, Princess Charlotte, but Caroline spends most of her time whoring on the continent, and from all reports, lives a most dissolute life, taking many lovers of unsavoury background. From the moment I first set eyes on her ugly face and figure, I knew we could never be happy together. Is it any wonder that I forced myself to go through with the marriage ceremony fortified by drink? I am so attached to Maria, but since my father's mental health is in decline, I expect I will need to spend more time at Court. There is also the king's fading eyesight and violent rages, which terrify my mother. They lead me to believe that it is only a matter of months before I assume the regency. By the way, Ponsonby, who is that lovely lady you introduced to me earlier?"

"Sire, I made her acquaintance in Rome when we both sat for our portraits by the celebrated painter, Batoni. By chance, we met again in Bath at the Assemby Rooms. We share your pleasure in cards and gambling, Sire. I hope to make her my wife. However my mother is not favourably disposed to her at present."

"I see that you and I share similar difficulties," replied the prince, rising to bid the company farewell. To the soft strains of "Greensleeves," Lady Ponsonby led the ladies into the drawing room for tea and gossip, while the gentlemen retired to the library for cigars, fine French brandy, and politics.

Parson Bray told Archibald Feathers he planned to preach to his congregation from his prepared sermon about the terrible social conditions prevalent in the land. As a man of the cloth, he felt it his duty to bring attention to further changes needed in the working lives of young children and recounted a recent visit to an isolated cottage along a rutted cart track. The interior of this dank hovel, home to one of his parishioners, boasted a smelly earth floor, continually damp from a leaking thatched roof. On a dirty straw pallet lay a sickly daughter, Lucy, soon to end her journey here on earth. Her frail body was racked by violent spasms and dry cough. Yet when he entered, a radiant smile spread over her pale features, reminding him of one of the stained-glass angels in the church window. "Lucy took a simple delight in the pleasure of my visit and enjoyed the nourishing broth Emma had prepared. I held her hand and read a few verses of scripture. She sighed and turned away from me to face the wall, declaring that she was 'done for' and would I arrange a decent Christian burial in St. Mary's churchyard? I pressed some coins into the mother's wizened hands and bade them farewell. As I rode away, reflecting on my promise to fulfill the dying girl's wishes, I thought about the lot of some of my poorest parishioners, comparing them with those of greater means, able to afford a decent way of life. It was no use telling mother and daughter 'the meek will inherit the earth' and 'blessed are the poor for theirs is the kingdom of heaven' when they did not know where their next meal was coming from. Church folk are much more inclined to pay attention to my sermons if they arrive with a full belly: that is, unless they fall into a sound slumber as old Sir Harry usually does. By the way," he said, leaning closer to Feathers, "I think that Sir Harry will not be long in following Lucy to the grave."

"I am in profound agreement with your sentiments and commend you for your consideration and kindness," replied Mr. Feathers. "I see some sad cases too in my profession, but naturally from a different perspective. You know, Bray, there was not a great deal of relief promised the workers when the Factory Act was passed in 1802. It stipulated that children could work no longer than twelve hours a day and forbade the employment of those under nine years of age. Mark my words, sooner or later Parliament will be forced to pass better laws to protect the poor from exploitation. If not, we must brace ourselves for more riots. Discontent will be widespread."

There was silence as the gentlemen sipped brandy and gazed into the roaring fire blazing up the library chimney. Mr. Hugh Travers wondered what would happen if a family was unable to find a place in service for a child. Farm wages were a mere pittance and the alternative would be to seek work in one of the factories or end up in the workhouse. This often required the whole family uprooting itself and making the arduous journey by stagecoach to the dreary cotton mills up north. "I have a list of changes I think would benefit the country. When I see Edward in London, I shall present them to him. But for now I will bide my time," said Feathers.

"And I will continue to preach about Christian charity and our responsibilities to those less fortunate until my retirement," said Bray. "I must quote you a verse from a poem written in the fifteenth century before we rejoin the ladies, since it reflects on the situation then and as it is now:

> Whether men do laugh or weep,
> Whether they do wake or sleep,
> Whether they die young or old,
> Whether they feel heat or cold,
> There is nothing under the sun,
> Nothing in true earnest done."

"What a good subject for a lecture," thought Travers, as he followed the gentlemen into the drawing room.

CHAPTER 21:
LADY ARABELLA DIES

Mrs. Hatchett stoutly maintained that several recent events hastened her mistress's death from heart failure within weeks of the nuptial celebrations. The tragic news of her daughter's death, in childbirth, and of her infant grandson's, a week later, caused her immeasurable grief. For days, she was beyond consolation. In consequence, the housekeeper came to the conclusion that the time had come for her departure from the Hall. She wanted to receive her promised annuity and retire to a small cottage on the estate, in which abode she could comfortably live out her days, without totally cutting herself off from her former life. An added reason was Matthew's marriage to Lady Charlotte. She knew that Lady Ponsonby had had grave misgivings about future prospects for the young couple. How would she serve the new mistress as faithfully and with such devotion? All these circumstances were carefully weighed up after the solemn rite of burial at St. Mary's Church, Parson Bray officiating.

"How many sorrowful tears do we shed, and how closely intertwined are the strands of joy and sorrow. The grave is silent. The yews stand tall and on guard, their branches sheltering the numerous twittering birds—all God's creatures, who fly over the graves when we have long departed this mortal coil." Lady Arabella had been particularly fond of all wildlife.

As the final mound of earth was spread over the coffin, the peaceful seren-ity of the churchyard returned to await the sorrowing bereaved offering floral tributes and silent, yet anguished prayers. Matthew felt more affected by his mother's death than of Earl Ponsonby, his late father. He bowed respectfully towards the gravesite as the procession assembled at the lych Gate through which Lady Arabella had passed for the last time.

Miss Gaunt and Matthew were the last mourners to leave. Stepping forward to cast a rose onto the earth mound, she prayed that Christians united in death would receive their eternal reward. "The gates of Heaven have opened wide that all who embrace the true faith might enter in, unless, by ungodly living they are doomed to damnation in the fires of Hell. For what," she said looking directly at Matthew, "will it profit a man if he gain the whole world and lose his own soul?" Miss Gaunt was mollified when she noticed that Lady Charlotte was carrying the Bible presented to her on the occasion of her first marriage. Neither she nor Uncle Charles approved of Matthew's extravagance in expending a goodly portion of estate revenues on his nuptial celebrations and nostalgic honeymoon in Rome.

Rome had acted as a magnet. A new portrait of the happy pair was com-missioned. They had both echoed the sentiments of novelist Fanny Burney when she wrote "travelling here is the ruin of all happiness! There's no looking at a building in England after seeing Italy." A boat trip on the Tiber, a visit to the ancient catacombs and St. Peter's in the Vatican had kept the newlyweds occupied while fast depleting their stock of cash. It was as well that a sum of only three hundred pounds—half that spent on Lord Cecil's funeral—had been sufficient for the late Lady Arabella's funeral. It covered the cost of the flaming torches borne by villagers and tenantry in tribute, lining the proces-sional route before halting at St. Mary's Church. Aunt Cassandra, showing signs of increasing infirmity, lamented the passing of her sister. All the mourners agreed that her speech was both moving and sincere.

"My sister was, as you all know well, a loyal and devoted helpmate to her late husband, even though she knew that I did not always see eye to eye with him nor he with me. Arabella had a number of outstanding qualities which endeared her to the tenants and villagers. This was especially true of her younger days when she came to the Hall as a rather shy and reticent bride. I recollect her telling me how terrified she was of her introduction to the staff in the entrance hall. Each servant stood stiffly to attention on the Master's instructions, ready to greet her with a small curtsy or nod of the head. Charity to all was her guiding beacon. Many were the afternoons when she would drive with Tapper to needy families, distributing food and clothing. As she raised her three children, Matthew, Sarah, and Henry, she frequently deferred to my advice which, naturally out of sisterly love, I was always ready to dispense, not having any family of my own. She did not take kindly at first to strangers unfamiliar with the household and its habits, but those whom she loved will sorely miss her. As the Earl wished, she was careful in her management of domestic affairs, and saw to it that both Matthew and his brother received the best education possible." Aunt Cassandra paused to wipe away a few tears. "I do know how much she looked forward to the birth of her first grandchild, for whom, with loving hands, she diligently prepared a beautiful layette. Now she is reunited with her husband, Sarah, and her infant. My one chief regret today is that Henry is absent, owing to his duties overseas." Aunt Cassandra turned back down the churchyard path to her waiting carriage, escorted on either side by Matthew and Edward. It was evident to all beholders that walking was now very painful. Increasing infirmity foretold the end of her journeys from Norfolk.

Life returned to normal at Albatross Hall. The new housekeeper, Mrs. Dobson, was frequently called upon to arrange elaborate feasts. Lord and Lady Ponsonby entertained on a lavish scale, taking advantage of improved harvests and the purchase of new breeding stock, sheep, and poultry. Matthew ordered new vats for the brewery. Hetty was ordered out of the alehouse and the dairy, banished to Lady Charlotte's boudoir as her personal maid. Bentinck and Jed shared the task of storing lesser-known varieties of imported wine in the vast cellars. Several of the older bottles at the back were festooned with cobwebs. Charlotte decreed that they were not to be used, being likely to poison the guests. They reminded Matthew of the strange pile of dirty bottles reposing in the window of the Three Jolly Rodgers at Cobham. Having a suspicious mind, he would never touch them.

The cream of society made frequent forays to the Hall by invitation including the Travers and Greshams among other notable and worthy locals. As invitations suggested, they prepared for a masked ball, donning elaborate costumes. They came dressed in the manner of Roman and Greek gods; a special prize to be awarded for the most original attire. Throngs of Apollos, Plutos, Venuses, Ariadnes, and even the emperors Hadrian and Constantine, mingled together in the riotous, carnival-like atmosphere to dance the night away, pausing only to partake of the excellent supper laid out on large tables on the terrace. King Neptune caused some anxiety when his trident became stuck in the glass doors leading onto the terrace. In spite of Bentinck's offer to keep it in a safe place, Neptune declared that it was "part of his outfit," and therefore he wouldn't be separated from it.

Zeus (alias Sir Frederick) came dressed as a thunderbolt. He declared that he must be in league with the elements when distant thunder threatened the festivities, rolling ominously across the sky. The company was obliged to retreat indoors as the first drops of rain fell. Sir Frederick considered he was entitled to the first prize and was quite annoyed when Mrs. Travers, dressed as Venus in swirling chiffon, was chosen. However, he quickly brightened when she planted a kiss on his cheek, by way of consolation.

Blind man's Buff proved a popular diversion, made even more challenging by guessing not only the identity of the person "captured," but the legendary figure he or she represented. Charades amused everybody, including the servants who peeked through a door of the Great Hall. Some of the guests claimed that Parson Bray, with his considerable knowledge of literary works, had an unfair advantage. But all the same it was good fun.

During the London season, Lord and Lady Ponsonby indulged in a whirl of balls, plays, concerts, and parties. The most important event was their presentation at Court and renewed friendship with the Prince of Wales, appointed Regent for the remaining years of King George III's life—a result of his increasing mental instability. Since the Drury Lane Theatre had been destroyed by fire, they watched the final performance of Sarah Siddons in her celebrated role as Lady MacBeth at Covent Garden. The noted playwright, Richard Brinsley Sheridan, so overcome with emotion by Siddon's acting, sobbed throughout the performance in his private box. He served as under-secretary at the Foreign Office, receiving acclaim for a speech in Parliament lasting almost six hours. An undoubted test of endurance for elderly members hard of hearing.

Back at Albatross Hall, Matthew and Charlotte required several days to recuperate from their London excursions. They had picnics in the park and rides to the gentry in the neighbouring great houses. They toured the greenhouses whenever Mr. Choke sent word that a new crop of grapes or peaches was sufficiently ripe for the table. Pleasant walks were taken in the rose garden. Charlotte gave orders that bowls of her favourite varieties be placed throughout the house. August waned into September. Tom was sent to gather the ripe peaches, pears, and apples espaliered on the ancient brick walls sheltering them from frost, yet exposing them to the sun's beneficial rays. Blackberries and field mushrooms were gathered, made into jam, or pickled for winter use. Many cottagers produced elderberry wine, "put aside," so they said, for Christmas, but invariably consumed before Michaelmas Day in late September.

When it rained and the countryside was sodden for days, Matthew and Charlotte retreated to the library to play backgammon and cards. When interest in these pursuits waned, they explored the well-stocked shelves. Matthew was intrigued by the following essay written by Count Leopold Berchtold in 1787, listing the questions a traveller might ask in a foreign land:
Which are the favourite herbs of the country? Are there many examples of people being bitten by mad animals? Which food has been experienced to be most portable and most nourishing for keeping a distressed ship's crew? How much is paid per diem for ploughing with two sturdy oxen?

He chuckled over this passage as he followed Charlotte into the glorious gold and red damask, pink-carpeted music room to hear her play on the harp and sing sweet, haunting ballads. How quickly she had adjusted to her position as mistress of the Hall. Since there was further income at her disposal from the recent sale of the Greville property in Bath, Matthew encouraged her to hire more servants. Hetty, revelling in her new position, took great delight in examining the contents of Charlotte's jewel case when her mistress was absent from her boudoir. She felt very superior to Molly, still at work in the scullery. Charlotte was conscious of a growing attraction between her maid and Jed. Hetty's promotion as personal maid would keep her from indulging in stolen kisses in darker recesses of the house. However, Hetty was an old hand at concealing flirtatious behaviour and knew where every priest hole was located, offering concealment. Discovery was unlikely.

Charlotte was made welcome at the most desirable places in the vicinity, but never at Mulberry Court. Her frivolous, indulgent ways, manner of living and entertaining at great cost, and mode of stylish dress did not endear her to the inhabitants of Mulberry Court. While writing a letter destined for a distant "heathen" land where thick darkness brooded, admonishing the weary inhabitants to heed the teachings of the New Testament, Miss Gaunt said to Uncle Charles, "I don't believe Charlotte attends any church service from what I hear of her activities. She can never take Arabella's place, God rest her soul. Charles, you should go with me soon to the Hall and see for yourself what Matthew is doing. After all, he is your nephew."

CHAPTER 22:
MAY DAY IS CELEBRATED

Early the following year, blustery March winds tossed clumps of daffodils in every direction. Molly was greatly inconvenienced hanging out the laundry, before Jed came to her assistance with the few remaining pegs. Playful, strong gusts threatened to entangle milady's dresses with the sheets. With the threat of rain in the atmosphere, Molly was in haste to ensure that the laundry be finished before noon. Later in the month, as the winds changed, blowing from the south, dormant animals emerged from burrow and den to bask in the sun's strengthening rays and make trails along forest paths. Shy primroses and violets peeked from mossy banks nestling upon the sweet-smelling earth, succeeded in May by bluebells and marsh marigolds.

The first day of May was eagerly anticipated in Albatross Village and by many others the length and breadth of the land. In time-honoured tradition, a maypole was placed in the market square. To the energetic tunes of a fiddler, dressed in green jerkin, and pointed brown hat (bearing an uncanny resemblance to the Pied Piper of Hamelin) the children bobbed and weaved, each holding a ribbon attached to the top of the maypole. Those in the outer circle danced in the opposite direction to those inside, and so a colourful woven tapestry emerged, to the applause of all the onlookers, beating time to the music. The festivities concluded with the crowning of the May Queen with a garland of fresh hawthorn blossoms. From a bevy of young village maidens, Bess Bray was chosen for her pretty face and figure, so much admired and desired by squire Matthew.

He was preoccupied by further changes on the estate, hiring a small army of labourers to excavate and stock a second lake in an area of the park far removed from the original. Since his first encounter with the ghost of Lady Georgiana, he admitted to a profound terror. A new species of carp would be added first and later, at Mrs. Dobson's request, brown trout. As she put it in conversation with the squire, "We allus used to eat a deal of fish at Felbrigg Hall. Old Sir William were particular fond of anythin' that swam, specially as we lived near the coast. I well remember him tellin' me about some relative who put to sea and went to fish off Newfieland. Never heard on him no more neither." Matthew smiled to himself. Mrs. Dobson was not as refined as her predecessor, but her outspoken manner appealed to him.

From a written list, the squire noted that the repair of the stone balustrade supporting the terrace and stairs leading to the gardens below needed immediate attention from masons to mortar various cracks, some wide enough to insert a coin into. Charlotte asked for yew topiary clipped into bird shapes to be placed along each side of a new flagstone walk, and specified that one must be an albatross.

"Ma'am, it will be necessary to hire at least two under gardeners to assist me," Mr. Choke said. "I cannot rely on Tom. He was so taken with Master Henry's uniform he made up his mind to go to Spain soon and be a drummer boy in Wellington's army. He has some foolish notion that all one needs to do is bang away and scare the enemy. I tells him that he could be in front of the soldiers, exposed to artillery fire, but he will not be dissuaded. I suspect he intends to go in search of Master Henry. Mrs Dobson is not sorry to see him go. She says that he is eating more heartily each passing day, and rapidly growing out of his clothes. Another point, ma'am, for you to consider is the purchase of more tools, particularly shears. The knife grinder said the other day that constant use is wearing out the blades. Some of the estate workers need new pruning hooks, rakes, and spades. Perhaps I should inform the squire?"

"Please do your best, Mr. Choke," replied Lady Charlotte. "In the meantime, send Tom to me this evening. I wish to speak about his plans to leave us. I bid you good day, Mr. Choke. I have an appointment with Tapper."

The coachman wore his new, stylish black outfit, sporting a blue and gold band around his silk top hat. In the winter, he changed to a fashionable beaver, and was proud of his new whip, a parting present from Mrs. Hatchett. Inside the coach house stood two refurbished carriages, each painted with a large albatross, dazzling to the eye. The doors and lamps were blue with gold trim; plush interiors displayed corded red velvet upholstery. Molly always ensured that a cloth-covered stone hot water bottle be placed on the floor of the carriage before each excursion, so mi'lady's feet were kept as warm as possible.

The drive to see Lady Cynthia, now a companion dear to her heart, took Charlotte past Mulberry Court to Wingate Farm, set in the hollow of a deep, wooded valley and reached by a steep, tree-lined drive. She was especially gratified to find her friend awaiting her on the front step. Cynthia could not fail to notice her elegant equipage and Tapper's finery.

Charlotte embraced Cynthia and, turning around in a circle, asked if she approved of her new brown walking dress and cream bonnet. "Matthew says it is most becoming and I find it very comfortable to wear."

"Certainly it conceals your condition to perfection," replied Cynthia, inviting Charlotte to follow her inside, across the black-and-white tiled entrance hall, into the front parlour. There a gate-legged table in a window nook was set for two with a snowy white handmade lace tablecloth.

"Hannah will bring tea. You must tell me all about your recent shopping trip to London."

"I think you would have been pleased to stay at Kirkham's Hotel in Brook Street. I can highly recommend such a convenient location. As it was late on the day of our arrival, we were much fatigued and retired to rest. We drove the next day to service at St. George's in Hanover Square. Matthew loves to hear me sing and play, so we took a hackney to Broadwoods on Monday and purchased a grand piano for the music room. The London streets, lit by gas lamps, were very crowded. All the shops, gay with Christmas decorations. I expect that we will go to London again, but of course not until after the baby is born. I have been meaning to ask you, Cynthia, if you would do us the honour of standing as godmother?"

"It will be a great pleasure. Please let me have word if you require my assistance at any time. I would be happy to send Hannah in my carriage."

"Thank you very much. I am sure Dr. Palliser will take good care of me. As you know, he is getting older. There are rumours that he might give up his practice next year. If you can recommend me a suitable young woman to act as nurse, I hope you will advise me. I do not think the village offers any suitable prospects, but I shall make inquiries soon. Now it is time for me to leave. Thank you for your excellent hospitality." The two friends embraced. Lady Charlotte returned to Albatross Hall with Tapper driving at his usual brisk pace. His route passed by the rectory. A sudden thought occurred to Charlotte. If Mrs. Bray could spare Bess from her duties, perhaps she would like to be employed as nursemaid to the new heir?

One evening toward the end of May, Matthew mounted the stairs of the portrait gallery to hang the portrait of himself and Charlotte recently arrived from Italy by Pickford's barge. Beside it would be placed Raphael's Marquis of Mantua, also purchased in Rome. But where was the Batoni portrait of himself? How was it that the painting of Lady Georgiana hung in its place? A complete search of the house, including the servants' quarters, was ordered, not sparing even the servants' attic bedrooms.

"I really can't abide the master's prying eyes," said Hetty, carefully concealing an item of her mistress's jewellery underneath the petticoats lying in the bottom drawer of her dresser.

"He seems very suspicious, as if one of us had stolen his portrait," replied Molly. "I spend most of my time assisting Mrs. Dobson in the kitchen or the wash house and pegging out the laundry. We are forbidden from entering the portrait gallery on the master's express instruction."

Mrs. Dobson pointed out, while preparing breakfast the following morning, that if the staff knew nothing about the whereabouts of the painting, they had nothing to fear. All agreed that ghostly hands were responsible for an occurrence for which there was no explanation.

Charlotte was not told any details of Matthew's previous experience with the ghost of Lady Georgiana. As she confided on their walk up Beechen Cliff, she had an immense horror of the supernatural. "Not just ghosts, Matthew, but awful beings like poltergeists. I knew of a distant relative who lived near Bolton in a place called Haslingden Hall, now completely deserted. Her name was Lucinda Greville. On one occasion, she suffered a sharp blow on the head by an object thrown from the top of the stairs. There was no one visible. The spirit, if indeed it was a spirit, increased his noxious behaviour and threw her pet dog out of a second-story window. Then one night, all the bells in the kitchen rang loudly for several minutes. Since everyone was in bed, and Lucinda was lying terrified under layers of bed covers, no one could account for this incident. When fresh milk turned sour and furniture sailed through the air as if transported by invisible hands, Miss Greville took to her heels. Locking the door, she left instructions that the windows be covered with iron bars. She moved many miles away to a distant town in Yorkshire. The skeleton of a dead cat was found years later at the bottom of a disused well. To the best of my knowledge, the house remains unoccupied to this day." Though it was a warm day, Charlotte felt a sudden chill. She held tightly to Matthew, quite agitated at the recollection of the unfortunate Lucinda Greville.

Miss Gaunt offered her usual forthright opinion on the inexplicable events at the Hall, suggesting Matthew invite an exorcist into the gallery. "I feel strongly that you should also ask Parson Bray to sprinkle holy water on the floor as our Lord did. He can command the unclean spirit to depart. You are being forewarned of trials and tribulations to come. In my judgment you should take care you spend less money on the place and contribute more money to the poor. Remember that you have to keep Henry's portion of the estate for his return home. Now I shall return to mine and pray at my bedside for our nation and the speedy trial of John Bellingham. I don't suppose you have heard the shocking news? He assassinated our Prime Minister, Spencer Perceval, a few days ago!"

"There is also a very interesting report in the London Chronicle," said Uncle Charles, not waiting for Matthew's reaction to Perceval's death. "It states that your brother was given the distinction of being made aide de camp to the Duke of Wellington following the Battle of Salamanca, and praises his courage and foresight. The report goes on to say that the British achieved a resounding victory over the French. Marshall Marmont, who was gravely injured, lost many thousand more soldiers than Wellington. But I'm sure that we haven't seen the last of old Boney yet, don't you think so, my dear?"

"Charles, you always exercise such good judgment in these affairs. My chief concern though is you are aware, Matthew, that Henry is risking his life in service to his King and country. When you next decide to go to church, which I don't expect until the baby is christened, pray earnestly for his safe return as I do."

Matthew realized he could never convince Gertrude Gaunt that he felt more keenly his duties on the estate, especially now an heir was expected. For the present, he would set aside his investigation of the missing portrait. He adhered to a strict daily routine which included discussions promptly after breakfast with his new farm manager, Mr. Brooks. They roamed on horseback over the fields, pausing here, to examine a fence damaged by poachers, there, to replace the broken step of a stile. Orders were given that the tenants' wishes for new tools be fulfilled immediately. In the words of Mr. Brook's favourite poet, Mr. Hood, almost as well-known as William Cobbett for his charming rural verse celebrating the countryside:

> A spade, a rake, a hoe,
> A pickaxe or a bill,
> A hook to reap, a scythe to mow,
> A flail or what ye will,
> And here's a ready hand
> To ply the needful tool,
> And skill'd enough by lessons rough,
> In labour's rugged school.

CHAPTER 23:
MRS. DOBSON PREPARES
A HOUSEHOLD INVENTORY

Mrs. Dobson felt very much at ease as she sat, early one fine July morning, at the same pearwood escritoire, in the same chair as her predecessor, Mrs. Hatchett. Unsurprisingly, her occupation was of a similar nature, writing grocery lists for Bentinck to execute. She added to the Jordan almonds some extra sweetmeats desired by Lady Charlotte and then prepared the household accounts. At this midpoint in the Albatross year, she read a list in her mistress's own hand. There was to be an inventory of the entire contents of the house, taking several days to complete. The idea was first proposed by Matthew, who took care not to divulge the true reasons for this task.

Being several years younger than the retired housekeeper, who spent much of her time in the company of old Gillies, Mrs. Dobson was blessed with good eyesight and hearing. However, her rotund figure and prematurely greying hair bespoke a careworn youth spent in years of service. Her last employer, old Sir William Windham of Felbrigg Hall near Cromer, insisted that the bounty of the sea be served "at least twice a week, being excellent for the brain, as liver would provide iron for a weak heart." So it came to pass that dinners at Albatross always included fish from the lake. The new housekeeper was fond of brown trout. Spinach found its way onto the menu as soup, but on the whole, there were few changes to the fare. The ancient leather-bound record book kept from the last century was quite a source of inspiration to Mrs. Dobson, although she could not match the fine copperplate mastered by Mrs. Hatchett. Nevertheless, grammatical errors and misspelled words filtered in here and there, so the pages became messy with ink spots and breadcrumbs lodged in the spine. It was fortunate that Bentinck was able to decipher Lady Charlotte's wishes through the literary efforts of the new housekeeper.

"Do you always spell oysters with an H and herring without an H?" he inquired, about to fulfill his commission to purchase supplies in the village.

"I allus spells it the way I hears it said," replied Mrs. Dobson, quite unabashed. "Hoysters is hoysters, and happles is happles, and, my good man, 'errins is errins'."

"Then let us say I'm off to the willage," laughed Bentinck taking up a wicker basket hanging behind the back door. He missed Tom's cheerful whistle and hoped he had reached the Iberian peninsula in safety.

As he later confided to Jed, "Mrs. D. doesn't look very becoming in dowdy grey gowns and oddly shaped caps with inverted ruffles. She squints excessively with one eye, but she cooks well. Choke shows his appreciation by providing the best vegetables from the garden and greenhouse. He tells me she makes figgy puddings as good as Mrs. H. ever did, and really prefers her hare pies."

This conversation took place while Bentinck and Jed were engaged in counting the cutlery the next day. The rosewood cabinet stored numerous wine goblets, many of Italian origin, and added to the substantial collection brought by Lady Charlotte from her home in Bath. "I don't think I have ever mentioned it to anyone here before," said Bentinck, holding up a red crystal glass trimmed with gold for closer examination, "but the letter I took up to Master Matthew today from Master Henry reminded me that I had a famous uncle, Lord William Bentinck, also a soldier. He was born in 1774, quite a bit before my time, and became the governor of Madras in India."

"Where's Inja?" asked Jed. "I niver heard of it afore."

"You never had the opportunity to learn in school, Jed. It has a shape similar to one of Mrs. Dobson's pears and lies to the east of Africa. Unfortunately,

William Bentinck was recalled, being held responsible for the Sepoy mutiny at Velore a year later. He died somewhere off the Mediterranean coast."

"Cor, wish I had a realtive like that," replied Jed, impressed. "Is he anyways near where master Henry is a fightin? My realtives are 'umble folk an I niver heard of them doin' anythink special like that."

"No, no, Jed, I told you he died at sea. He was later given the traditional funeral of a distinguished diplomat and soldier. Here's Molly coming to join us, Jed. Take those cracked goblets to the kitchen and then go outside and lend a hand to Mr. Choke."

"Well guv, we might even find that missin portrait of the master's," said Jed as he left the dining room. How gloomy it looked, quite funereal. Protective dust covers lay over every damask chair. The Willement sideboard was concealed in like manner, its exquisitely carved figures invisible to the passerby. Venetian blinds eliminated any sunlight which might cause damage to the Flemish tapestries.

Jed had a guilty conscience, aware of rising colour in his cheeks. He muttered to himself as he entered the garden. He supposed his mistress would ask in addition that all the fruits and vegetables in the beds be accounted for, then the flowers. The cattle and sheep might be next, followed by the new pullets. Jed kicked moodily at the gravel path, tossing some overripe tomatoes at the broody hen which appeared from the other side of the hen house to nibble at Mr. Choke's early seedlings. There was never any love lost between himself and Molly. In the words of the nursery rhyme, he wished a "blackbird would come down and peck off her nose." The gardener was nowhere to be found. Jed tossed his straw hat high in the air and crossed the park to visit Gillies in the lodge. No doubt he hadn't heard the news of Tom's sudden departure. Before returning to the house, he went for a quick chat with Tapper.

"Now Molly, I am aware that the late Lord Cecil stipulated nothing be removed from the house unless in need of repair or refurbishment, but I have a strong suspicion that there are a few items still missing," said Bentinck, scrutinizing the list again. The linen cupboard was next.

"You are right, Mr. Bentinck," replied Molly, pulling out the remaining sheets from the bottom of the linen cupboard standing tall in the passage leading from the kitchen. "There should be several more spare for house guests. I certainly replaced them, and several more pillowcases. I remember that Jed helped me peg them on the line, but when I ironed them later, I didn't realize anything was amiss. I did not think of counting them when I removed all the linens from the clothesline."

"I hear the bell ringing for lunch," said Bentinck, "and so I will take my list to Mrs. Dobson. Thank you, Molly, you are a good girl."

Later that evening, the housekeeper rose from her chair after locking the records and inventory in the drawer of the escritoire. Taking a lighted candle, she walked slowly up the back stairs to her room, one floor below the servants' attic quarters. It was sparsely furnished with a low oak bed, on which rested a worn mattress covered with a checkered blanket. Next to it stood a small night table and tucked underneath, a heavy chamber pot decorated in a floral pattern. By the light of her candle, Mrs. Dobson prepared for bed. Then sat at her kidney-shaped dressing table, brushing her long hair which fell abundantly around her shoulders as she undid the tight coil, held in place by a few pins. Next, she removed her gown and petticoat and donned a flannel nightgown, before kneeling at the foot of her bed to recite a few prayers. She humbly asked God to sustain her in all her duties, and take care that she not overcook the meat or burn the bread.

Most of Mrs. Dobson's family had long since departed this fragile earth. Only one sister, Jessie, remained out of a family of twelve. Jessie was many miles distant, working in some obscure Lancashire cotton mill. Since the northern newspapers reported a strike by the workers, Mrs. Dobson feared for her sister's safety. Violent clashes had taken place between the militia and labourers. Some of the latter had lost their jobs, replaced by imported Irish men. An angry crowd assembled outside Harding Mill, demanding that the mills be set on fire unless their request for higher wages was speedily dealt with. In vain, the mill owners pleaded that higher wages would result in loss of work as revenues were falling, owing to strong competition from overseas. A minority of mill workers knew dues collected by the unions would not go far enough to keep most families from certain starvation. Stealing was a capital crime or at the very least a sentence of transportation to Australia.

The sorry sight of a worker hanged for stealing a loaf of bread acted as a severe deterrent. Even for very minor offenses, convicts were transported to Tasmania. The housekeeper sighed, folded up a copy of the Daily Gleaner, snuffed out her candle, and lay down in bed. Barely asleep, Mrs. Dobson was aroused by strange noises coming from the courtyard far below her window. She threw back her bedclothes and looked down on the wet cobblestones. There was a faint light from a flickering lantern. She could just make out the bulky form of Tapper scurrying in the direction of the stables. A low, piercing whistle followed and none other than Jed emerged from the shadows of an archway. He crossed to the open stable door and entered, glancing furtively over his shoulder. Soon afterwards, the buxom figure of Hetty ran with all speed in the same direction.

The housekeeper waited no longer. She put on her dressing gown and went down the corridor to awaken Bentinck. He quickly descended the stairs, exiting through the servant's door and across to the stable to find Jed, Tapper, and Hetty inside, conferring in low whispers, unaware of the butler's approach. The mystery of the thefts was revealed. The missing portrait covered by piles of sheets in one corner lay underneath a horse trough full of feed for Rajah was discovered by Bentinck, who walked the stable floor with his own lantern. The guilty servants huddled together nearby.

"So why did you conceal my portrait beneath the oats in Rajah's stall?" asked Matthew in a stern voice while interviewing Jed, Hetty, and Tapper in the library the next morning. "Did you really believe you could sell it, Jed? As for you, Hetty, I think Mrs. Hatchett was quite right to inquire of your old employer, Lady Chadworth, 'whether or not you were honest and could be trusted in a house of fine goods.' We sent you out of the brewery because of your persistent habit of sampling too much ale above the daily ration set out for all my household staff. We gave you a position of trust in my wife's boudoir as her personal maid. You have broken that trust by the theft of certain pieces of her most valuable jewelry which you artfully wrapped in a sheet and then deposited at the bottom of your underclothing drawer. It was timely that Bentinck, accompanied by Mrs. Dobson, discovered your misdeeds. I have no option but to dismiss you both immediately from my service and, of course, without any references. You may look for work in the cotton mills up north, where Mrs. Dobson can tell you from her sister's experience that you will suffer from the deafening noise of clanking machinery and hissing steam engines. Breathing will be difficult as your lungs absorb cotton fibres. That is, provided you can adjust to a damp, unhealthy climate and frequent fogs. You have no regard for Lady Charlotte's delicate condition, Hetty. As for you, Jed, I suggest that to repent of your despicable behaviour, you follow Tom's example and go to Spain. Offer to be a camp cleaner or assist with the baggage trains. Learn what real men do in the service of their king. Bentinck brought me a letter from my brother, Master Henry. Many brave men lost their lives in the Battle of Salamanca. You are not worthy to act as a bearer of arms. But I am wasting my time. Both of you begone from my sight, never to return to a home that has sheltered you both and provided you with sufficient food and clothing." Matthew looked with great scorn on the pair of sinners and as they left the library, warning Tapper that if ever he became associated with such acts in the future, he would suffer the same fate.

Matthew re-read the letter from Henry, sent from Spain.

July 22nd, 1812.

My dear brother,

You will probably have read in a dispatch sent to the London Chronicle from the battlefield here that I am now aide de camp to the Duke of Wellington. He is such a fine leader of men, even though he expresses reservations about the abilities of some of my fellow officers. There was notable lack of confidence when I overheard him say while examining the list, "I only hope that when the enemy read this list of names, he trembles as I do!" He also gave his opinion in a most forceful manner about the indiscreet behaviour of the officers attached to the 9th cavalry regiment. "They have acquired the bad habit of galloping at everything in sight and then galloping back as fast to our own lines as they gallop on the enemy. They never think of manoeuvering before an enemy, so little in fact that one would think they cannot manoeuver at all except on Wimbledon Common."

In spite of his contempt for some poorly trained officers though, I am sure you will be as happy as I am to learn that we have secured a major British victory. The weather has not helped us. Both armies crossed the River Tormes in a violent thunderstorm. A tent in Marmont's lines collapsed when stampeding horses caught its ropes. Still, it is troublesome that casualties continue to mount on both sides, yet Wellington shows such heroic courage and coolness in the field. At breakfast in our farmyard headquarters, he discussed his plans. Then mounted his charger and while devouring a chicken leg, he observed with his telescope the carnage as the Frenchies and our men hurled themselves at each other. What happened next, Matthew, was an astonishing event which will go down in history. Still gazing through his glass, Wellington noted a fatal gap had appeared in the French line at Ciudad Rodrigo. General Marmont was attempting to cut our commander off from his base. Wellington pronounced Marmont ruined. Turning the head of his horse, he deceived the French completely by feigning retreat. He reminds me of a cunning fox! I do tell you, Wellington is a humane man. He seemed genuinely concerned when Marmont was grievously wounded by cannon shot which destroyed an arm and two ribs.

I was quite impressed with the Portuguese cavalry supporting our right flank. Within a matter of minutes, the dragoons struck hard at Marmont's soldiers marching down the road, causing a cloud of dust to rise in every direction and blotting out all movement in their path. During this final stage of the battle, Marmont sent a force of experienced men into the attack. Wellington was ready for him, ordering our troops to send a withering volley of musket fire into their ranks. Finally the cavalry, whooping and yelling, plunged into the fray with deadly bayonet charge. This was a good day's work for us. I think our leader is well pleased with the results.

And now I have a surprising bit of news. Toward the evening, when I retired to my tent feeling very weary, whom should I spy loitering outside but young Tom! How he managed to make his way to Spain I shall find out later after our meal. At least it will be hot this time. Wellington has given permission for fires, but only for cooking purposes. I suppose Tom will tell me that he crossed over from Portsmouth in a merchant sailing vessel, hitching rides on farm wagons and carts. His clothes are ragged and dirty. I will get him a drummer boy's uniform soon. His heart is set upon beating the drum. Now that he is here, he will be most useful to us in other ways. He has already polished my spare pair of top boots. Captain Moreton has designs on him too!. I verily believe his drumming performances will alternate with polishing Moreton's sword and brass buttons. Of course he is eager to mount a horse and brandish a sword; so eager in fact, it is hard to curb his enthusiasm. I don't think he realizes how deadly war can be.

I don't know yet when I can take some leave in England. Napoleon is determined to drive us all back into the sea near the River Tagus. It is rumoured one of his generals, Loison I believe his name, massacred every single inhabitant of the Portuguese town of Evora: men, women, and children. Who knows what further atrocities will be committed by Boney's soldiers as they rape, pillage, and ravage the plains. Can you imagine such terrible cruelty, Matthew?

I would compare them to Cromwell's men. They deface all Portuguese shrines that lie within their path. Such beasts! Such savages! We have been badly harassed by Boney's skirmishers. Wellington showed great foresight by placing a line of his own roustabouts in front of the soldiers, so we could pay them back in their own coin. What a sight to see a thin red line of grenadiers opposing the French with wave after wave of rolling musket fire, sending them all reeling back down the hill.

This is a long letter, but at least you have all our news. Send me yours soon, Matthew, and let me know how things fare with my sister-in-law.

Ever your devoted brother, Henry.

P.S. Tom sends his regards and says it won't be long before he becomes a real soldier. I reckon that one English soldier is worth three Frenchies any day.

CHAPTER 24:
SON AND HEIR,
LORD CECIL PONSONBY ARRIVES

Matthew felt in need of a diversion from his duties on the estate. He read the contents of his brother's letter, postmarked Belgium, 1813. There might be danger abroad from Napoleon's army, but the prospect of excitement and an opportunity to make money at the gaming tables was attractive. His destination would be Belgium as soon as time permitted. There was already a large English community in residence in the capital. Many years had passed since he travelled on the continent with Everett—his old tutor now teaching history and the classics at Winchester public school. Since it bore a reputation for scholastic excellence, Matthew felt it might serve his son well. Thus he applied for admission even before the birth of Cecil Thomas Ponsonby. Now two years of age, a robust, sprightly lad, Cecil could be safely left in the care of Fanny, his former wet nurse, now in charge of the nursery, replacing Bess who had, at Mrs. Bray's request, returned to the rectory.

Fanny was a simple farm girl living a few miles from Albatross Village. Fortunately for Fanny, it was not known by the gossips she was the mother of a child now raised by her parents. Given the climate of the times, her parents had informed her of their extreme displeasure. She had born a child out of wedlock without confessing the paternity of their grandchild. Fanny had further incurred their wrath by refusing the face-saving offer of marriage made by a neighbouring farmer, well respected in the agricultural community. A position at the Hall with the local squire would effectively rid them of an embarrassing situation and prevent ridicule in the village on market day. They were relieved when their errant daughter took up her duties in the Ponsonby nursery. It boasted a rocking horse with long black mane and tail, partially mutilated when Cecil attempted to pull it off. He was a vigorous fellow, tugging at the red leather reins while shouting "Gee up, gee up." Before long, dobbin lost one glass eye.

Cecil exhibited an insatiable curiosity about his surroundings, trotting down to the lake to feed the ducks or visiting the falconry, always in the company of Gillies, brought out of retirement on such occasions. Gillies kept Cecil enthralled with tales of his years spent at Albatross as gamekeeper. "Afore long, young un, you'll be snaring rabbits just as I did, but mind you don't chase the ewes."

His father would never accompany him to see the enormous falcons. Matthew invariably told his son that he had more urgent business to attend to, but expressed delight when Cecil declared his ambition to mount a real pony and join Papa in the fox hunt. Blessed with golden locks and clear blue eyes, Cecil reminded Matthew of his late sister, Sarah. There was a strong resemblance to his grandfather, the same determined mouth and purposeful step as Cecil ran to his mother's arms squealing with delight. He particularly enjoyed gathering bouquets of wildflowers blooming in the meadows. Charlotte doted on her young son, and frequently took him in the carriage to visit his godmother, Lady Cynthia. Before Cecil went to bed, Charlotte played and sang sweet lullabies on the Broadwood piano. Guests were frequently invited to the Hall to play cards or listen to music, especially during the long winter evenings. Molly lit fires and candles to offset the growing chill and fading light.

One morning in February, Mrs. Dobson requested an urgent interview with her mistress, rearranging books in the library to fill in spaces which had recently appeared. "Ma'am, to put it plain in a manner of speaking, it will be necessary for you to grant me permission to go to the spring hiring fair next month. We have not replaced Hetty or Jed, and although Molly is a very hard worker, bless her soul, she needs an assistant scullery maid. Mr. Choke assures me that an under-gardener would be useful. He is having such difficulty planting the early peas. The ground is very wet. Betinck can no longer manage to carry heavy cases of wine down the cellar by himself. Why, only last week he complained of a sore back.

I called in Dr. Palliser. Another pair of hands to help lay and serve at table is needed as well. I'm sorry to trouble you ma'am, but without extra help, I shall be obliged to give my notice."

Lady Charlotte was well aware that good housekeepers were not easily obtainable. She recognized, by Mrs. Dobson's frank conversation, she was seriously considering leaving her service. "Very well, I will speak to the master later this morning, Mrs. Dobson. I believe he had an appointment with Mr. Brook after breakfast," replied Charlotte, leaving the housekeeper alone in the library to study her "hiring" list. At least Mr. Brook, in his capacity as estate manager, did not have to concern himself with the shortage of domestic staff. She noted, according to her record books, he had been in the Ponsonby's service for two and a half years. Looking through the windows, she observed him with Matthew inspecting the packhorse bridge. It had been heavily damaged in the floods last autumn. The central span was in imminent danger of collapse. Swirling waters had risen well above their normal levels, tearing out mortar and threatening the remaining four arches.

While Matthew remounted Roamer, Brook pointed out another problem. "Sir, the steps leading down to the River Avon from the rear door of the Hall are also badly affected. The last step has crumbled away, allowing waters to seep into the cellars through crevices in the stone foundation. I don't think Bentinck will be pleased when he finds the wine bottles floating around! I must also report to you the dire position of the tenants. Their crops and animal forage have been spoiled by heavy rains. Like Mrs. Dobson (who had taken the farm manager into her confidence) quite a few are thinking of giving notice of intent to leave a life of hardship for what they falsely assume will be a better life in the industrial towns. Another grievance, sir, is a number of their common grazing lands outside the estate boundary have been enclosed to form part of larger estates. Might be better for the gentry. However, the labourers look upon the enclosures taking away their traditional rights to graze livestock. Not to cause you any worry sir, but there could be riots. I learned from Billy Grogg that some disgruntled folks two villages away set fire to some ricks during a brief dry spell. It is hard to understand their motives, and we don't have sufficient militia stationed in the county to prevent further occurrences. Billy Grogg is one of the few trying to cope with a bad situation. He still occupies the old cottage with his mother and is showing great promise, with excellent knowledge of husbandry. When Mrs. Grogg dies, I respectfully suggest that we hire Billy as a ploughman and cattle drover. Some of the fields have been neglected. Some left fallow when they were due for new planting. We really should engage in crop rotation. How do you propose to deal with some of the tenants' requests for a reduction in their rent payments, sir?"

"It is a difficult question to answer just at the moment," replied Matthew. "I do not wish to foreclose on those in arrears, but need income to cover the cost of all those repairs you have drawn to my attention. In the meantime, please ride over to each cottage and farmhouse and talk to the tenants. They then might have a better understanding of our state of affairs and be willing to stay until next year. Try to encourage them to be reasonable. I must ride to Mulberry Court to make peace with Miss Gaunt. She sent me a disturbing message that Uncle Charles is acting very strangely, showing signs of increasing senility."

Later that day, the squire entered the grounds. He was astonished by a strange sight at the end of the drive which curved to the rear of the mansion, ending at an old cemetery. Mounds of earth resembling mole hills were heaped about, due to the labour of Uncle Charles and Miss Gaunt. Both were dressed in the oldest and oddest assortment of garments, loose-fitting and flapping in the wind. Matthew gained the strong impression they were imitating scarecrows, but in a cemetery? Moving forward for a closer inspection, he observed they were stooping low around shallow pits, digging in such a manner, either hunting for treasure or burying objects placed on a large sheet nearby. On it lay a collection of feathers, skulls, two complete skeletons, and an assortment of bones either from animals or humans. It was hard to tell. But undoubtedly, they had been removed from the display cases kept inside the house. Indeed, the very same items that Sarah had been afraid of during her stay at Mulberry Court. Now it was obvious to Matthew that a burial ceremony was underway, made certain by Gertrude's recitation of verses from a little blue book she held in her hand:

Let these bones lie where they fall,
In times of trouble, in times of toil,
Release them from their earthly bonds,
To cast no more spells on those here or beyond!

Was this witchcraft? thought Matthew, walking towards his uncle and Miss Gaunt. She promptly closed her book at the sound of his approach.

"Well, it was really my idea," said Uncle Charles. "I couldn't recall where Lady Georgiana's skeleton lay in the house. I am getting a bit forgetful, you know. So my sister and I thought we might as well give her a decent Christian burial. You know we first came across her remains in the lake while fishing for trout. We didn't have any luck that day, but dragged up Lady G. instead, or at least what remained of her. The mud at the bottom seems to have preserved her bones. She has been resting in the house in one of our largest glass cases on a bed of sand ever since. Despite Parson Bray sprinkling holy water in your portrait gallery, we knew she might return to haunt you. Ghosts are not laid to rest so easily. This is a good solution to the problem, don't you think, nephew?" Uncle Charles tilted his battered straw hat onto the back of his head, leaning heavily on his spade. "See here, nephew," he said, pointing with a long, bony finger to a depression underneath the oak, "we have laid Lady Georgiana to rest. Now you should have some peace of mind from any further hauntings by her spirit."

Matthew was amazed at his uncle's words. He had not told a soul about his first encounter with Lady Georgiana following the reading of his father's will. Did Charles Ponsonby operate by some means of unnatural telepathy?

"Do you remember the wicked crocodile of the Nile, Matthew? He can join the rest of the stuffed birds, fossils, and minerals. Thus I will be saved the bother of finding the lot of them a new home. You look surprised Matthew. Did you imagine that we knew nothing about your meeting with Lady G.'s ghost? Perhaps you have not heard the news of our discovery, being so busy with that sweet little boy of yours. We are moving to Bramble Cottage in the village before next winter. This place is too big. Anyway the house is always damp and cold. Needs a lot of work."

Matthew finally found his tongue, "Uncle, I appreciate your good intentions, but shouldn't we bury Lady Georgiana in the hallowed ground of St. Mary's churchyard? I know Parson Bray would express concern that you have buried an ancestor of mine in unconsecrated ground. After all, this seems rather undignified for human remains."

"Not a bit of it, "replied Charles, heaving the Nile crocodile on top of the pile of skulls. "Saved you some money, haven't I? Look what it cost to bury your father and Lady Ponsonby. I hear that you need plenty of brass to repair Albatross. Anyway, when we buried your parents they still had some flesh on them didn't they? These creatures here are in the same condition as they bury men, women, and children in India. The vultures fly down to peck at their bones after they are laid in circles in the temple, so they are no different! Think they belong to the Pharisee sect. No that must be wrong," said Charles, correcting himself. "It was the Pharisees who were such hypocrites!"

"I think you mean the Farsis who arrived in India from Persia," laughed Matthew. He realized he was not about to convince his uncle of the impropriety of digging a grave at the back of Mulberry Court, even if it was for a two-hundred-year-old skeleton. Remounting Roamer, he rode away shaking his head at this evidence of his uncle's growing eccentricity. But on second thoughts, it was expedient to let Miss Gaunt and Charles have their own way, provided Parson Bray did not get wind of their questionable activities.

CHAPTER 25:
MATTHEW AND CHARLOTTE
SAIL FOR BELGIUM

An invitation to
the Duchess of Richmond's ball

Matthew pondered the scene just witnessed, wondering whether Uncle Charles was truly losing his mind or simply attempting to put his fears at rest by burying Lady Georgiana's skeleton. These thoughts lingered in his mind as he rode home, barely giving the new stable boy a nod of thanks as he dismounted and strode into the Hall. He was not altogether convinced that the ghost of Lady G. would no longer haunt him. Neither could he forget the legend of the black falcon, foremost in his mind when Cecil asked to visit the falconry. How uneasily unwonted thoughts lie on a troubled breast. Still, he talked to his wife about their forthcoming visit to Belgium as if nothing were amiss. Fanny was given detailed instructions for the proper care of Cecil in their absence,

"You must never let him out of your sight, Fanny. Make sure that when he goes on an outing, he is attired in warm clothing. Mrs. Dobson will see to it that he is fed properly. Tapper will guide him on his pony around the park on fine days for half an hour. His godmother takes a great interest in Cecil, and has promised to look in on him."

The packet boat, laden with mail for Belgium, rode at anchor in the port of Dover. Brisk winds pushed her against the wharf, straining her moorings and giving promise of a rough passage to Ostend. The gangplank creaked in an alarming fashion as families thronged onto the heavily laden deck. Coils of hemp, barrels of tar, one rusting anchor encrusted with barnacles, and assorted seafaring paraphernalia lay strewn about. Charlotte glimpsed an empty cage, several pieces of broken glass, and the most primitive toilet imaginable on the lower deck from which issued the foulest of odours. No cabins were available. Nothing seemed orderly, nothing provided for the comfort or safety of the S.S. Middie's passengers. The crew, concerned only with draining the contents of any rum bottle close by, neither answered questions or paid the slightest attention to the decks, through which salt water, mingled with oil, oozed and ran down in rivulets underneath the rails. Boisterous carriers lurched up the gangway hoisting enormous sacks of grain, followed by porters heaving chests of weapons and what Matthew took to be contraband bottles of spirits, bolts of silk, and wads of 'baccy. The Channel coast was infested with pirates taking advantage of passenger sailings to carry on illegal trade. Just a few bribes to customs officials and one could carry goods without fear of being searched. It took a very righteous individual to resist the lure of easy profits. As Matthew remembered from Aunt Cassandra's stories, even clergymen such as Reverend James Woodforde had not been prevented by their scruples from joining the ranks of smugglers. These individuals who violated the country's excise laws earned the utter condemnation of Dr. Samuel Johnson. He described them as "wretches who in the defiance of the law, import or export goods without the payment of customs." Aunt Cassandra's sudden death in November of 1814 caused Matthew deep regret. No longer would his guests be entertained by the doughty old lady's tales from the Norfolk coast.

The Middie gave three short blasts of its steam whistle, gently nosing into the choppy waters of the English Channel. Matthew and Charlotte stood at the rail, watching the familiar white cliffs receding into the distance. For the next few hours, Charlotte lay on a tattered, smelly divan below, very sick and very miserable, assisted by her new maid, Felicity, who sponged her feverish brow until the shores of Belgium were sighted by the scruffily dressed captain through the window of the wheelhouse. The Middie zigzagged into port on the incoming tide. Most of the passengers decided Captain Hicks was half drunk, and resolved to make the return journey on another ship. Hicks' desire for alcohol as a stimulant to aid his skills at the wheel was confirmed when the ship lurched, striking the pier with great force.

"My love, I will hire a carriage as soon as you have rested from your ordeal," said Matthew, supporting Charlotte as she walked unsteadily down the gangway on to the wharf, followed closely by Felicity, carrying her mistress's case and a basket of provisions assembled by Mrs. Dobson for the long journey across the flat plains of Flanders.

Before leaving the port of Ostend, Matthew found himself agreeing with comments overheard from a fellow passenger. "The port was a dismal place with narrow, dirty streets, gloomy, old-fashioned, low, mean houses, the whole surrounded by marsh, sandhill, or restless sea." The Ponsonbys had no desire to stay in town, urging the hired coachmen to drive on as quickly as the horses could canter. They passed numerous abandoned farmhouses where late-blooming poppies provided a gay splash of crimson around sagging barns, no longer repositories for cattle fodder, but roofless and neglected, testament to the absence of former occupants. A stray pig, or mangy fowl scratched among weeds or poked listlessly at grains of wheat in overgrown farmyards, watched from the back doorstep by thin, starving cats too weak to chase after their natural prey.

The population wisely fled any possibility of being embroiled in future hostilities. They listened to the distressing news, brought by hard-galloping relays of messengers, that Napoleon had escaped from his prison on the island of Elba. He was about to march across the border with France, thus defying the weak Bourbon king, Louis XVIII. The wearying miles, the dull thud of the carriage wheels on the muddy surface of the highway, a brief but drenching shower brought a misty landscape. Charlotte could no longer read the signposts. Overcome with fatigue, she fell asleep in a corner of the swaying coach. In the distance, Matthew could hear echoes of cannon fire. Scraps of conversation from the driver filled him with alarm.

"Hope we can get to Brussels before nightfall," said Noakes to his companion. He urged the team of four horses to a brisker pace by lashing them with his whip. "Won't do to be out on the road when there's soldiers hanging about. I'll stop in a few moments and light the two side lanterns. Besides we could meet robbers. I don't think those foolish English passengers inside have the slightest notion of the dangers that could leave them penniless or deprived of their fine clothes and jewellery. The gent is attired in a braided frock coat, white trousers, and peaked cap sporting a red cockade. His lady mounted the steps of the carriage wearing a crumpled green silk dress. Her bonnet was crushed as if she had been lying down somewhere."

"I can see Brussels about three miles away," said Noake's companion, remounting the box seat after lighting the lanterns. "Won't it be interesting if old Boney's lying in wait for us?"

Soldiers speaking Dutch, German, and English—the vanguard of Wellington's vast army—swarmed the streets of the capital, many of them escorting their ladies. To the travellers, the populace appeared gay and festive. But the question on everyone's lips was, "Where is Boney likely to attack next?" Urchins urged passersby to purchase flags of the various combatants, and scrambled to the cobbled pavement to collect coins thrown at them. The waterways were congested with supply boats. Some English civilians took good care of themselves by hiring luxurious barges, well-stocked with the finest of foods and wines sure to sustain flagging spirits if the dogs of war were about to be unleashed. Matthew eyed his countrymen with contempt.

"Charlotte, my love, my dearest wife, you would think those rascals were coming to enjoy a theatrical performance at Vauxhall Gardens. The way they are indulging themselves and making merry is just preposterous. Are they not aware that the 'great monster' has, according to Noakes, arrived on Belgian soil, ready to throw his armies against Marshall Blucher's Prussians and our own brave lads? My love, we might spot Henry marching down the street. I told him he would recognize me by the red cockade in my cap. Since, my own, you have not yet made his acquaintance, I will let you know if I catch a glimpse. He might be with his old comrade, Captain Moreton."

"It is truly amazing how many of our countrymen have made the same journey, Matthew. Especially at such a time of unrest, with armies on the move. One could easily imagine that we are to join in a seaside picnic at

Brighton. See those groups of bystanders on the opposite corner idly gossiping? They give no heed to the dangers which might overcome us. I know you came to see Henry, Matthew, but perhaps it would have been wiser for us to stay home. I miss my little boy." Charlotte shed a few tears. She was hungry and greatly fatigued by the long journey.

Matthew patted her hand. The carriage turned into Rue Fauchon, a street of fine gabled brick dwellings, some a century or two old, leaning toward each other in such a crazy fashion that a householder could conduct conversations with his neighbour through an upper window. Men doffed their caps when Charlotte peered out of the window, looking for the Hotel Belmont. It had a fine reputation as a respectable hostelry favoured by aristocrats, full of heavy Louis XIV-style furniture, crowded with large potted palms hanging over tables and sofas stuffed with horsehair. The desk clerk gallantly stepped forward to welcome Lord and Lady Ponsonby to the Belmont. He handed Matthew a note from Lieutenant Henry Ponsonby.

Dompier Barracks, June 14th, 1815.

My dear Charlotte and Matthew,

It is a pleasure for me to know that on receipt of this letter you will have arrived safely in Brussels. I enclose an invitation from the Duchess of Richmond requesting that you attend her ball, to be held at her mansion on the Rue de la Blanchisserie tomorrow evening, June 15th, at 8 o'clock. By way of introduction, I mention she is a dear friend of my commander, the Duke of Wellington. Such a wise lady. She asked the Duke whether it was desirable to give such a ball, considering the presence of Napoleon and the alliance of armies assembled to do him battle. Said Wellington without a moment's hesitation, "You may give your ball with the greatest of safety ma'am, with no fear of interruption. I am not certain of Napoleon's plans, but rest assured that since many of my generals and officers will be dancing under your roof, it will give me great opportunity to consult them if necessary." You can appreciate, Matthew, how decisive and capable Wellington is. I look forward to our meeting with eager anticipation, and, dear Charlotte, my first introduction to my new sister-in-law.

Until tomorrow, warmest regards,
your devoted brother, Henry.

P.S. Tom is now wearing a soldier's uniform. Says he is tired of being a drummer boy and wants more action! I warned him that his ears might be creased by flying rifle bullets, but he pays no heed. With the bravado of youth, everything I tell him makes no impression. He is so keen to learn "soldiering." Let us hope he survives long enough to return to England. For my part, I wish that peace was already declared and I could see dear Albatross again. You must give me all the latest news.

The Duchess of Richmond's ballroom, part of a converted stable, was a short carriage ride from the Belmont. Charlotte remarked to her husband that everyone appeared to be going in the same direction; there were so many conveyances jostling each other with wheels in danger of collision. A carnival atmosphere prevailed as flower sellers offered their wares to anyone with a few coins in his pocket.

"Would milady like to place these sweet-smelling blossoms in her hair; would the genl'man take this rose for his buttonhole?"

"No one would ever believe that this property belonging to the Duchess had once been a coach house," said Charlotte to Matthew, entering arm in arm into the elegant ballroom. They saw their likenesses in heavy baroque-style mirrors, reflecting the flickering glow of chandeliers ablaze with myriads of candles. Ornate pillars were twined with ribbons and fresh flowers. The walls hung with rose-trellised paper. Rich draperies in red, black, and gold partly covered huge windows, opened to allow the revelers relief from the hot, oppressive air. Through them wafted loud shouts of an excited citizenry, watching troops mustering in the Place Royale nearby. Totally concealed behind one of the pillars, coolly surveying the scene—as the nobility, officers, and gentlemen mingled, chattering animatedly, eager to see and be seen, self-assured, and basking in the glory of Wellington's recent victories—stood

Lieutenant Henry Ponsonby, A.D.C., smoking a fine cigar while rocking on his heels. His dress uniform well became him. His boots gleamed to perfection, showing Tom's eagerness to please. He darted forward and seized Matthew by the hand.

"Now brother, it is delightful to see you here. Pray, tell me what you think of the duchess's skills as a hostess? Bet she would be an ornament to any field of battle! It is a great honour for me to make the acquaintance of my beautiful sister-in-law, at last. Madame, allow me to kiss your dainty hand. How pretty you look in your long yellow silk gown, with primroses and sprigs of violets adorning your corn-coloured hair." Henry made Charlotte a sweeping bow. A deep blush rose to her cheeks.

"You are really much too kind. Don't forget I'm an old married woman with a son now," laughed Charlotte. "I'm sure we will come to know each other better soon. I do hope the forthcoming battle will not cost too many lives, Henry. May God keep and preserve you. By the way, who is that distinguished gentleman standing with his back to us, wearing a handsome uniform?"

"He is the son of King William of Holland, the Prince of Orange, Charlotte. If you recall he intended to marry the Prince Regent's daughter, Caroline, but she refused him. Now he has been made commander in chief of the allied troops on his father's orders. Next to him is Arthur Shakespear, an officer in the light dragoons. He was badly wounded at Bussaco. Then standing just beside the orchestra is Admiral William Lukin from Aspling House in Norfolk. He must know Mrs. Dobson. As he does not live far from where Aunt Cassandra used to reside, maybe you would like to meet him?"

Lukin's opinions of the capital were decidedly negative. "You know Ponsonby, Brussels might be gaiety itself, but I am tired to death of it. Mrs. Lukin likes it well enough." He shook hands, bowed to Charlotte and, taking Mrs. Lukin by the arm to lead her onto the dance floor, adding, "I will be glad to return home and see how my bullocks and sheep are faring. Nothing like England's green and pleasant land, eh what?"

"Poor darling, he always gets morose when he is not roaming around his beloved Norfolk." Mrs. Lukin whirled her moody husband into the seething mass of dancers. Charlotte and Matthew joined in the familiar strains of a waltz. There was no shortage of gallant partners here either. The next quadrille on her dance card was reserved for Henry.

Chapter 26:
Lt. Henry Ponsonby
Joins the Party

Waterloo
There was a sound of revelry by night,
And Belgium's capital had gathered then
Her beauty and her chivalry, and bright
The lamps shone o'er fair women and brave men;
A thousand hearts beat happily; and when
Music arose with its voluptuous swell,
Soft eyes looked love to eyes which spake again,
And all went merry as a marriage bell;
But hush! Hark! A deep sound strikes like a rising knell!

Did you not hear it? - No; twas but the wind,
Or the carriage rattling o'er the stony street;
On with the dance! Let joy be unconfined;
No sleep till morn when youth and pleasure meet
To chase the glowing hours with flying feet-
But hark! That heavy sound breaks in once more,
As if the clouds its echo would repeat;

And nearer, clearer, deadlier than before!
Arm! Arm! it is, it is the cannons opening roar!
Lord Bryon

And still the festivities went on without pause at the Duchess of Richmond's ball. In blissful ignorance, some of the participants would partake of their last supper. And a very handsome supper it was too, laid out on small tables in a candlelit anteroom, raised by several stone steps above the ballroom. Charlotte was surprised to read one of the gilt-edged placards placed on a table tucked away in an alcove. It bore the name "Robert Greville," a member of the Royal Artillery and, on inquiry, proved to be a distant relative of her late husband, Rupert. Colonel Greville showed no recognition of the fair lady as she moved gracefully to the table reserved for the Ponsonbys.

"I wonder if Napoleon still has a taste for opium and belladonna," said Henry, seating himself between Charlotte and Matthew. He helped himself to a serving of oysters and pronounced them absolutely delicious. "Boney has made a bold move, Matthew, but we will repel him. He will live to regret leaving the care of Colonel Campbell on Elba, and the scent of juniper and myrtle. It is regrettable that he is making such a nuisance of himself by re-entering France across the Alps at the head of a large rabble of soldiers. I reckon King Louis must be alarmed. He is plagued with gout. From what I hear he is as heavy as the Prince Regent. Still, he must find refuge—and perhaps cross the border into this country."

"Well there might be sweet-smelling plants on Elba, but from reports reaching England, I believe it a pretty hostile place. It has deep quarries, mined since Roman times. The stone was used in the building of Pisa's cathedral and the Medici Chapel in Florence, which I visited when in Italy with my tutor, Everett," said Matthew, offering Charlotte a plate of pastries.

"Yes, I remember your journey to Rome and how father became distressed on account of your riotous way of living at Oxford. Isn't Rome described as the 'eternal city,' the place where you both first met and declared 'eternal' love for each other?" asked Henry turning to Charlotte with a twinkle in his eye. "You know, Charlotte, things might have turned out differently if I had been there instead of Matthew! Truly, I cannot imagine how Napoleon managed to escape from such an isolated island as Elba. He is reported to have approached his captivity as a prisoner with the bearing and manner of a sovereign emperor. He had the gall to hoist his personal standard: white with three bees and a band of orange. Such audacity, such wit; I almost begin to admire the man. I don't think that we will ever see his like again."

"The London Gazette opined that Elba had become a tourist attraction and many spies were among the travelers flocking there," said Matthew.

"I don't have much feeling for those Whig sympathizers, anyway," replied Henry, sipping another glass of hock. "Silly fools! Just imagine taking busts and portraits of that monster back to England as souvenirs. They should all be hanged as traitors."

"Come to think of it though, Tom would have made a good spy. Do you see the young rascal over there lurking behind one of the pillars? And he hasn't even been invited," commented Matthew.

"Ah, leave him alone. He might die before his time anyway, Matthew. He has served me quite well. But there still remains the burning question of why there was so much support for Napoleon among the English aristocracy before he made his escape from Elba. He strutted around his palace like a little bantam cock, when not driving around in his carriage giving orders as if he were still a true sovereign. Every person he meets comes under his spell, including the captain of H.M.S. Undaunted who sailed Boney to Elba. The captain received a thousand bottles of wine, one thousand Spanish dollars, and a portrait of the 'emperor' edged in diamonds. And in a speech to the ship's crew, the bo'sun thanked Napoleon, saying, 'Sir, I'm sure we all wish you better luck next time!'"

"I would say the captain was a traitor and should be treated as such," said Matthew, placing a white silk shawl around his wife's shoulders.

"I know Viscount Ebrington paid Boney a call and came away utterly charmed with the man. But Napoleon committed such a gross error when he blockaded our ports to prevent us from trading with the continent. No wonder many respectable merchants have gone bankrupt. Still, in the end, the good people of Elba showed some sense when they tired of Boney's schemes and his oppressive taxation to pay for roads, hospitals, and a military academy. They no longer greeted him with enthusiasm when he entered their villages crying 'Vive L'empereur.' At that time, he was saying to anyone who would listen, 'I was born a soldier, I mounted a throne, and then I descended.' Now he has changed his tune, telling the good burghers of Paris he is a 'messiah of peace and protector of the people's rights.' His proud boast was that he intended to take Paris without a shot."

"Some messiah," replied Matthew, as they re-entered the ballroom at the stroke of midnight. A hush fell upon the gathering. The Duke of Wellington presented himself without his wife, Kitty Pakenham. He'd sent her back to Ireland prematurely, the gossips said. There were whisperings that since both husband and wife had nothing in common, he sought the companionship of other ladies, partly out of boredom and a lingering sense of dissatisfaction. A highly favourable relationship was formed with Harriet Fane, wife of Charles Arbuthnot, a political man of consequence in Lord Liverpool's government. Harriet, twenty-six years younger than her husband, delighted in Wellington's company as he did in hers. Poor Kitty remained faithful to Wellington all her life, which cannot be said to have been entirely happy. Wellington, accompanied by his chaplain, the Reverend Samuel Briscoll, and his chief liaison officer, the Prussian Baron von Muffling, mounted a small dais to make a solemn announcement.

"Napoleon intends to march on Charlerois. We will give a good account of ourselves. Let every officer present rejoin his regiment and prepare to march at dawn." This terse announcement caused confusion both within and outside the house on Rue de la Blanchisserie. The battle cry was sounded by buglers in nearby Place Royale. The news of Napoleon's plans spread rapidly throughout Brussels. Everyone knew the supreme moment was at hand to rid Europe of Bonaparte. Loud knocking resounded on doors, rousing sleepy soldiers (some groggy from an excess of ale) from their slumbers.

"Come Tom," said Henry's old comrade in arms, Captain Moreton, shaking him by the shoulders, "put on your new uniform as quick as you can. We have orders to march in two hours."

Tom rubbed his eyes. "I dreamed I was at a ball last night. So many lovely people a dancin' in a bootiful ballroom. Such charming decorations; so many fine genl'men in uniform."

"Well if so, you'll soon be dancing to another tune. Hurry, my lad, be brave. The first streaks of dawn are in the eastern sky, Tom. I hear, in the distance, the firing of muskets and the sound of booming cannons, the rattle of creaking baggage trains."

The armies of Wellington and Napoleon clashed on the field of Waterloo in a deadly embrace, leaving many thousands of dead and wounded on both sides. The life of a drummer boy turned soldier was snuffed out in the initial engagement. Tom was killed by a skirmisher's bullet and left bleeding on the muddy ground. Cavalry swerved their mounts to avoid what appeared to be a mere bundle of rags, not resembling the torn and soiled uniform of a brave new recruit. Moreton, coming upon the fateful scene, dragged Tom on top of a hillock above the ranks of combatants, gently closing the eyes of the lifeless boy, murmuring a prayer in which he thanked God that the lad had not suffered too long. For his epitaph he ordered a stone with the inscription: "Tom died before he truly lived in the service of his king and country aged eighteen in the year 1815. Birthplace unknown. He will rest in peace, gathered into the bosom of his forefathers."

Moreton wiped away tears, unable to restrain his feeling of loss. He picked a roadside poppy, placing it carefully on Tom's chest, bidding him farewell. The rain came down in torrents as he rode after his regiment. A few hours later, Moreton too would suffer the same fate on a blood-soaked battlefield. Not even the gravely wounded were spared a final thrust from a bayonet, delivered by the enemy under orders to take no prisoners.

"And to think I will never see that poor boy again," said Mrs. Dobson to Bentinck as she and Molly wept at the kitchen table after Matthew recounted the sad news on his return. "I would have put up with him a growin' out of all the clothes of creation if only I could see him 'ere eatin' his vittles and a polishin' Master Henry's boots. To think of him lyin' buried, stone-cold in a foreign field, with nothin' but the stars above to keep him company. Mr. Choke will miss him too. He is not so pleased with young Simon in the garden." The good housekeeper sobbed into her apron. Molly fled to her bedroom. She had a soft spot for Tom and had hoped to marry him one day.

"Well, you know," said Bentinck, placing a comforting hand on Mrs. Dobson's shoulder, "war in 1815 is a family affair. I take solace in the fact that Tom followed the star of his destiny. You must not be too sad, for, at least,

Master Henry is still alive. He had the honour of bringing the glad tidings of Wellington's remarkable victory to the Prince Regent."

All of England rejoiced at the news of Europe's deliverance from Napoleon Bonaparte, congratulating themselves on his exile to the remote island of St. Helena, where he died in 1821 (some say of poisoning by arsenic). But there was a price to pay. The economic principles of war, which brought prosperity to arms manufacturers, now spelled disaster for steel and iron workers, gunsmiths, and clothiers. Farmers faced ruin through the import of foreign corn. As the price of corn fell, they could not afford the rents charged by landowners.

Edward de Lazlo introduced a bill in the House of Commons asking that foreign corn not be imported until the domestic price rose to eighty shillings a quarter hundredweight.

To Gillies' consternation, a punitive measure passed in 1816 condemned a person found in possession of a snare for catching rabbits to seven years transportation. He made a vow that he would not ask Cecil to go rabbit hunting when he was older. "Well if the rabbits are not kept in check, they will eat all Mr. Choke's lettuces. Mark my words, Mrs. D. you will be sorry if there are none for the master's table!" Gillies was paying his weekly visit to Albatross kitchen and never left without partaking of Mrs. Dobson's special game pies.

The new laws were of great concern to Parson and Mrs. Bray as they sat at breakfast, a few weeks after peace had been declared. "Just think, Emma, there are many crimes dealt with by capital punishment. I will preach a sermon on God's forgiveness and how He shows mercy to sinners, next Sunday morning. Too many harsh laws are not good for the populace. I feel reform is essential. I am even in favour of emancipation for the Catholics. They have a right to participate fully in public life and vote, don't you think so, my dear? At least they should be able to stand for a seat in Parliament."

"You are right," replied Emma, reading a report in the London Chronicle. "Listen to this, the poor souls. Seventy-five thousand of the convicts have been transported to Botany Bay in Australia. One such chap, by the name of Dunshea, was sent for the crime of stealing two pigs. He pleaded with the court that he had paid for them, but to no avail. No doubt lawlessness is everywhere, but we are paying a high price for victory. It is sad to read that poverty and disease are on the increase."

"There is a constant cry for reform heard throughout the land. The social system must be changed. It is high time the criminal code is revised and more humane laws passed. I am pleased that Jeremy Bentham is taking a close look at every punitive law to see if it can be taken off the statute books," said Bray, lowering his spectacles to the end of his nose and taking a generous pinch of snuff. "I think very highly of him, Emma. He is a good Oxford man, like me. I must say he has achieved greater success than Matthew, although to give him his due, I believe he is improving. Then there are the views of William Cobbett, for example. He is a man very much concerned with the present deplorable state of affairs. Although I cannot agree with his avowed hatred of my fellow clergymen, I feel that to a certain extent he is right in disliking some of the manufacturers, because they are encourage peasants to leave the countryside. He is also against the 'rotten boroughs' because corrupt, greedy landowners and men with powerful influence control all affairs of the nation. I dislike towns myself, Emma. I found Cobbett's ranting most amusing. He wrote that, as he rode through Calne on his horse, 'he could not come through that villainous hole without cursing corruption at every step.' In another ten miles, he came to another 'rotten hole', Wooton Bassett. This is a mean, vile place,' he wrote."

"My dear, you are quite a radical yourself," said Emma pouring out the remains of the teapot and signaling to Bess to clear the table.

"Before you go, my dear, I would like to read you a poem by Shelley. I think he sums up the present climate of this country in a very succinct manner." Parson Bray bustled off to his study and returned with a slim book of verse from which he read using his "preaching" voice, a habit developed from years in the pulpit:

> Men of England, wherefore plough,
> For the lords who lay you low?
> Wherefore weave with toil and care,
> The rich robes that your tyrants wear?

Mrs. Bray looked thoughtful. "I think he expresses himself well. Now if you will permit me, my dear, I will pay a call on Miss Gaunt and Charles at Bramble Cottage. I am sure they have made the place as comfortable as they can. I trust that Charles has found new interests to replace his specimen collection."

"Fine, Emma, but take care that Gertrude doesn't try to convert you to her chapel way of thinking. She is zealous and I don't want her encouraging you to go out and become a missionary in what she calls 'darkest Africa.'" The rector chuckled as he retired to his study to prepare for Sunday service. He shook his head. Parliament had no real insight on how to address the country's economic grievances. Lord Liverpool's government was saddled with a massive war debt of eight hundred and sixty million pounds. Bray sighed as he sat down at his desk. He felt thankful not to be among the dissenters who wished to take the Church in a new direction. Some of them had been forced to leave their livings and seek employment outside the Church. For the present, both he and Emma would benefit from a decent living until the local bishop decided otherwise.

Chapter 27:
Bramble Cottage Charles
Searches for Skeletons
in the Garden

Bramble Cottage was tucked away at the far end of Mill Street, so named for the old watermill on the Avon, downstream from the Hall. It was in full operation grinding corn into flour, if the harvest had been sufficient to keep the miller well supplied to ply his trade. When constant rains spoiled the local crop, the miller was forced to import more costly grain. It was thus the village baker who bore the brunt of his customer's complaints. A penny was one thing, but doubling the price of a loaf made them too expensive for some of the poorer villagers. Miss Gaunt was seen walking to her new abode with trepidation. She knew her brother's frugal habits. The two-penny loaf in her wicker basket would certainly raise objections. She consoled herself with the thought that Charles might be working in the garden, as she entered through the front door of Bramble Cottage.

Their new home could have been named "Wisteria Cottage," for in the early springtime, long cascades of trailing vine with luxuriant purple blooms obscured the view from the small upper window, underneath the thatched roof. The roof was a fine example of the thatcher's art, being embellished by two roosters at either end, keeping distant company with the thatched cat in the middle, next to a thatched mouse whose tail dangled over the neat edge. Smoke from a tiny brick chimney indicated cooking from a kitchen fire within. The remaining windows were shielded from the sun by dainty lace curtains, while the wooden front door appeared only designed to admit those of small stature. Tall people, including Charles, were obliged to stoop low or rub a sore head.

Emma Bray pushed open the white gate set into the picket fence and noted that Charles was in the little garden at the back.

"It's too early for the blackberry blossoms to set, but the bees are already active.

As you can see, we are delighted to have the wisteria in full bloom. Good day to you, Mrs. Bray. You will observe that I am busy digging to find any fossils, bones, Roman remains, and suchlike. The Romans had quite a number of settlements in this part of the country. Because they governed for four centuries, they left behind objects for us to discover, belonging to their civilization." Charles jerked his spade and once more plunged it into the black earth. "This could be an ancient barrow where they buried their dead and most of their possessions. Come to think of it, if I dig deeper, I might find a few more coins."

Mrs. Bray couldn't suppress her laughter. "But I understand from Miss Gaunt that you have buried your collection of skeletons, skulls, stuffed birds, and animals, not even sparing the Nile crocodile. So forgive me, Charles, I thought you would be content to plant a few vegetables and flowers."

"Not a bit of it," retorted Charles. A few worms slithered away, too close to the spade's sharp end. "You never know what you might come across when you're least expecting it. I did find a fragment of pottery the other day. I'm sure it showed part of the face of a Roman goddess. Then see this coin," he continued, pulling a piece of silver from his pocket. "This is the face of Julius Caesar. I will take it to the museum in Bilsbury, together with this segment of tessellated pavement. See how bright the colours are after all these centuries and how intricate the design. Might have been once the floor of a Roman bath. We find this place small after Mulberry Court, Mrs. Bray, but there are greater chances to find hidden treasures. Besides, we are closer to the shops, and Gertrude already has a favourite butcher. We never miss one of your husband's excellent sermons."

"I must leave you now, Charles. I have promised the rector that I will look in on Mrs. Grogg and take her some honey and homemade remedies. She is not well. Billy spends most of his time at the plough or performing odd jobs up at the Hall." With a cheery wave of her hand, Emma closed the picket gate and walked in the direction of Mrs. Grogg's little cottage, murmuring a prayer of thanks that tranquility had returned to Albatross Village after Waterloo. The good folk resumed the familiar rhythms of pastoral life, continuing their daily tasks of spinning and weaving, baking and shoe making. The farm labourers maintained that to do a full day's work from dawn until sunset they required plenty of good, wholesome food, none of "that there fancy stuff as is only fit for the gentry's tables." Elderly villagers were sitting outside the Albatross Arms, on low wooden benches, gossiping or passing the time of day with the postmistress in charge of the tiny post office. Miss Gaunt had sent another parcel to Africa, conveniently hidden in a bag, under her loaf of bread. It was a time to sow the good seed—the good news of the gospel. In the fields, heavy Shire horses paced slowly in front of the plough, in preparation for hand-broadcasting of seed in the deep furrows of newly turned earth.

"Drat those birds, they swoop down the moment Billy has thrown the seed from his basket," said Mrs. Dobson looking across the fields, past a ragged scarecrow, to where the master and Mr. Brook had paused in their inspection of the tenant farms to compare notes underneath a large oak tree.

"I trust that we will have a much better harvest this year, Mr. Brook, as my expenses are very likely to exceed my income otherwise. I have decided to hire a tutor for my boy to prepare him for the time when he becomes a scholar at Winchester. He is showing such aptitude for country pursuits, and sits his pony well. I predict he will be ready to join the hunt before long. Just look how he has a natural instinct for chasing the lambs in the pasture yonder. Why, Mr. Brook, the collie can hardly match him for speed! I am pleased the housekeeper will allow him to collect eggs. Last week, he only let one slip from a basket of a dozen newly laid brown speckled ones. He told me they looked as if they had the measles, which I suppose he will pick up as soon as he gets to school."

"He has sturdy legs, Master Matthew. I'm sure he will grow up to be a fine boy," replied Mr. Brook, as both men passed through a five-barred gate and down the narrow lane to see the new barn at Spinney Farm.

When not running after the lambs, Cecil chased the ducks to the far side of the lake, clapping his hands gleefully as they paddled furiously away from their tormentor. Bird nests were always popular and could be discovered in the dense hedgerows. Cecil placed the small blue robins' eggs inside his cap. It was a good idea to take them and show the housekeeper. Cecil was not welcome in Mrs. Dobson's domain. As she said to Bentinck, "That boy needs a firm hand. He is very spoiled. I expect when he gets to boardin' school, he will find hisself one of many to be a taken care of, not gettin' all the lavish attention as he does now."

"Winchester will be the making of him. My ancestor, Admiral William Bentinck, was educated there. He received a good grounding in the classics before he went out to India."

"Fancy that, Mr. Bentinck. I niver knew you had sich a famous person in your family 'afore. To tell you the truth, I haven't traveled above a few mile away from Kettledown where I was born, but I think I knows abit about life and my dear old mum, bless her soul, taught me all I needed to know 'bout cookin' and sich. She even showed me how to make polish from beeswax scented with fresh lavender. Molly uses it every day on the dining room furniture. She also taught me how to churn butter from cream off the top of the milk. There's other uses for beeswax than just for makin' candles, you know. What bothers me most, Bentinck, is when we have to light a thousand of 'em for special occasions. I only hope that the gas lightin' in London streets spread all over the land. It'll be a while afore it gets in the village." Mrs. Dobson sighed. "Lady Charlotte is expectin' Walter Scott to come here shortly and wants the best of fare on his plate. I tells her ladyship that there might be a few brown trout. Gillies promised to get me a hare or two—which reminds me, I must remove the stones from last year's plum jam, as I know Henry can't abide 'em. He will be arrivin' tomorrow. I wonder what he intends to do with his life, now that Wellington no longer needs his services."

"Perhaps he will go into the Church or become a lawyer," said Bentinck. "Quite a few second sons born to upper class families are obliged to find a way to support themselves, although I believe Master Henry will be on half pay as a former army officer."

A few days after his joyous homecoming, celebrated with a special cake inscribed, "Welcome Back to Albatross Hall, Henry," Henry could be found early in the morning, deep in thought, seated in the library. One arm supported his head as it rested on the table, set a short distance from the globe on which he had traced the voyages and expeditions taken since his departure. His ancestral home was a dear place, full of innocent childhood memories and the occasional rough and tumble with his brother, which had irritated the old earl, who had condemned it as "foolish horseplay." But he knew that a cloud hung over his future. It did not help Henry to realize he was falling in love with Lady Charlotte, from the time he first met her at the Duchess of Richmond's ball and the time spent in her company escorting her around Brussels with its splendid monuments to past heroes, equestrian statues, and shady, elegant squares where the park benches were so restful, so conducive to intimate conversation.

During this interlude, Matthew found his way to the gaming tables and spent time fox hunting in the forest of Soignes. Thus Charlotte and Henry were together during his long absences. Romantic ideas of love must be banished from his thoughts. While Henry adjusted to a slower pace of life at the Hall, he should heed his conscience. He believed in the sanctity of marriage—unlike the Duke of Wellington, who sought the company of other ladies, especially married ones such as Harriet Fane. With the full acquiescence of her husband, Charles Arbuthnot, Wellington remained a devoted friend and lover until her premature death in 1834 from cholera. Why, Henry mused, did English heroes engage in affairs with other gentlemen's wives? There was the sordid scandal of the late Lord Nelson and his much-publicized relationship with Lady Hamilton, wife of the British ambassador to Naples, who mourned the dead hero of Trafalgar. It is said she kept a lock of his hair in a small box on her bedside table, refusing to receive visitors for months afterwards.

And yet there was something so alluring in Charlotte's dress and manner, something so appealing in her stately beauty, that prevented Henry from making definite plans to leave Albatross and seek another profession. Henry's plight was no different to that of other ex-army officers. Many were unemployed, roaming the streets of towns and cities, struggling to support themselves on a meager pittance. The general populace quickly forgot their bravery in battle and rarely showed compassion for amputees or those who had lost their vision. Many were reduced to the indignity of begging, holding out shabby military caps at street corners. Henry decided to pay a visit to Parson Bray and seek his advice. He might suggest suitable employment. He knew that the good rector and near neighbour would recommend the Church. But this possibility had no appeal to an ex-soldier who did not feel spiritually inclined after fighting in the Peninsula Wars and witnessing carnage on a vast scale. Neither did his experiences during the American Revolution incline him that way. Henry remembered affectionately the late Colonel Billop. As poor Billop prophesied in his last letter to Henry, consumption had "carried him off." How could he bring messages of peace to worshippers with sincerity when he questioned his own faith? Was it his imagination that his elder brother was trying to avoid him? He was always in Mr. Brook's company. Besides, there was little opportunity to discuss Henry's future at meal times. The servants were always present, watching, waiting, listening, and gossiping.

Could it be that Matthew's lack of attention was due to the fact that the Albatross estates were not providing sufficient income and the squire had been obliged to reduce Henry's share from one-third to one-quarter? Was this the reason related to Matthew's sudden return to the gaming tables? Henry's thoughts raced wildly from one topic to the next. It did occur to him Matthew might have some suspicion of his feelings for Charlotte. There really was no evidence to anticipate that anything unpleasant would happen, either now or in the future, to sever his relationship with his brother. Henry rose from the table and took up his hat. A walk to the rectory could be helpful. He had known Parson Bray since his early childhood, so he felt confident that the rector would give profitable advice. It was fortunate that, as Henry passed by the terrace, he did not notice Charlotte strolling among the yews. Otherwise his heart would have been beating even faster than from the exertions of his walk.

CHAPTER 28:
HENRY SEEKS ADVICE
FORM PARSON BRAY

Bess opened the door of the old brick, ivy-clad rectory. Taking Henry's hat in one hand and his walking stick in the other, she ushered him into the study. Just as he remembered it, thought Henry, noting the familiar well-stocked bookshelves bulging with literary masterpieces dating from the Reformation to the early nineteenth century. A pervasive, musty, damp smell issued from these volumes, used by Parson Bray for writing pamphlets and Sunday sermons. The comfortable leather chairs were more worn than before. Henry could not recollect there being so many papers strewn over the desk, which still held a familiar glass inkwell in the shape of a round Saxon church, brainchild of early East Anglian glassblowers. Beside it rested a quilled feather pen and a much-used snuff box. But as the parson rose to greet his visitor, Henry couldn't help noticing that instead of a draft for a sermon, or a list of the lessons to be read and hymns to be sung, there was a recent copy of the London Chronicle.

"I have been reading an article about the poor negro slaves working in dreadful conditions in the sugar plantations, Henry, and I pray that this evil will soon be abolished. Read this old account dated Monday, May 1st, 1788. Bray pointed to the second page with the heading:

To be sold at public auction, if not previously disposed of at private sale-from forty to fifty valuable slaves and families, mostly born in Carolina and Florida and unexceptionable property.

"Were you aware Henry that even Thomas Jefferson, third president of United States, kept slaves on his Virginia plantation and gave some of them to his daughter, Martha, as a wedding gift?"

The article also reports:

Just arrived in the brigantine Favourite, Captain Lane from Barbados brings a consignment of seventy-two Windward coast negroes. They are in high health, consisting of prime slaves, men, boys, women, and girls, who will be sold on said vessel Nassau, Bahamas, May 1st, 1789.

"I heartily agree with your opinion," replied Henry, "and predict the day will come when all men will be free, and not chained in bondage. I did see a slave ship sailing to the West Indies when I was returning home on the Bellerphon."

The kind-hearted rector removed his spectacles. "But I do get carried away so by the subject, Henry. Do forgive an old man his ranting. Welcome home, my dear boy. You have changed quite a lot since I last saw you and I'm sure you have many tales to tell about your military service. I trust that everything at the Hall is to your liking. If I can be of any assistance, you have only to ask. I can see by the expression on your face there is something on your mind, perhaps more serious than I can guess. I pride myself on my ability to read men's minds after all these many years of devotion to the church. You have my solemn promise Henry. I will respect any confidence you care to place in me. Have you fallen in love, my son?" Seeing Henry's startled look, Bray paused. "My humble apologies. I must not intrude in your affairs. As you can see from these newspapers, my feelings and thoughts have been much engaged in prayer for the deliverance of poor wretched souls from captivity and ill usage, unless the merciful Creator takes them to his bosom first."

"I have come to seek your advice," said Henry, as Bray gestured him to the same deep armchair he had often sat in as a boy. Then, his legs had not been long enough to reach the floor, so Henry swung his legs to and fro muttering to himself until a rebuke from Lady Arabella caused him to stop. "Children must be seen, but not heard, Henry. And don't fidget so!"

"There is some concern regarding my future, both on my part and I'm sure on Matthew's too. I must consider how long I should remain at the Hall before I apply to one of the professions."

"Quite right, my boy. You have to make the transition from military to civilian life. I can sympathise with your dilemma. You are caught between two footstools. Could I suggest you enter the Church? This is the first solution that comes to mind. I will be retiring shortly with the bishop's approval. Emma and I have set our hearts on a little place on the Norfolk coast at Sheringham, there to dwell pleasantly among the many clergy that favour the county for their retirement. This living would become vacant. However the major drawback to this proposal is that the living is at the sole discretion of the local squire—in this case, the squire of Albatross Hall. As he is your brother, there might be conflict of interest and disagreement. Although I recognize that Matthew pays little attention to church affairs, problems could arise between you. Have you considered the law or standing for member of Parliament as your brother-in-law did? I hear Edward is introducing bills to bring in overdue reforms which the Tories oppose. Change will be forced on them if, like the proverbial ostrich, they bury their heads in the sand. No man can stop the march of progress. Of course, you would need to find a wealthy person to sponsor you. Most of the pocket boroughs are in the hands of titled people who have certain landholdings which enable them to influence those eligible to vote. It is shameful that Catholics are still barred from exercising their right to elect a member in Parliament. I am aware of a strong movement to remedy the situation."

Bray rang the bell hanging at the side of the fireplace. Bess reappeared bearing a tray of cakes and tea. The refreshments provided a welcome pause in the conversation. "Have you given any thought to leaving England and setting yourself up in the farming way, say in Canada? It would serve two purposes. The first is that you would gain some measure of independence, using your estate income to 'seed' your venture and secondly, you would be far removed from the object of your desire."

"Why sir, you have the gift of reading my innermost thoughts," said Henry, greatly astonished. "How came you to such a conclusion so soon?"

The rector chuckled. "I saw you looking at Lady Charlotte in church with deep affection last Sunday. And begging your pardon, I couldn't help overhearing your conversation as you both waited for Tapper to bring the carriage round to the lych gate. I believe that her ladyship likes you very much, but bear in mind you are related through marriage. Remember she is the mother of the heir to Albatross Hall. Matthew is frequently absent on what he calls 'business affairs.' Very mysterious, I must say, although I imply no criticism. The village gossips are already wagging their tongues. And so there is plenty of opportunity to spend more time than is advisable in Charlotte's company. This is in confidence, Henry. I know there are rumours spreading in the village about the squire's comings and goings. It is not for me to comment. In the meantime, you must follow the course which best suits you, Henry. Do call on me again when you care to, but heed my advice. The Devil lies in wait and lures the unwary with temptation … Remember the words of our Lord, 'Thou shalt not covet another man's wife …'"

"Nor his oxen, nor his ass," replied Henry, laughing in spite of himself.

"It is getting near lunchtime, and I have lectured you enough, my boy," said Bray as the two men shook hands. "By the way, I would very much like to meet Sir Walter Scott when he comes. Goodbye, Henry. Bess will show you out." The maid had a curious expression on her face, unnoticed by Henry, as she returned his hat. He was oblivious of the emotions he aroused in her. It was his striking resemblance to his brother. To this day, no one but Bess knew of her chance meeting with Matthew on her return from Rowan Grange and unfortunate tumble into the nettle patch. Neither did anyone except Bray know Henry's secret passion for Charlotte. It burned in his soul as he walked slowly through Saint Mary's cemetery, pausing to linger beside the tombstone of Lord and Lady Ponsonby. The inscription, "United in death as they were in life," had a profound effect. There was no doubt in Henry's mind that his parents remained faithful to each other, despite the Earl's frugal habits and obstinate ways. That he had fulfilled his role as the hospitable squire of Albatross Hall, there was no question—at least in the minds of guests partaking of excellent fare and good wine.

Henry took the path that led through the woodlands. He cut a sturdy hazel switch, aimlessly brushing the fallen leaves and beech nut husks from the path, which finished at the last turnstile before the road to the Hall. The road surface, Henry noted, was a major improvement from the former muddy cart track. It now boasted a wear-resistant surface, consisting of successive layers of small stones, compacted smooth by the wheels of numerous carriages, and was impervious to rain. This new road spoke to the genius of one John Macadam, a Scottish engineer. Matthew had signed a contract to surface all the roads around the estate in this manner, only specifying that gravel was to cover the drive heading up to the Hall. This was quite in keeping with the approaches to an historic Elizabethan mansion, thought Henry. He mounted the steps into the Great Hall and up the second flight leading to his bedchamber, unobserved by any member of the household. Shortly afterward, the dinner bell rang. Henry quickly dressed in a velvet jacket and green trousers. He cast a nostalgic eye at his regimentals still hanging in the large mahogany wardrobe. The military phase of his life was well and truly over.

"Yes, of course, we will invite Parson Bray to breakfast with Sir Walter, Henry," said Charlotte, passing him a plate of soup. Both Molly and Felicity had permission to take the day off and go into the village. Thus Charlotte was assisting Bentinck at the table. "I'm glad you mentioned it. Since Walter was trained as a lawyer, we should also invite Feathers. He has not been one of our company since Lady Arabella's death"

Mrs. Dobson did not take such a sanguine view of the extra guests, offended by the work necessary to ensure their comfort. She was aggravated by her discovery that Simon had been caught in the village, selling surplus vegetables for small change. It was hard to think Molly might have put Simon up to this deed, but she knew Simon was unreliable, not worthy to be Mr. Choke's assistant. On reflection, she thought that if the master paid better wages there would not be the temptation to steal.

"If only Tom were still here," she said to herself, shedding a few tears at the memory of her "poor boy," never to return. The kindly housekeeper vowed that one day she would visit Belgium and seek out Tom's final resting place.

Sir Walter Scott arrived punctually at nine o'clock on a wet June morning with his second daughter, Anne, immortalized by a portrait of her by Sir Henry Raeburn. Since early childhood, Scott suffered from lameness—a disability noted by young Cecil who whispered to his mother that Scott had a "funny leg and walked with a limp."

"But my young man, it did not prevent me from giving a good account of myself when the local boys made jokes and took to flying at me with open fists," said the poet as he leaned on Anne's arm, climbing the steps with difficulty into the Hall. "It would be remiss of me not to offer my sincere condolences to you all on the passing of Lady Arabella."

"You look quite splendid this morning, Walter," said Charlotte, complimenting her famous visitor on his cocked hat trimmed with lace, scarlet waistcoat, and white knee breeches.

Over the substantial meal of cold beef, hare pie, assorted cheeses—all washed down with endless cups of tea and tankards of ale—Sir Walter regaled the company with many fine stories and anecdotes. As was his usual custom, he wrote for three hours before breakfast. Since this was his principal meal of the day, he was well pleased by the bounteous spread. Lady Charlotte expressed her heartfelt praise for two of Scott's most famous works, "The Lay of the Last Minstrel" and Marmion, which held pride of place in the Albatross library.

"Pray tell me, Walter, how is your new home at Abbotsford progressing?" asked Charlotte.

"Perhaps you mean in the sense of my being able to find the necessary funds to pay the labourers? It is quite simple. The more I apply myself to writing, the more my publisher receives from the sale of my works. We have an agreement whereby he forwards advances from future novels to pay for the considerable expense of building on lands which originally belonged to the monks of Melrose Abbey. To be very frank, I own that in order to acquire such a handsome dwelling, there is constant drain on my purse. One of my associated publishing houses in London is on the verge of bankruptcy. So there is a need to work at my craft with great assiduity as new ideas and plots percolate in my brain. The two books you mentioned sold several thousand copies. As they are printed by hand, the proofs require minute scrutiny. You might be interested to know Henry, that as you have served in the Peninsula

Wars, I am studying the life of Bonaparte. I intend to write a book about him. Although I can't profess to being a military man, I did spend time serving as a volunteer in a Scottish regiment."

Here was a subject Henry could discuss with some degree of expertise. "Sir Walter, what was the name of your regiment?"

"It was a cavalry corps, the Royal Edinburgh Light Dragoons. I was refused as a candidate for active service, owing to my disability, but I could ride a horse well. Did you happen to know of a General John Burgoyne when you were away fighting in the American War of Independence, Henry? I once knew a fellow named Dalgetty who served under Burgoyne as an ensign."

"What an extraordinary coincidence," exclaimed Henry, much enthused. "He was my commander and a very able general too. Now, Sir Walter, if you wish to have any first-hand accounts of Napoleon's campaigns on the battlefield, I would be delighted to supply you with any relevant information to your purpose. A book about Napoleon would attract many buyers, and enhance your literary reputation."

Scott bowed politely and said he would be pleased to receive any material from Henry. Charlotte smiled at her brother-in-law and Sir Walter. "Do tell us more of your life at Abbotsford. You mentioned on the last occasion of our meeting that your writing desk is made of pieces of wood taken from some of the galleons of the Spanish Armada wrecked off the Irish coast, and that we both possess furnishings from the Borghese palace in Italy."

"I also have a clasp of bees from Napoleon's cloak. You told me that you have great difficulty, Charlotte, in finding domestics suited to your needs. I will tell you the story of how I acquired one of my servants. During my legal career—and this narrative will be of interest to you, Mr. Feathers—I defended a poor prisoner at Jedburgh, at a time, you understand, when my clients were mainly poachers and sheep stealers. I know that poaching is commonplace and the penalties high. Imagine my surprise when the presiding judge, instead of convicting my client, Tom Purdie, let him off with a warning. I took a liking to the rough and ready ways of Tom. I felt he was really an honest chap, and so I gave him a job as general help around Abbotsford."

"And no doubt he has remained loyal and faithful to you ever since as a mark of gratitude," said Feathers.

"Aye, that he has. There isn't any task either small or large that he would not do for me. Why, he even offered to forgo his wages when he got wind of my financial troubles! You are quite right, Mr. Feathers. Sometimes when you give a man a second chance, he is so thankful, especially if he has a wife and bairns to feed, that he won't go astray again."

"Some of my parishioners would do well to follow Purdie's example," said Parson Bray, taking a good pinch of snuff. "I regret to tell you that a few find themselves in the workhouse or the debtor's prison at Marshalsea. My good wife, Emma, tries her best to help, but as the good Lord says, you can't help those who won't help themselves. What I dislike above all, Sir Walter, is that the families of the insolvent father are forced to take up residence in the prison too, a place of misery and degradation."

"Well, it is not easy to keep oneself from going into debt," said Matthew. "I can barely afford the upkeep of this place, particularly if the harvest is bad again this year."

"Matthew, you know I was in Stratford recently. I read in an old book placed in the Shakespeare museum, the account of his poaching expedition here with a few lads from the grammar school."

"You will remember our walk through the Great Hall on your arrival, Walter, and the portrait of my Elizabethan ancestor, Sir Thomas Ponsonby. He was a magistrate and justice of the peace, appointed by her majesty, Queen Elizabeth I. In addition to his zeal in seeking out Catholic priests, obliged to go into hiding after the death of Queen Mary, he was very severe with poachers. When young Willie Shakespeare killed one of the deer in the park, Sir Thomas ordered a sound whipping. In revenge, Shakespeare had the audacity to place a notice on the gate, on which were written some bawdy verses, before he prudently retreated to London. You can read the references in his play, The Merry Wives of Windsor. Shakespeare makes fun of a coat Shallow (Sir Thomas) is wearing. Sir Thomas was proud of this old coat because it was embroidered with pike or 'luces,' referred to by the bard as 'louses.' Such a wicked wit!"

Everyone laughed at this story, and vowed to read the play. Scott rose and kissed Charlotte's hand. Charlotte offered to take Sir Walter and Anne into the library to show him the rare first edition of Shakespeare's plays. However Scott graciously declined.

"We have a fair distance to go before we reach the village of Somerby for the night. It is still raining. God bless you all. It is my earnest desire that you find a new path in life, Henry. It is a pleasure to meet you again, Charlotte, in your new home. I believe it was in Bath where we first met? I thank you and Matthew most sincerely for your warm welcome and this fine breakfast. Henry, since you have faced Bonaparte, I leave you with this thought. What would the future of Europe have been if he had followed his first idea of becoming a bookseller? He might have done wonders for my trade! With your kind indulgence, Lady Charlotte and all the assembled company, I will read you the opening stanza of the "Lay of the Last Minstrel" and sign a copy for you to keep:

> The way was long, the wind was cold;
> The minstrel was infirm and old,
> His withered cheek and tresses gray;
> Seemed to have known a better day,
> The harp, his sole remaining joy,
> Was carried by an orphan boy,
> The last of all the bards was he,
> Who sang of border chivalry.

Loud applause and fond farewells greeted Scott's recitation. Little did Charlotte know that when Scott departed Albatross Hall with his daughter, she would never see him again.

CHAPTER 29:
1820 - DEATH OF GEORGE III

The year 1820 marked the death of George III and the accession of George IV. "I do wish my ole man was still alive to see this procession of all them fine folks a followin' King George's coach. I niver thought I'd see the likes of this kind of day agin, at any rate not since the old King's funeral. All this pageantry a takin' place afore my very eyes, it fair dazzles me, it do. A pity that poor Jane Dean, God rest her soul, is not 'ere to see the guv pass by, a wavin' to all the crowds a millin' everywhere. What a crush, an' some foolish folk a gettin' too close to the 'orses 'ooves. Why it's even more difficult to keep a space on the pavement, than to git a decky chair on the beach at the seaside!" Our old friend, worthy Mrs. Fowey, addressed these observations from her well-guarded position to her companion, a middle-aged, rather coarse-looking man known to her as Quentin (but also by the alias Smokey to others less inclined to be awed by the coronation of a new monarch, despised by many an Englishman). This gentleman—tall, athletic and wiry, overdressed in a heavy greatcoat despite the mild weather—did not appear to pay much attention to Mrs. Fowey's remarks. His sharp, piercing brown eyes scanned the crowded streets in the vicinity of Westminster Abbey, watching, waiting, searching for certain individuals in whom he had a keen interest.

So intent on the business at hand was Quentin, keeping his brown woolen cap well pulled down over his eyes to avoid detection, that he barely noticed a fashionably attired gentleman pushing his way through the throngs past various Jewish pawnbrokers lining the streets. This high-born gentleman had recently sailed up the Thames by barge. His servant made vain attempts to keep up with his master, labouring under the weight of several large parcels, before depositing them on the counter of a shabby shop in need of repair. The proprietor of this popular establishment was a Mr. Cheatall. His doorbell tinkled. The pawnbroker rubbed his hands together at the inviting prospect of further lucrative dealings with his regular customer, none other than Matthew, Lord Ponsonby.

Meanwhile, Quentin continued his search, showing no sign of recognizing any particular person, even by the flicker of an eyelid. Mrs. Fowey gave his elbow a sharp nudge. "You didn't hear me a speakin' to yer, Quentin? I was a sayin' that the golden state coach is nigh abreast on us, bearin' the fat figure of George IV. Do you see 'im?" The words had scarcely passed Belinda Fowey's lips, when she started back in surprise, almost falling into Quentin's arms.

"Well, in all my born days, I 'ave niver seed urchins a peltin' the king's carrige wi' stones afore. Such troublemakers," gasped Mrs. Fowey, as a burly constable gave chase. But the lads were too nimble for him. "They're the ragamuffins who live by stealin' happles from horchards, knock o'er pails of milk and drownded all the stray cats. You knows, Quentin, I am but a poor widder woman and I can't abide stealin' at any price."

"I don't approve of the little rascals any more than you do, Mrs. Fowey. I would punish them severely, but like many of George's subjects, including myself, they don't intend to offer the new king either loyalty or respect. He doesn't signify much as a man, much less as a sovereign. Who in his right mind would exclude his wife, Caroline, from the crowning and refuse to acknowledge her as his rightful queen? The scandal of putting her on trial, accusing her of the same sins of misconduct and unfaithfulness (when dallying in Europe with an ill-assorted bunch of courtiers) as he himself is equally guilty of? He even introduced a bill in the House of Lords, petitioning them for a divorce from Caroline. This request did not make the members very popular with the general public, I can tell you. Many still sympathize with her royal highness and forgive her continental indiscretions." Quentin spat on the ground. "Just look at the king's immoral behaviour, Mrs. Fowey, and ask you'self if Georgy Porgie is fit to be a ruler. Remember how he scandalized his late father by associating with Maria Fitzherbert, and her a Catholic too … Perhaps the only time in his life when he stopped whoring and gambling for a short time was when his only daughter, the princess Charlotte, died in childbirth. He cuts such a gross figure, and I believe that his health can't be any the better for all his eating and drinking and gambling."

Kind-hearted Belinda Fowey shed a tear for a princess, too young to die at the age of twenty-one, born to ill-matched parents who fought over her future as a dog fights over a bone. "My old man lasted many more year than her. Quentin, I must be off soon a visitin' his grave, and mebbe Jane's too arter I've bin to Margate. I will pay for mi' oliday by a pickin' some 'ops in Kent on mi way back. Might bring you back a nice bag of happles too."

As the early morning sunshine gave way to clouds and rain, Quentin disappeared. He darted in front of the now empty Abbey, vanishing in the direction of Bird Cage Walk. "Not King's weather, it ain't," said Mrs. Fowey to no one in particular, joining other spectators, sheltering as best they could in doorways or spilling over the threshold of numerous public taverns.

"Mine host" was only too eager to take advantage of the inclement weather to engage his patrons in idle gossip, refreshing them with a steady supply of drinks, watered down if he was unscrupulous enough, or suggesting they partake of a weak broth, very nourishing, but at least two days old, and more suited to moisten pig swill. Such sly habits were degrading and without merit, but rarely was a complaint registered. A nod here and a wink there; a toast to the new king's health or his speedy demise, depending upon one's point of view. Which was the more popular sentiment of the two, it was hard to say. Did the nation have cause to rejoice? According to the garrulous landlord at the Cog and Wheel, "the bunting and flags is all sodden through. So is King George and so will be my regular customers if the rain keeps up another hour." It teemed down in torrents. The gutters overflowed with remnants of horse manure and other foul-smelling refuse; the drains were full to capacity.

Still the merrymaking went on. So did the elusive Quentin, a spy driven by ambition and past success in rooting out and apprehending radicals in the final days of the old king's reign. George III, increasingly frail, blind, and deaf, died in 1820, a milestone in Quentin's remarkable career, also notorious for the infamous Cato Street conspiracy. Everyone had marveled at the late king's stoicism as he submitted to agonizing treatments for a condition not fully understood by his learned doctors, who prescribed a barbaric combination of restraints and leeches and cruel separation from his beloved Queen. Turmoil at the palace and turmoil in the country, oppressed by legislation which decreed harsh punishments for relatively minor offenses. One statute forbade assembly of more than fifty persons!

Lord Liverpool's government feared that such a meeting would produce agitators such as one Arthur Thistlewood, the most dangerous of a gang of desperate men, bent on reform and resistance to authorities by force, if necessary. Thistlewood was, on Quentin's list, likely to pose a formidable threat to the security of public buildings which, according to his carefully written notes, included the Bank of England on Threadneedle Street, military barracks, and the Tower of London. The Chronicle printed an announcement of special interest to Quentin, acting in the capacity of paid government informer.

"From the Calendar of our correspondent: A cabinet dinner will be held on Wednesday the twenty third day of February at the residence of Lord Harrowby in Grosvenor Square. All the leading members of Lord Liverpool's government are expected to be present." This information gave Quentin a rare opportunity to put his considerable skills to work on a disguise by which he intended to infiltrate the group of conspirators. Thus "Smokey" was born, attired in typical working man's clothes, comprising shabby corduroy trousers, sturdy leather lace-up boots, jacket with baccy stains, missing a few buttons, faded yellow shirt, and a black cap, much larger than its predecessor. A pair of old spectacles and pocket watch, suspended on a gold chain, completed Smokey's new outfit. Surveying himself in the mirror of his lodging house bedroom, he felt supremely confident that he could so ingratiate himself with the leaders and thus be in a position to learn their secret plans. When the time was ripe, Smokey would alert the local constables at Bow Street. He had reason to suspect a plot to assassinate the cabinet as they sat at dinner, given the widespread publicity (courtesy of the London Chronicle) and his powers of deduction.

Perhaps Smokey had Guy Fawkes and his aborted attempt to blow up the Houses of Parliament in the reign of King James I in mind when he agreed to such a risky enterprise. The same newspaper reported the following day:

"This plot was quite clever. One of the conspirators was chosen to deliver a parcel to the Earl of Harrowby's home. Upon the door being opened by one of the servants, the rest of the gang were to rush into the hall, kill everybody, not sparing the butler, then speedily mount the staircase to the dining room. All the cabinet were to suffer the same fate as the unfortunates 'below' stairs." Furthermore the report stated that hand grenades were lobbed into many of the mansion's rooms, causing confusion and panic. The heads of my lords Castlereagh and Sidmouth were to be stuffed into a sack, presumably for the entertainment of the public at some later date, to be mounted on pikes attached to Tower Bridge. Then, with no other possibility than a successful outcome, the conspirators were to form a revolutionary government with thirty patriotic souls.

These traitorous deeds might have been accomplished, but for the timely information released to the militia and constables by Smokey. He gave them the address of a property on Elm Street—a shabby, disused hayloft not far from the Edgeware Road, where the criminals were holding a meeting—of more than passing interest to the Bow Street Patrol. The loft was accessible by a single ladder, which would be withdrawn at the least hint of danger reported by the posted lookout. Unfortunately, Binkie had enjoyed too many libations at midday; he was sound asleep by an open window. The patrol ascended the ladder and discovered Dr. James Watson, his son, Thomas Preston, John Hooper, and others arming themselves for battle with knives, swords, and grenades. Evidence of an act of high treason lay on the bench for all to see.

"Quite an impressive stock of ammunition, don't you think?" said one of the officers as he picked up a number of cutlasses. Another Bow Street constable removed six swords and some fully loaded pistols. During this moment of discovery, Thistlewood signaled one of the plotters to extinguish the lanterns. In fading light, he plunged his drawn sword into the breast of officer Ruthven, a well-respected member of the force and father of two. He died instantly. The plotters took full advantage of the situation. Many, including Thistlewood, escaped. But their freedom was short lived. Arrests and capture by the Bow Street Patrol occurred a few hours later. At a trial, presided over by a stern, incredulous judge, it was stated that the gang had also raided the shop of a Mr. Beckwith, a gun maker at Clerkenwell. They had taken as many arms as they could carry, accompanied by an increasingly unruly mob intent on taking possession of the Tower of London. Gasps of amazement were heard through the packed courtroom, when Graves, counsel for the prosecution, confirmed they had offered the soldiers guarding the tower one hundred guineas each if they would leave their posts and join the "reformers." Further, it was stated by the learned lawyer that they regrouped, then marched down the Strand, looting more shops for goods deemed necessary to their cause, "… in which, my Lord Beagle, they fervently believed. Our chief witness for the prosecution, Smokey, whom you see before you, will testify how he felt himself, carried along by the mob as if on a tidal wave of humanity. At this time, My Lord, he wore the ill-fitting clothes favoured by the conspirators and bore a rifle with such ease, that prisoner Thistlewood signaled him to lead the way into an obscure side street, known as Fetter Lane. Once inside a tavern known as the Black Dog, of ahem, ill repute …"

"You mean a house of whores," interrupted Judge Beagle, gazing at the prisoners with such severity that Hooper turned away, terrified at the sight of the forbidding figure in black robes and white periwig.

"Exactly so, My Lord," continued the counsel for the prosecution. "You put it very well."

"Go on, Mr. Graves, what happened next?"

"It appears, My Lord, that the plotters made a unanimous decision to flee to Northampton. At this critical moment, our brave man, Smokey, showing great heroism, slipped away unnoticed through the back door of the tavern to join our chaps in the next street. According to plan, they waited at Highgate to arrest the men. I suggest on behalf of the Crown, My Lord, that there is only one possible sentence for these wretched prisoners standing before you today. They are guilty of the most vile act of treason."

"Thank you, Mr. Graves. You may resume your seat. Is anyone prepared to speak on behalf of the accused?" The court fell silent. "I agree with you, my learned counsel, that this is an open and shut case."

Judge Beagle leaned over to confer with the court clerk. All in the court were commanded to rise as Beagle rose majestically to his feet and placed a black cap on his wig.

"Have you anything to say before I pronounce sentence?" The prisoners at the bar did not utter a word, but stared blankly at the judge—with the exception of Thistlewood, who remained defiant, tapping his fingers impatiently on the wooden ledge of the dock as if to say, "Let's get it over with. We are as good as dead anyway."

"Then it is my solemn duty to sentence the ringleaders among you to death by hanging, namely Mr. Arthur Thistlewood, Dr. Watson, Thomas Preston, and John Hooper. May God have mercy on your souls. The rest will be detained in the Tower at His Majesty's pleasure. Constables, I charge you with the safe conduct of these foolish, misguided men to await execution one week from today. I order the courtroom cleared."

The hero of the day, Jonas Quentin, shed his alias and resumed his former identity, remaining incognito until the government deemed sufficient time had elapsed after the trial to give him a substantial reward. This Mrs. Fowey acknowledged a few months later, when both she and Quentin took up occupancy of a little cottage in a remote part of the Welsh hills: "Jonas, you was a good man to help the p'lice and sichlike and you must promise me that we will niver part agin. I thought I wouldn't niver find you agin in the crowds a gawkin' round the Abbey. I looks high and low fer you, but you wos nowheres to be seed." Quentin gave the new Mrs. Jonas Quentin a tight squeeze. Together they looked forward to a quiet retirement at "Rose Cottage," at a secret location.

CHAPTER 30:
LORD PONSONBY VISITS
THE PAWNBROKER, CHEATALL

Would it be possible for Matthew to keep his mysterious journey-ings to London a secret too? Not a few of the early risers in the village questioned why the squire had such urgent business that he needed to gallop through at such high speed in the Ponsonby coach on his way to the capital. Even Tapper grumbled privately that he was becoming wearied of the regular visits to Mr. Cheatall. He considered the pawnbroker to be greedy and unscrupulous, ready to take advantage of his gullible master by driving a very hard bargain. Since he was sworn to strict secrecy, he could not confide in Mrs. Dobson.

Only Tapper knew the squire was either selling or pawning some of the Albatross heirlooms; he imagined it was to defray his expenses on the estate and give Henry what portion of his inheritance his straightened circum-stances would allow. In reality, it was to pay off creditors for mounting debts incurred at the gaming tables. Parcels of various shapes and sizes, all care-fully wrapped in sacking, were transported to London by coach and barge and into the hands of eager dealers. Cheatall occupied premises larger than most, employing several clerks in the upper rooms of an old dilapidated brick house. It was their job to maintain exact accounts for each customer doing business with the firm. Day after day, they sat perched on high stools, quill pen in hand, scratching away as if their very lives depended on giving satisfaction to an employer known for his astute transactions in a very lucrative trade. Benjamin Cheatall was a shrewd judge of character. Lord Ponsonby was easy prey, just another delinquent English noble, a poor example of his class of society, who neither knew nor cared about the needy. In aligning himself with the worthless Mr. Cheatall, Matthew gave no consideration to his family or the future of Albatross Hall.

Matthew was quite ignorant of those individuals on the floor above the shop who laboured so diligently in an unheated room, wearing half mittens to protect cold fingers, presenting themselves at seven in the morning for work from which they could not seek release until the evening street lamps, now converted to gas, were lighted. They were bound to a master who provided only the most meager nourishment to sustain them throughout the day. The alternative, so he never failed to remind them, would be the workhouse.

On his return to the Hall, usually in the early evening, invariably in low spirits and without a great deal of ready cash to show for his efforts, Matthew desired that no supper be saved for him. Could it be that the empty liquor bottles lying in the coach left him with little appetite?

"I really don't know what the master is a comin' too," remarked Mrs. Dobson, as Bentinck returned to the kitchen with a tray of untouched food. "I niver knew the squire not to eat my hare pie afore. He'll waste away and get poorly. Try and see if you can get him to sip some of my chicken broth, Bentinck."

But all that Matthew would accept was a glass of whiskey, a drink consumed infrequently in the Albatross household since the demise of Aunt Cassandra. Taking it in his hand, Matthew went in search of his wife in the music room. Charlotte was playing the pianoforte, and singing a few verses of her favourite sonnet in such a plaintive voice that Matthew paused to listen behind the door before entering. Unsuspecting, he was quite flattered to hear the following words:

How can I leave thee!
How can I from thee part!
Thou only hast my heart, dear one believe.

Thou hast this soul of mine, so closely bound with thine,
No other can I love, save thee alone.

It did not occur to Matthew that his wife's affections were no longer his
to command.

Lady Charlotte informed her husband that "since Cecil is away at school
and Lady Cynthia absent from Wingate Farm, attending to her sick mother
in Devon who is not expected to live, I must confess that after Sir Walter
and his daughter departed for Abbotsford, this place has become dull. Apart
from my needlepoint, music, and books—which seem to be disappearing
from the library at an increasing rate—I can only ride out in the park when
the weather is fine or receive a few visitors. They express surprise that you,
the lord of the manor, are not here to entertain them. I hear the servants
whispering about your frequent absences. Unlike their old master, the late
Lord Cecil, you take no interest in their families, being much too preoccupied with your own affairs. We have a pleasant young girl called Matilda
now in our service. I don't suppose you have met her, but she came highly
recommended by Mrs. Dobson."

Matthew fidgeted and moved to the chair closest to his wife, looking
contrite. "My dearest love, my own sweet wife, it grieves me to find that
you are in any way discontented with life here. I will give Mrs. Dobson and
Choke instructions to prepare a special dinner in honour of your birthday
next week. You can sit at your writing desk and issue invitations to all our
acquaintance, not forgetting old Sir Harry if he is still alive, and others of
your choice. Forgive me. I thought you were happy. May I suggest that you
go and visit other local residents, especially Cynthia when she returns. It will
be too late to invite Henry, as he sails for Canada on Monday—I wish you
to arrange to have a parcel addressed to him delivered to Liverpool before
the Isadora departs." Matthew finished his whiskey, unaware of Charlotte's
deep blush and visible agitation at the mention of Henry's name, concluding
that an intimate dinner party would be all that was necessary to improve his
wife's humour.

Charlotte found solace in Henry's company. With sadness in her aching
heart, she helped him with arrangements for his new life overseas. He planned
a second visit to Parson Bray, who was with Miss Gaunt when Bess ushered

him into the rector's study. "My dear boy, what brings you here on this fine, sunny morning?" said Bray, greeting Henry with warm affection. "Is there anything I can do for you?" Before Henry could reply, Miss Gaunt observed that not much could be done for poor Mrs. Grogg. She had just been buried in St. Mary's cemetery. Billy, being now an orphan, yet a grown man, would need both prayer and support.

"No one in the wide world to care for him. He is a good worker, a very agreeable fellow, full of energy and a desire to please," continued Miss Gaunt.

"I apologize for the intrusion. I came to see you without an appointment, sir. I am truly sorry about Mrs. Grogg. If I am interrupting any business concerning her funeral, I will take my leave."

"Not a bit of it my boy. You are welcome to stay. Mrs. Grogg was one of my oldest parishioners, and had been in a bad way for months, suffering with gout and a weak heart. It was a blessing that God saw fit to call her home. Now Henry, I can see there is something on your mind."

"I came to let you know that I have decided to take your advice and will go to Canada to farm. My time here is short. The captain of the cargo ship Isadora is sailing soon. He has accepted me as one of the passengers, on the condition that I work part of my passage as a deck hand. He made this concession when he learned that I had sailed on the Bellerphon and knew something of a seaman's way of life. You were quite right. It would be improper for me to stay longer at Albatross Hall. Both Charlotte and I admit to strong feelings for each other, deeper than is desirable between two close relatives. Although I know little of the land—or the country, for that matter—having spent my life as a soldier in His Majesty's service on the battlefield close to Boston and in the Peninsula Wars, I will try to make the best of it. When I am settled, I promise to write to you." Henry saw that Miss Gaunt wished to speak again. He offered his hand to Bray before turning to the door.

"Now don't you go getting in touch with those heathen Indians, Master Henry. But if they should cross your path, I have a package of biblical tracts you can carry with you. If the opportunity arises, you can use them to preach the gospel and so bring them to a knowledge and love of Christ."

Parson Bray marveled at Gertrude Gaunt's words. She was a master at exploiting any given situation. "Wait a bit, Gertrude. You forget that Henry has been in North America before. I'm sure he will have no trouble in establishing friendly relations with the natives. I understand from my readings that they do observe some form of spirituality and talk about a 'great being' that watches over them. They hunt, fish, and make the most wonderful canoes out of birch bark in which they navigate vast rivers. They set trap lines for fur-bearing animals such as the beaver. I possess a beautiful beaver hat which Emma gave to me as a Christmas present. Now all my congregation want one too! The hat is very becoming, and moreover very practical."

"That may be so, my friend, but I have heard from my missionary sources what the savages have done in the past to some Jesuit priests who were martyred while delivering the good news. I am horrified that white settlers have been scalped in defense of their homesteads. The savages burn them to the ground before whooping and hollering back to their settlements in triumph," said Miss Gaunt, looking at Henry with misgiving.

"Please do not trouble yourself on my account. I have no fear that I will be sacrificed as part of an Indian ceremony," laughed Henry. "I intend to settle in a place called Pakenham in Ontario, reported to be a small village on the banks of the Mississippi river. Apparently, the grist and sawmills were built by early Scottish emigrants, who have made an admirable job of clearing the untamed land. They acquired large tracts of forest. The trees served them well for log cabins and fenced pastures for cattle and sheep. If you have any further advice to give me, sir, I would be happy to listen. Otherwise, as my time is growing short, I must bid you good day."

"Just one last word, Henry. If you do find any hostile Indians, and they capture you, try to escape and go to live with the Hutterites. They are a God-fearing people, very thrifty and hard working."

Henry retrieved his hat from Bess, who gave him a little curtsy as he walked through the rectory door, almost invisible with creeping ivy trailing down it and across the stone porch. He had a strong premonition he would see neither the parson nor Miss Gaunt again. But who can foresee the future? His chief worry was his imminent departure from Charlotte. He would miss conversations with Billy Grogg and Mrs. Dobson's delicious fare. Miss Gaunt looked after him, making his way slowly down the rectory path.

"There goes a young man with a troubled mind. What a pity he has fallen in love with his brother's wife. I refrain from using the word, 'covet,' Parson, but no doubt he will find a suitable young lady when he arrives in Canada.

I only hope he is spared the perils of the deep as well as the temptations on the other side of the Atlantic. 'Sufficient unto the day is the evil thereof.' May God grant Henry a safe journey and a prosperous life."

"Amen to that, Gertrude. I see Emma coming through the cemetery gate, just in time for tea."

Meanwhile, Matthew's sojourn in London bore good results. Several paintings exchanged hands. One notable piece of art was a portrait of an ancestor. His distinguished naval career during the reign of Queen Anne rivaled that of his contemporary, John Churchill, first Duke of Marlborough and confidante of James II. The Gainsborough painting of Admiral William Ponsonby now rested forlornly against the wall of Cheatall's shop. A stuffed Central American parrot lay in front, obscuring the admiral's handsome buckled shoes. The rest of his imposing figure was dressed in a long-buttoned silk jacket, dark blue cloth coat with gold braided sleeves, and a tricorn hat befitting his rank perched at a jaunty angle on his grey powdered wig. His left hand held a long brass telescope. The other rested on his coat pocket while contemplating the sea. His rugged face expressed contentment—a man pleased with his recent naval victory and the reward of an elegant country home, The Briars in Hampshire; a gift of her most gracious majesty Queen Anne, and a grateful nation.

Back at the Hall, Matthew had no satisfactory explanation to offer his wife concerning the removal of the two Chinese pagodas. They had been purchased at a reputable London auction house, and now returned to a sleazy pawnbroker's shop! Charlotte's timely ramble through the portrait gallery alerted her to a large empty space, where a frame had hung on the faded silk wallpaper. This was the very spot where Admiral William Ponsonby's portrait had hung, a tribute not only to the fame of an illustrious forebear, but to the celebrated artist Gainsborough, darling of the English nobility. Charlotte was very distressed at this confirmation of her suspicions.

"Matthew, you are parting with our son's rightful inheritance. Did you realize the value of the Meissen vase which no longer graces the hall table? Can it be that you have designs on the priceless collection of ancient medieval leather-bound volumes in the library?" Charlotte had strong reasons to question her husband. He had, without discussion, disposed of her own considerable fortune. Moreover, his generosity to her had ceased shortly after the birth of Cecil.

In the early years of marriage, Matthew had played the part of an ideal husband. After Henry's return, everything changed. The atmosphere was strained. Matthew, always tired and short tempered, was rapidly losing interest in the day-to-day affairs of running the Hall and estate. Charlotte found herself thinking constantly of her feelings for Henry, but the date of his departure was at hand. No time for regrets or what might have been.

A crisis arose late one evening when Matthew returned home, the worse for excessive drinking. He was put to bed at once by Bentinck, obliged to support his master as he staggered up the stairs to his room, muttering incoherently about a diabolical, evil individual. At breakfast the next morning, Matthew was banished from his wife's presence after a stern lecture. His erratic behaviour and theft of Albatross treasures must cease at once. More attention must be paid to her needs and their social life. The proposed birthday party no longer interested her. Neglect of the estate should end. Charlotte knew Brook was doing his best to attend to the livestock and tenant farms with Billy Grogg's help, but the master was frequently absent. "As for Cecil, he writes every week for funds to spend in the Winchester school tuck shop and expresses sadness that we do not visit him. I have said before, Matthew, remember you are only custodian of Albatross until the day of your death. Mr. Feathers has paid me a visit and reminds us that according to the provisions of your father's will, the house and all its contents are to be passed intact to your heir. I entreat you to acquire funds by honest diligence, working to improve the lot of the estate workers to raise their income, and, in turn, yours. Bad harvests do not occur every year! We can do without costly dinners and lavish entertainments, even for my birthday dinner celebration. I'm sure Mrs. D. won't grumble as much if the meal is cancelled."

"My dear, I did hope you would understand my difficulties as a truly loyal wife. I have given Henry a portion of the income to which he was entitled to assist him in his new venture. The measures I have taken, so reprehensible to you, are calculated to sustain the estate and pay off the servants."

"Can you promise me that the monies obtained by sale of certain heirlooms are not used to gamble and drink? What can you tell me about your condition last night? What assurances can you give me that you are not associating with characters of ill repute?" Charlotte's scorn and anger were heard by Felicity, eavesdropping behind the door. She feared her angry mistress capable of doing violence. But Charlotte hid her face in her handkerchief and fled sobbing from the room.

"Why my lady, whatever is the matter? Are you feeling unwell?" inquired Felicity, entering her mistress's boudoir in response to the clanging of Charlotte's bell on the kitchen wall. Charlotte gave no reply. She lay on the floor in a deep faint. It was some time before her maid could revive her with smelling salts and help her to a comfortable couch. There she remained for the rest of the day, refusing Matthew permission to enter. Dr. Palliser was sent for. He prescribed complete rest, no unwanted visitors, and diagnosed a weak heart aggravated by nervous exhaustion. The housekeeper would oblige him by sending up nourishing hot broths and a small glass of Mrs Hatchett's old recipe, sure to revive Charlotte's flagging spirits, even if it had done nothing for the late Earl. As his patient improved, Mrs. D. was to provide her favourite dish of lake trout. Palliser believed that fish was ideal food and would fortify the brain of anyone wise enough to eat it. Matthew, on the good doctor's orders, was forbidden to see his wife for several days. Palliser had heard rumours of village gossip. If true, they put the master of Albatross in a very poor light.

A reliable confirmation came from Parson Bray, not prone to spread tales as Palliser well knew. It was quite apparent that Lady Ponsonby was pining for Henry. He was certain that she no longer loved her husband.

CHAPTER 31:
MATTHEW RETURNS TO BATH

Life—including the relationship between Lord and Lady Ponsonby at Albatross Hall—was never to revert to its earlier pattern of parties, evening entertainments, and picnics in the park. Intimacy, ease of purpose, domestic bliss, were never to be regained. Charlotte no longer had confidence in her husband. Recovery was slow and it was not surprising that she refused to drink Mrs. Hatchett's special concoction which Mrs. Dobson assured her would "buck up Your Ladyship and help you enjoy life as you used to, ma'am." For hours on end, Charlotte lay on a sofa by the window, admiring the splendid view of the pastoral countryside, though Henry was constantly in her thoughts. She pictured him on his journey, tossing on the heaving seas, suffering from illness caused by lack of cleanliness or virulent disease. That infections could spread with extreme rapidity on sailing vessels was well known. Many a ship was labelled a "floating coffin," carrying dead men, women, and children, whose solitary grave would be in Neptune's bosom or washed ashore into some obscure cove, ravaged by the surging foam.

As days lapsed into weeks, Charlotte was concerned Henry might have been shipwrecked. Or the Isadora boarded by privateers searching for booty among the cowering passengers, especially those with iron-bound chests, well-locked and secured with stout rope. They would be an inviting target for a ruthless bunch of worthless brigands who did not fear death, swinging at the end of a yardarm. Such brigands would come aboard so well-armed with cutlasses and pistols that the captain would readily agree to their demands. In fact his position would be made redundant by the mere obligation to "walk the plank."

Felicity was a comfort to her mistress during the times when Charlotte was low in spirits. Under instructions from Dr. Palliser, she tried to persuade the patient to resume her social activities. Charlotte firmly declined any such suggestions. "It would be pointless to converse with the guests when I do not feel cheerful in their company. They talk of mundane matters. When is the cow belonging to Violet Gresham to give birth, or the tenant's pigs to be slaughtered? Then Horace Travers speaks of the hunting season and how the fox population must be exterminated. I become exceedingly bored and would rather be left to myself. Please ring the bell for Mrs. Dobson, Felicity, and leave me now."

Charlotte lay back on her cushions as the housekeeper entered her boudoir, prepared to discuss her mistress's weekly list of housekeeping supplies, from which Charlotte had crossed off any item considered extravagant. The housekeeper expressed surprise when her mistress advised that Bentinck was not to be sent to London for the ingredients required for Christmas cake and puddings for the time being, even though September was fast approaching. "We must wait and see how plentiful the harvests are and if there is a market for our corn and barley which will provide sufficient monies for the purchase of a fat goose and some warm clothing for the servants. I am relying on our new gamekeeper to organize a pheasant shoot so you can restock the larder. Before you return to the kitchen, Mrs. Dobson, there is another matter on my mind. I saw Matilda scurrying down the back staircase yesterday. She bears a remarkable resemblance to you. I called her name, but she did not come. Is she shy? Pray tell me what you know about her and how she came to be here?"

"Well to tell you the truth, ma'am, I might as well be honest. Matilda is my daughter, born, I am sorry to say, out of wedlock. One of my former masters took advantage of me when I was a young servant girl. With your Ladyship's kind permission, I have put her to work in the dairy where I understand Hetty used to be employed. She seems to like making butter and is good at bringing me milk. She lifts the heavy jugs of ale which I can no longer carry from the brewery. I must tell you, mi'lady, that she is most obedient to my wishes. I beg your kind indulgence, but she has no other home since my sister Jessie passed away a few months ago. I sent Matilda to be taken care of by Jessie as I knew tongues would wag if I did not send her away from the village."

"You were quite right to take the steps you did, Mrs. Dobson. If Matilda proves to be as useful as you say she is, I welcome her into the household and will send for a new uniform and pay her a small wage. It is understood between us that I will not reveal to Lord Ponsonby her true identity."

"Thank you so much, ma'am. I am deeply indebted to your Ladyship and promise that I will supervise my daughter and love her as a mother should." The housekeeper paused as she turned to open the door. "Begging your Ladyship's pardon for taking such a liberty, but will the master be home later tonight?" Charlotte did not reply. Mrs. Dobson retired to her domain, shaking her head.

"You know Bentinck, all is not well between master and missus. Who knows where it will end up? Then what will 'appen to you and me?"

Parson Bray visited Bramble Cottage that same day, listening to Miss Gaunt's rambling account of her brother's penchant for cluttering the tiny dwelling to the point where an empty seat was hardly to be found. Most of the chairs held an assorted jumble of odds and ends which Charles termed "collectible" items. He developed an annoying habit of misplacing items such as keys, spare change, and eyeglasses, only to find them hours later lying hidden beneath fragments of pottery on the kitchen shelf or a flowerpot in the tool shed. Much to his sister's despair, Charles's peculiar habits caused problems when she had to pay the baker or milkman. The latter tradesman would sometimes pass Bramble Cottage without stopping to pour milk into her pail, knowing that payment was unlikely soon. He could not go to the trouble of writing overdue accounts in a ledger since he was illiterate, having never attended St. Mary's village school. "It bothers me so," said Miss Gaunt, as Bray removed some newspaper clippings from a chair, assisting her in a fruitless search for the only piece of gold jewellery in the form of a cross and chain which she possessed. "You would think a magpie lived here instead of a human being."

"Eh, eh, what's that?" interjected Charles, cupping a hand over his ear. "There ain't no magpies in here. I can't see any. Just one came near my spade afore the parson arrived as I was digging for some ancient fossils."

"I'm surprised there are any more relics for you to find, Charles," replied Bray.

"Parson Bray, my brother's odd hobby has reached the ears of the editor of the local Daily Gleaner. It reported in some detail on Charles Ponsonby's latest excavations. They opined he must be an eccentric old man, continuing to look for specimens just as he had at Mulberry Court. However they concluded that he really was harmless, not a danger to himself or anyone else and this 'hobby' is filling his days which, like all of us, are numbered anyway!"

"As in the biblical prophecy of three score years and ten," replied Bray, taking off his spectacles and placing the cuttings back on a nearby table, which showed signs of a recent meal. A soiled napkin, covered with food stains, overhung a chairback nearby. Miss Gaunt determined that since she could not keep Charles spotless, she would replace his linen once each week.

"What I am really frightened about is that Charles will lose something of importance and we won't be able to find it—be it in the garden, in the shed or in here."

"Do you remember the story of the widow's mite, Gertrude? Seek and ye shall find. Do not worry about your brother. Apart from some loss of memory, I don't see he is in need of special care at present. I can always ask Dr. Palliser to look in on him if you desire. I must get back to the rectory now. The headstone for Mrs. Grogg arrives this afternoon and I want to make sure that the stonemason places it securely in the ground. As you know, there are many old ancient headstones in the cemetery, most covered with lichen and weathered so the names of the deceased are illegible. After several centuries they develop a precarious lean, a danger to passersby if they should fall down, especially along the path leading to the church. Good day to you, and may the Lord be with you."

"Amen," said Gertrude as she closed the door quietly, leaving Charles to doze in his chair. It would not be long before she followed the parson, ostensibly to look for a grave site for her brother's future needs, but really to linger near her favourite headstones, each carved with stone figures of the

Grim Reaper. Not far away at the top of the path, lay an early martyr of the Christian church, Thomas Tyndale.

Billy Grogg was in attendance at his mother's newly dug grave when the parson returned. It had a beautiful aspect, facing toward the lych gate. For most of the day it would be bathed in sunlight. Billy mourned her death as the nation mourned the untimely death of uncrowned Queen Caroline, also in the year of 1821. It was universally felt that the queen had been unfairly treated. Charlotte moped inconsolably in her room, recognizing a similarity between herself and Caroline. Both had produced one child. Both had spouses addicted to gambling. However there was one essential difference between George IV and the squire of Albatross. The king could draw on the vast wealth of the crown, and remain solvent, despite substantial losses at the gambling tables. Matthew, on the other hand, was ensnared in a vicious cycle of wins and losses, mostly the latter. Creditors were constantly driving at his heels, demanding that he repay loans by a certain date or face unpleasant consequences.

"To put it in plainest terms, mi'lord, you will be obleeged to sell or pawn yet more of the contents of that fine ancestral home of yourn. It is not that many miles away from London, that we won't be able to reach you. By fair means or foul, we can use remedies which might deprive you of your liberty. Our friends, the constables, will escort you to Marshalsea debtor's prison, an old institution for sure. There you will be obleeged to stay, watched over by a stern beadle. It will be hard to avoid the opium sellers. They swarm outside the walls of Marshalsea. If you fall to the pavement in a stupor from the evil effects of this powerful narcotic, thieves will take advantage of your senseless condition to relieve you of anything of value they might find on your body, including your clothes. But look on the bright side, mi'lord. You could be spared all this trouble, inconvenience and ultimate disgrace if you repay us in full a week from today. We can't say fairer than that now can we, sir?"

Mr. Cheatall, Mr. Crickshaw and his amiable partner, Josiah Finch, walked away from their intended victim. Matthew had to admit he was in the sure grip of three cunning rogues, planning to separate him from all that he owned. He turned into the Green Dragon for a pint of ale, pondering his next move to keep a step ahead of his persecutors. Should he go home empty-handed and be coldly received by his wife? Charlotte had recently adopted a method of communication pioneered by Matthew's uncle, Charles. She wrote little notes to her husband, notable for their brevity and lack of warmth. These were given to Bentinck and handed to his lordship if and when he decided to return home. Was it possible that this pair of jackanapes, Crickshaw and Finch, could make such a fool of him? Had Mr. Cheatall sent them as part of a dastardly plot to bring him to a state of total ruin? Matthew drained his glass and sent for the hostler's boy. Tapper drove the Ponsonby carriage up to the door of the inn, ordered to drive at once to Cheatall's shop. The pawnbroker, as was his custom, sat placidly before his counter, a jeweller's loupe fixed into one heavy eyelid. He barely looked up from his careful scrutiny of a diamond ring when the musical tinkling of the shop bell announced his customer's arrival.

"I thought you would be back, my lord. Getting short of funds, are we? What do you want with me now?" Cheatall removed his magnifying glass, rubbed one hand over the other, and leered at Matthew. He knew Matthew better than Matthew knew himself. He had seen it all before, born of long experience, the gradual descent of a man into pliable submission—at the command of those he considered inferior. His rank could not save him from ultimate disaster. Those of high birth were not as the common people, whose dreary existence was a daily round of unremitting drudgery, uncertain where the next meal was coming from. Yes, Cheatall did know his client. He patiently waited for Matthew to name his business.

"Ah! I see you have brought me a gold pocket watch and chain. Any inscription on it? Good, my lord. Might be able to give you an advance of twelve guineas on it, but not a penny more. Already got four in the window, and there's not much demand in these here parts. Have you brought anything else I can use?" Matthew placed Miss Gaunt's gold cross and chain on the counter.

"You really are a man without conscience, Mr. Cheatall," he replied, strongly inclined to strike the pawnbroker with his gold-topped cane. "The watch is worth at least thirty or forty guineas. Now sir, you have already disposed of a great number of my paintings, chinaware, and some Georgian silver—practically half the contents of the Hall. I will not part with my time-piece for such a miserly sum!"

"In that case, suit yourself. Let us not waste anymore of each other's time. You are in too deep my lord to act independently. If you should change your mind, you know where to find me," said Cheatall, fully cognizant of his customer's desperate plight. With great shrewdness, Cheatall had taken into his confidence the two aforementioned villains. On his explicit instructions, both Crickey and Finch (known to the pawnbroker as "Gold" Finch for his uncanny ability to turn a profit on all outstanding accounts) would pay close attention to the squire's movements, following him along any route Matthew chose to take.

Matthew slammed the wooden door of Cheatall's shop so violently that the tinkling bells of the two Chinese pagodas trembled as if they truly foretold an impending earthquake. Matthew felt quite ill, but determined to drive away from the clutches of his creditors. Instead of returning to Albatross Hall, he ordered Tapper to turn the horses' heads in the direction of Bath.

It was as well Matthew did not return home for a few days. He would have witnessed a remarkable change in Charlotte's appearance. Her full recovery, much more beneficial than any of Dr. Palliser's medicines, was the result of a letter from Henry, to be read and re-read, then tucked safely out of sight in her bosom.

Pakenham, Ontario, Canada.
Bank of the Mississippi River.

My dearest Charlotte,

You will be pleased to learn that I have arrived safely in Canada after a tiresome journey of seven weeks. The voyage on the Isadora was very arduous indeed. We were buffeted constantly by high seas. The waves so huge they threatened to overturn our vessel, and would have done so but for the superb seamanship of the captain and his willing hands. He put me to work assisting the ship's doctor at minor operations. Sadly, one of the women died, giving birth to a sickly baby. A kind-hearted passenger offered to take the boy when we reached our destination. Many of my fellow passengers were sick, and although the captain did his best to make all as comfortable as possible, there is no gainsaying the awesome power of the elements. But God in His mercy brought us to port. I must tell you how excited I was to sight a whale off the Grand Banks. The fishing is very rich. The captain told us that Portuguese and Spanish fishermen have taken vast stocks of cod and herring into the holds of their boats. They are so heavily laden that I do not know how they return to Europe without sinking.

After landing, I hired a coach to take me part of the way. When the rough road ended at the edge of the bush, I joined other travellers in a boat and crossed lakes and rivers the size of which would amaze you. Shortly after I arrived in Pakenham, an attractive little place with a five-span stone bridge, I made straight for the office of the land agent. He greeted me in a most cordial manner and gave me my papers, signed and registered, entitling me to a tract of one hundred acres. This parcel is known as a 'land grant' which, by decree of King George III, is awarded to all ex-British army officers now on half pay. I have inspected a small section of my property on horseback and note that there will be much to attend to. Many trees will have to be felled to clear the land ready for spring ploughing and the seeding of crops. This land, my dearest, is much wilder than Albatross estate and will take months of hard work to tame.

Still, I am not discouraged, especially when I think of you and Cecil. I will need to hire suitable domestic help when I take up residence in the log cabin. With the assistance of other settlers, it will be finished in two months, built at the edge of a forest of maple, hickory, and spruce. The maple trees can be tapped for syrup. I will try my hand at it in the spring. Many trees and plants are strange to me, as is the case with birds. The American robin is much larger than those in England. Everyone goes to the aid of his neighbour and all participate in raising barns for cattle and storage of hay (a very social event, so I understand). Since the river is close by, I do not need to dig a well for water. My fellow settlers tell me that the forthcoming winter will be very harsh, with snow and ice for a period of four months. Still, I look forward to my new life, and will inform you of my progress.

Please send out a chest containing warm clothing, and some domestic items such as chinaware, serving dishes, pots etc. I'm sure Mrs. Dobson and Bentinck will be glad to assist you. I think longingly of my regimentals, but of course there is no opportunity for their use unless the governor invites me to a ball! I miss you very much and feel quite homesick when I remember those left behind. Still, my first impressions of Canada are quite favourable. Please don't worry about me.

With my fondest love,
Henry.

CHAPTER 32:
MATTHEW VISITS
SIR MILES STANDISH

atthew's journey to Bath was in the nature of an ignomini-
ous retreat and it was particularly humiliating to pass by The
Dolphin, knowing that the price of just one night's accommodation was no longer in his wallet. All it contained was a mere five guineas,
hardly sufficient for three nights of food and lodging in Mrs. Clegg's cheap
boarding house situated on Cheap Street, frequented by Mrs. Fowey and
Jane Dean. Dusk was falling and overcast skies promised more rain. Matthew
directed Tapper to drive down Milsom Street to the residence of his old
friend and possible benefactor, Sir Miles Standish. A loud clanging of the
doorbell at number thirteen Laura Place brought Greech, Sir Miles's aged
butler, shuffling to see who could be visiting at such an unusual hour. It was
now raining heavily. The stray cats of the town began their nightly prowl,
taking advantage of shelter afforded by tall yew hedges or open cellars, where,
undetected, they engaged in playful skirmishes with unwary mice.

"I was not aware that Sir Miles expected any callers tonight," said the
butler in a querulous voice. "He is presently away seeking legal advice from
his solicitor. I do not think he will return until six o'clock. Is there anything
I can do for you?"

Matthew handed Greech his card of introduction, suggesting it was possible the butler did not recognize him, since it was a few years ago when
he had first visited Sir Miles. He consulted his gold watch (apart from the
gold-topped walking stick, the only item of value in his possession), saying
he would await the return of his friend, if the butler would kindly give
him permission.

"My humble apologies, sir. Forgive an old man for losing his memory.
Allow me to show you into the reception room and hang up your wet cloak
and hat. You can rest from your long journey. It is a night for neither man
nor beast to be out. I will bring Your Honour refreshments right away."

The butler ambled slowly to the kitchen after ushering Matthew to a
comfortable leather armchair. The spacious room brought back memories,
unchanged from the time of his first meeting with Sir Miles—a happier time,
when the squire's life was all he could wish for: the prospect of a beautiful,
charming bride, and a mother conscious of her son's need to take his rightful
place as heir of Albatross estate, source of a handsome income for himself
and Charlotte. Taking stock, his present position, mired as it was in debt,
appeared bleak. Instinctively he moved his chair closer to the fireplace. A
cheery blaze of crackling logs warmed cold hands and feet. The ornate carved
mantle supported small, delicate statues of frisky Irish wolfhounds, ardent
swains, and a miniature Irish harp. Resting against the harp was a mischievous
leprechaun, a tiny elfin cobbler celebrated in folklore and reputed to own
hidden treasure. Matthew, acquainted with the leprechaun's history from Sir
Miles, who claimed Irish ancestry, fervently wished that the elf would give up
his secret.

Sir Miles was not proud of his forebears overseas who abandoned their
holdings when they no longer paid rents sufficient to maintain the absentee
landlord in his accustomed lavish style. Unscrupulous agents, employed by
English masters, without fear of challenge, refused to renew tenant leases
on any pretext, stating that evictions were legal by signed document, often
blatant forgeries, delivered from England. In fact, the greedy agents coveted
the land for themselves and sold property rights at will. Miserable peasants
were forced to live in mud hovels, warmed only by peat cut from a nearby
bog, bemoaning the undeniable fact that their lot had not improved since
the union of Irish and English Parliaments in 1801. Thus, the wearing of the

green was an anathema to Sir Miles, even though Greech presented him with a shamrock every St. Patrick's Day. Matthew smiled, noticing several forlorn dried bunches of the plant lying next to the harp.

One of Sir Miles's best loved paintings, mounted in an enormous gilt frame, hung on the opposite wall. It was a large landscape by Nicolaes Bercham, showing a mystical, mist-shrouded scene of shepherds grazing their flocks underneath long shadows cast by the ruins of an ancient Irish castle, probably the old seat of nobility no longer interested or able to keep it in good repair. A few stones had been carted away for road-building by the peasants, if not brazenly stolen to build the land agent a more desirable dwelling. Matthew was still contemplating this painting of rural decay when Sir Miles entered, apologizing profusely for his untimely absence when his friend arrived.

"Do not think of it," said Matthew, rising to shake Sir Miles warmly by the hand. "The lateness of the hour requires an apology, my dear sir, and the reason for such an inconvenience will be related shortly. Perhaps it would be wise for me to come quickly to the point," he continued, as Miles expressed his surprise that Lady Charlotte had not accompanied her husband. He urged his friend to take some refreshment before stating the nature of his business.

"Your friendly offer of hospitality cannot be refused," said Matthew, accepting a glass of wine and some cold pheasant and ham pie from a tray proffered by Greech. The butler bent with difficulty over the fire and stirred it into a roaring blaze before retiring, leaving the two companions to discuss news and business in private. "I have come to ask your help, Miles. I am urgently in need of a loan to cover unpaid debts. To be very frank, I have come upon hard times, partly owing to my foolishness at the tables. Thus I owe my creditors, bloodsuckers that they are, some guineas amounting to several hundred. The names of these human leeches are Cheatall, Crickshaw and Goldie Finch, my sworn enemies. They are pressing me for repayment within a week and support their demands by undisguised threats that I will end my days in the Marshalsea debtors prison. The beadle in charge bribes notorious ruffians, who guard the gates with due diligence to see that none escape until full payment has been rendered. All visitors are carefully searched on entry. Prudently, they never fail to grease palms, so that 'gifts' to friends and relatives be not confiscated. Such a vile place, Miles, is not to be contemplated. Whole families live there. Some get sick and die, some are born. Only a few, perhaps resorting to further bribes, manage to live out their days away from the Marshalseas' precincts. I don't think that I would fare any better in the King's Bench Prison, Miles. I must explain that I have, through rash decisions, fallen into the clutches of a rogue Soho pawnbroker, Mr. Cheatall. Finch and Crickshaw are his accomplices and do his dirty work.

"Over a period of a few months, I have put at his disposal certain of the Albatross paintings, statuary, and other valuables in order to pay estate accounts. Some still remain in his London premises, scrupulously accounted for by his legion of grasping petty clerks, all ill fed and clothed. I long for the day when I might be able to retrieve them and restore them to the Hall. I could never part with my Batoni portrait. It is a fact that Cheatall has sold some of the best paintings, so I don't expect to see them again. The gaming tables are my downfall, Miles. You might look upon this tale of woe as the confession of a penitent sinner, fallen far below his station. When my late father, in reference to myself on his deathbed, besought my mother 'never to leave the scoundrel a penny,' I confess it would have been better had the estate not been bequeathed to me as the firstborn. I think my brother Henry is better suited to be squire of Albatross. However he has gone to seek his fortune, farming in Canada. My purse contains the miserly sum of five guineas. I am firmly in Cheatall's snares. The two rascals mentioned, Mr. Crickshaw and Mr. Finch, follow me wherever I go. Even as we speak, it is highly probable they know my whereabouts in Bath and plan to detain me at the first opportunity. I thought we had left them far behind on the journey here. I urged Tapper to whip up the horses to such a pace that we almost left the highway and narrowly avoided the ditch. This brought to mind the terrible accident on my return to the Hall from Bath the first time, when poor Jane Dean was killed by the coach wheel. I did not let Cheatall deprive me of my watch. But apart from this ring and my gold-topped cane, it is the only piece of jewellery in my possession."

"My dear fellow, allow me to say how deeply distressed I am to hear of your present misfortunes. You look quite gaunt, and, if I may say so without offense, but a shadow of your former robust self. You need take care to restore your body and spirits. Talking of spirits, Matthew, were you ever troubled further by the ghost of what was her name … ah, I remember, Lady Georgiana?"

Matthew forgot his troubles for a moment, recounting how Lady Georgiana's remains had been resurrected from the lake by his Uncle Charles and under his sister's supervision, given a decent burial. The squire shifted uneasily in his chair, placing his empty glass on a small marquetry side table. The conversation was drifting from his intended purpose. Sir Miles asked his friend if he still kept falcons at the Hall, forgetting how frightened Matthew had been of the legend of the black falcon. Matthew turned very pale. He felt so fatigued from his journey that he was grateful when Miles offered him a room for the night. "Greech will show you to a bedroom on the second floor and provide sufficient candles for your comfort. We will discuss your affairs on the morrow. Good night and rest easy, my friend."

Matthew's sleep was disturbed by wild visions of Lady Georgiana, floating in a white burial shroud near his body and sitting in various mournful attitudes underneath the canopy of the four-poster bed. Her tormented spirit changed into the shape of a grotesque black falcon, descending with open beak on Matthew's outstretched arm. He thew his hand across his face to fend off the bird of prey circling ever closer. He awoke in a cold sweat, calling out in terror, not yet fully conscious of his safe haven in Sir Miles's home. No one heard him. Daylight brought little relief. His dreams boded ill and Matthew was superstitious by nature. He thought, as he dressed, that it was unlikely that his friend would grant his request since he had declined to discuss it the previous night. For a brief moment, he consoled himself with the conviction he had nothing to lose except the entire estate and the contents of the Hall. All that would be left to him, his wife and son.

Breakfast was served in a sunny conservatory filled with exotic plants, overlooking a garden with neat flower beds and manicured lawn, shaded by trees which thrive in the warmer climate of the southwest. "I have given your desire for a loan very careful consideration," Sir Miles began. "In the past, we once shared the pleasures and pitfalls of playing Faro and other games of a similar nature in the Assembly Rooms. I well recollect that we were unsuccessful in making any profit. That is, with the exception of your future bride, who either had much greater skill or was favoured by lady luck. She had a considerable fortune of her own when she became Lady Ponsonby. Am I correct in surmising that you used her monies to make vast improvements to Albatross?" Matthew did not answer. "As you will observe, you see before you all the comforts of life which I enjoy, Matthew. I do not wish to risk them for a loan which could cause a break in our long friendship. My position is complicated by the mere fact of my ancestry, coming as I do from a line of absentee landlords from Ireland. Although at present my landholdings are being looked after by a most congenial and honest agent, which I take the liberty to add is a rarity these days, he is unable to procure the necessary income from my tenants.

"To put it in its bluntest terms, Matthew, many tenants under the jurisdiction of corrupt agents have been evicted as undesirable paupers, with the substitution of more servile parasites in their place. This occurs even after the agent's equally corrupt wife has accepted gifts of chickens, eggs, and butter. It may surprise you to learn that cows are bartered to secure a signature on a lease due for renewal. Cowardly though it may appear in your eyes, Matthew, I have been unable to bring myself to travel to Dublin and see for myself the current state of my holdings. In a sense, I am trying to protect myself from unpleasantness. Besides I would find the probability of being forced to sell ancestral lands quite reprehensible. As you know, they once belonged to a more prosperous generation of Standishes, partly due to the fact that they successfully opposed Cromwell during the bloody rebellion of 1649. Cromwell terrified the local populace, especially in Drogheda and Wexford, through wholesale massacres and harsh repression. And he called himself the Lord Protector! I wish I had inherited their courage. But my dear friend, without boring you any further with my family history, I can only say once again how sorry I am not to be able to help.

"I am mindful of the fate of my fellow countryman, the famous playwright, Oliver Goldsmith. He died heavily in debt. It is very remiss of me, Matthew, but I forgot to ask you how you slept last night. You still look weary. Greech, another cup of coffee for our guest! Now, do tell me all your news. How is your little boy? And pray tell me how Charlotte fares. Is she in good health?"

It was several minutes before Matthew answered, so deeply did he feel his disappointment. "Our present impecunious state has placed our relationship under great strain. Thus she is under Dr. Palliser's care, although my housekeeper and her maid both agree that her illness is the result of a nervous condition. Naturally she is most upset that I have been obliged to remove some of the heirlooms from the Hall. She is in constant denial of the reality of our present plight. She accuses me of denying our son, Cecil, his rightful inheritance. I don't think we can ever be reconciled to each other again. I suppose Miss Gaunt would compare me to Jacob, when he stole Esau's birthright."

Later that morning, Matthew reluctantly bid Sir Miles farewell. His visit to Bath had not gone according to plan. He was both destitute and friendless; his pride had deserted him. In a sullen frame of mind, not heeding the pouring rain or where his steps would carry him, he wandered down Fairlie Street and into the nearest ale house. Here he would spend his last guineas, reserving two for the coming night's lodging at Mrs. Clegg's worthy establishment. He was about to turn into the Harrow and Plough when he was accosted by an unknown assailant and knocked to the ground.

"Your life is in my hands, Lord Ponsonby. Now, sir, what explanation have you to give for your hasty departure from London. Did you truly believe that you could escape your creditors so easily? Whether you live or die, it's all the same to us ..."

Matthew heard no more of Crickshaw's lecture. He lay senseless on the wet pavement, face down, with his feet in the gutter—a sorry sight for all passersby, who determined he was just another worthless drunk. One beggar rolled Matthew's prostrate form over, hoping to steal anything of value, but found only a sodden wallet containing two guineas. A trickle of blood emerged from the squire's white shirt, testifying to some grave internal injury. But the passing crowds, on their merry way to the Assembly Rooms or Baths, looked the other way.

There were no Good Samaritans in the town.

CHAPTER 33:
1822 – LORD CASTLEREAGH
COMMITS SUICIDE

There was almost as much consternation over the circumstances surrounding the unexpected death, by his own hand, of Lord Castlereagh, foreign secretary in Lord Liverpool's government in August 1822, as there was in Albatross Village over the near fatal attack on Lord Ponsonby. The news of Matthew's attack by an unknown assailant was speedily conveyed to the Hall by Tapper, obliged to return with an empty carriage on the instruction of Sir Miles Standish. Crossing Westminster Bridge and the vicinity of St. James's Square, Tapper became aware of crowds milling near the residence of Lord and Lady Castlereagh. The mood was sombre, yet respectful, although some bystanders mocked Castlereagh as a man who once fought an illegal duel with his rival, George Canning.

A week later, agitators mounted hostile demonstrations outside Westminster Abbey as Castlereagh's funeral cortège made its dignified approach to the entrance, accompanied by soldiers of victorious "Peninsula" regiments, beating a slow march on drums muffled in black crepe. Those inside interpreted the jeers of the mob as cheers in praise of the Duke of Wellington, who served as a pall bearer. It was the dead minister who appointed his friend commander of the army in Portugal. Some mourners remembered Robert Castlereagh as a foreign secretary of great ability, who had assisted in building the final coalition against Napoleon at Vienna.

It seemed to Tapper as he dismounted, parking the carriage in a nearby hackney stand, that some shed tears of grief, but others clamoured loudly for reforms long overdue. They felt Castlereagh did not merit their full confidence as a politician, although, to his credit, he was an ardent supporter of Catholic emancipation.

"Was it really true," they said, whispering and pointing to the house of Lord and Lady Castlereagh with the large black silk wreath attached to the massive oak door, that the minister was blackmailed for homosexuality? They knew he was overworked and very tired, but did this scandal bear any credence? It was a known fact that deplorably low standards of morality were commonplace during the reigns of the two Georges. Promiscuity was acceptable in the upper ranks of society. Tapper entered into conversation with another coachman whose acquaintance he had made while awaiting completion of his master's business at Cheatalls.

"You know, Tapper, I wouldn't have thought that Castlereagh was capable of committing suicide, anymore than I would believe this 'ere hoss o' mine would refuse a bag of oats at the end of a long day's work a pulling me and my passengers," observed Welkins, a burly individual in gay red tartan cloak and traditional black top hat, lighting his pipe while the emaciated beast of burden lowered his shaggy head to accept a stolen apple offered by one of the ragged street urchins. These unfortunates were homeless waifs, forced by their poverty-stricken families to fend for themselves. They frequented Covent Garden fruit and flower market, bold enough to creep up to an unwitting vendor's stall before being chased off again, leaving a trail of overturned wheelbarrows, scattering oranges and apples in their wake.

"Such goings on in the government," continued Welkins, drawing mightily on his pipe, sending curls of smoke in Tapper's direction. "As you know, and this is a piece of irony if ever I heard one, instead of meeting his end dueling with Canning, for which crime both men were relegated to the back benches of the House, he finally decides to take his own life. Before you arrived, one of the crowd told me the Duke of Wellington visited him last week and apparently was so alarmed by his friend's nervous state that he went immediately afterward to summon Castlereagh's doctor. A few months back, another person reported that he saw the minister and an unidentified trollop enter a brothel. Ever since, Castlereagh was afeared that he would be unmasked as a practicing homosexual. What a pity Dr. Charles Bankhead arrived too late to save him, even tho' he obeyed Wellington's instructions. Castlereagh fell back into the good doctor's arms, still clutching the small white-handled knife with which he had stabbed himself in the throat, severing a main artery. Such a loss to Lord Liverpool's government. However, since he supported the prime minister's repressive measures, it is not surprising that some in the crowd revile him."

"Poor Lady Castlereagh. I am as much moved by her husband's untimely death as I am by the sad news I convey to my lady Charlotte. My friend, since I last met you in Soho, you will be shocked to learn that Master Matthew has been stabbed by some vagabond, who savagely attacked him outside the Harrow and Plough in Bath, leaving him near death. I must leave you now, Welkins, as I intend to reach Bedfordshire by nightfall and Albatross early tomorrow. It ain't safe to be on the roads after dusk, running the gauntlet of highwaymen, when there is a snug bed to be had for a pittance in a convenient wayside inn, though I grant you that the mattress is generally crawling with fleas which torment all night. If the chambermaid is slovenly about her work, the slop pots haven't been emptied and the room smells rotten. Still the hostler is efficient and the horses well fed and watered. Otherwise, as you know, Welkins, they refuse to budge after breakfast!" Welkins nodded and patted Tapper on the back as he turned the carriage in the direction of Woburn Village.

Not since Henry's departure for Canada had the Albatross villagers been roused to such spirited debate. All the highly exaggerated stories about the late Lord Castlereagh and Matthew whiled away a great deal of time in the Albatross Arms. The recent arrival of Tapper, conveyor of both London and Bath intelligence, gave him added status in the patrons' eyes. They paid close attention to his account of his master's attack, some nodding their heads as if to say they knew the squire's frequent visits to the capital would end in trouble. He was the author of his own downfall.

Others insisted Matthew maintained a secret mistress in Bath in a house purchased especially for her, that Brook must have knowledge of this unseemly behaviour, but was, in all likelihood, sworn to secrecy. To further loosen Tapper's voluble tongue, the villagers plied him with hefty tankards of ale. How had Lady Ponsonby received the news? Would she be preparing for a funeral? Was there any truth to the rumour she was passionately in love with Henry? Was this the obvious reason for his leaving for the colonies? Had Cecil been summoned from Winchester? Had Lawyer Feathers received a request to visit Lady Ponsonby?

Coming to Tapper's rescue, and thus momentarily disabusing him of his celebrity status, the landlord pointed out he had it on Mr. Brook's good authority that the squire was very preoccupied with estate affairs. So speculation as to his reasons for trips to London and Bath were none of the villagers' business. It was premature to talk of funerals. If Mr. Wick had not yet received instructions from her ladyship to make arrangements to open Lord Cecil's tomb, it must be assumed that his lordship might recover. Parson Bray was visiting a parish some miles distant, Dr. Palliser, busy with Charles Ponsonby, so no news from Bramble Cottage. Anyway, the regulars in the pub would be better off attending to their own affairs than sitting for hours drinking and gossiping. Mr. Morgan, the portly mayor, who had imbibed more of the contents of the Albatross Arms' cellar than anyone present, supported this admonition and led the company in a hearty round of applause. Mr. Cob and Mr. Carver, not to be outdone, both stood, tankards held high, and swore an oath of loyalty to Lord Ponsonby who provided, as they put it, "Good employment on the estate. May he recover his health sufficient to give us the benefit of his patronage in the village and the Lord in His mercy grant us good harvests for all to share."

"And so say all of us," said the villagers in unison, as they took the hint and dispersed. Tapper, basking in the glory of being hero of the hour, remounted his box and urged the horses forward at a brisk trot.

"Do you really mean to tell me that Matthew fell wounded among thieves and whores and no Good Samaritan came to his rescue, Dr. Palliser? Although he never attends church services and has not encouraged his wife to do so, it is hard to believe he lay unaided in the gutter for a few hours before being found by Sir Miles's servant. I have a very uncharitable opinion of those low people living in Bath. Their minds are wholly occupied with bathing in the hot springs, or gaming and dancing in the Assembly Rooms, just like the characters in Jane Austen's novels, written while she lived there. She showed such skill in pricking the vanity of pompous matrons, there only to see and be seen in all their gaudy finery."

Miss Gaunt could be accused of hypocrisy and self-righteousness. She was not at all concerned with Matthew's fate, having washed her hands of him as a candidate for salvation. No reward of eternal life after death, available only to true believers.,

She raised the distasteful subject of the errant squire with Dr. Palliser while tending to her ailing brother, persuading him to drink a concoction of burdock and lime to restore his energy. Charles Ponsonby was in declining state of health, no longer interested in searching out and hiding various objects that took his fancy. He was content to spend his days as an invalid, dozing in the doorway of Bramble Cottage, wrapped up in a checkered blanket, admiring the pretty village wenches passing by the picket fence. An occasional glimpse of Bessie Bray, the fairest of them all, would stir the old man into an upright position for a brief moment. As Bess would soon be lost to view, Uncle Charles would lapse once more into a semi-comatose state.

"Give him some beef broth with a little sherry in it, Gertrude," advised Palliser, as he examined his patient for signs of bodily weakness and failing heart. "As far as his nephew is concerned, I'm sure it would not be wise to divulge news of his attack until the time when it might be necessary. I only hope the surgeon in Bath dressed Matthew's wounds properly, and his attackers were arrested. It is time we had a police force worthy of the name. Those Bow Street Runners are not up to the task."

"In the meantime, we must pray for him. Prayer can move mountains, you know," said Miss Gaunt, handing the doctor his black broad-brimmed hat and medicine bag.

"Take comfort in the fact that you can now pay the milkman," laughed Palliser, mounting his horse.

Lady Charlotte paced her boudoir re-reading the letter from Sir Miles:

My dear Madam,

I am sending this letter to you directly, to deliver news of your husband for which I am heartily sorry. Tapper will have informed you of the unprovoked assault by two scoundrels who left him lying in the street, bleeding from a serious wound. I suspect that the cowardly attack was the result of certain unpaid debts accumulated by Matthew, for which repayment he was hard-pressed by his creditors.

Forgive me, Charlotte, but I was unable to comply with Matthew's request for a loan. I feel guilty that I am partly responsible for what happened. However, now that he is in my house under the care of Dr. Fortescue, I will do what is humanly possible and offer him every comfort. At times, your husband is quite delirious. He murmurs something about being pecked by a black falcon with a sharp, hooked beak. He did mention the bird to me on an earlier visit, and whispers in more lucid moments that it is a harbinger of evil, a premonition of death. I believe there is a connection with Albatross Park, but whether it has to do with the time of his father's funeral, I am not clear. Then he also murmurs something about a ghostly spirit-I believe of Lady Georgiana.

Dr. Fortescue's assistant has bled Matthew twice, and directed that his room remain darkened with no visitors admitted. A search of the area in which the Harrow and Plough is located for evidence of the weapon used in the crime has so far proved fruitless. I respectfully suggest that you do not attempt the journey here, but await more news from me in a day or so.

With my deepest sympathies,
I remain ever your true friend and humble servant,
Miles Standish.

Charlotte fell onto her couch, deeply affected by what she had read. This time she grasped the significance of the letter. If Matthew were to survive, what would be her position in society if both she and her husband found themselves unable to meet their financial obligations? Looking to an uncertain future, without Henry to help and advise, was unbearable. The last paragraph of his second letter indicated that he found his new way of life quite congenial, but so unlike those privileged to live in the great houses of England. Henry wrote,

Sometimes, the master is on an equal footing with his servants. They insist on eating at his table and won't consider employment otherwise. You could describe this as democratic, not approved of in England with the exception of radicals like William Cobbett. On the subject of my requirements, Charlotte, I do not wish you to send out any heavy mahogany furniture from the Hall, as the cost of transporting by sea and thence overland from Montreal is so very high. Besides, there are black walnut and oak trees here in abundance. They can be turned into capital tables, chairs, beds etc. I am at present busy working the land with a team of oxen. I find these placid and docile animals very different from the Shire horses on the fields at the Hall. Do write and tell me your news, my beloved. I miss you very much.

Adieu, your only Henry.

P.S. Give my fondest love to Cecil and tell him to write me about his progress at Winchester.

Charlotte refolded the letter, unaware that it did not reveal Henry's true state of mind. He had written with enthusiasm of his new experiences, of his feelings of being a true pioneer. He made continuous reference to a pocket-book written by the Reverend James Croxton for the guidance of immigrants willing to challenge the hardships and dangers of the bush. "It is essential to carry a pocket compass, an ax, some nails, one kettle, some flints, and a frying pan. A firearm will come in handy if you encounter a bear which, if slain, will provide grease to ward off ferocious mosquitoes and blackfly. If lost in the bush (here I urge you to mark each tree with the blade of an ax or some other such recognizable mark), take care to find a trail which will lead you back to the road. For I warn you, dear reader, that many a woodsman has found himself tramping further away from the settlement, never to be found again, unless happened upon by a local native band either inclined to remove his scalp or take him as one of them, and oblige him to go through some form of marriage with a dark-eyed squaw. Finally, my brethren, I exhort you to give thanks to God for the blessings he has bestowed in bringing you in safety to this vast and promising land. Always be on the best of terms with your neighbours. They could provide the key to your survival should you require assistance or the need to borrow oxen, build cabins and barns. Always respect nature. She will provide for those ready to accept her rules."

Henry replaced the book in his jacket and sighed as he resumed chopping firewood. This land was not for the weak of body and spirit, but only for those who could bear the loss of sick children with stoicism—hardy survivors of cramped, foul-smelling immigrant ships.

It was time, thought Henry, to add to his meager stock of food. When, with the approach of winter, fresh trout for dinner (that he'd triumphantly caught himself) had to replaced with salt fish, Henry's diet became monotonous. It consisted of potatoes, salt pork, and bread, with the occasional feast of venison, baked porcupine (rather different in flavour and texture to the baked hedgehogs of Shakespeare's day), and a few blueberries. He thought nostalgically about the splendid fare at the Hall and Mrs. D's. excellent pies. But with extreme cold and snow predicted by "old timers," it was essential to purchase snowshoes and heavy clothing, to protect the extremities from frostbite, and to build a rudimentary sleigh for transportation. For the first time since his arrival, so full of promise, Henry sat alone inside a log cabin well-chinked with moss. A crude stone chimney had been inserted into the roof, cemented with loam and stones, for the emission of smoke from a rough iron stove which served for cooking and heating. He heard the wolves howling their nightly chorus. How long would it take the energetic beaver to dam up his nearby stream before hibernating? No wonder one of his neighbours had described the beaver as "nature's master builder." His former military career and Charlotte were but distant memories. On retiring for the night, Henry lay down on a straw mattress. His dreams, at first pleasant with visions of Charlotte, turned into nightmares of battle scenes in America and Portugal.

He saw the imposing figure of the French Marechal Soult commanding a vast army, facing the British across the river Douro on the opposite bank to the city of Oporto. How stealthily came the surprise attack by the Grenadiers under cover of darkness. Henry found himself crossing with the soldiers in four wine barges converted into ferry boats. But instead of retreating, as history books record, the French, acting with vengeance, rounded on the stragglers, bayoneting those struggling in the current or scrambling up the steep banks. Henry's life was about to be ended by a drawn sword, when he awoke in a cold sweat.

CHAPTER 34:
HENRY'S ADVENTURES
IN CANADA

Was the winter of 1823 to become Henry's winter of discontent? He had the sense to realize he must replenish the iron stove without delay to warm his chilled body. He heard gruesome stories of settlers freezing to death in their beds, their bodies solid as blocks of ice, cold as the waiting tomb. These gravesites were a prominent feature of the local community, scattered in forlorn groups across the landscape. They bore mute witness to those who had perished, some at a very tender age, from fatal illness or starvation due to an unforgiving climate or poor knowledge of sound farming practices. Cholera and dysentery stalked the land. Henry knelt down before the stove, rekindling the embers by vigorously blowing through the small open door until the grey ash glowed red. Some kindling stored in a crude box nearby was almost depleted. Henry made a mental note that its replenishment would be his first duty of the day. His neighbour, Mr. Tewksley, assured him that hardwood trees such as maple and oak were far superior to spruce. They must be well seasoned, otherwise they hissed and spat with evaporating sap, giving off smoke rather than an agreeable flame. The room was now sufficiently warm. Henry lost the numbness in his fingers.

Over a frugal breakfast of cold ham and bread, he recalled the warning given by Parson Bray.

"Life in the wilds of Canada will not suit everyone, my boy. I know that you served in North America as a military officer and came face to face with danger and some hardship, but you had the support of your regiment and those employed to look after your physical needs. I have read accounts of the lives of early settlers in Upper Canada reported in journals lately published in this country. Some emigrants write of vast, trackless forests, burned to clear land for agriculture—a task of almost unimaginable scope, as the charred roots and stumps of trees make the sowing of seed, except by laborious work with a hand rake, very difficult. I only bring this report to your attention, Henry, my dear boy, as you are by birth a member of the aristocracy, an ex-British army officer. I do not share Gertrude's opinion that you should take no thought for the morrow, but live only by faith and trust in the Almighty for His protection. I would merely observe that the Lord helps those who help themselves. Since you have firmly made up your mind to establish yourself overseas, Henry, the Lord bless and keep you." The good rector had turned away, his eyes moistened with tears. Copious tears were shed later as the fortunes of the Ponsonby family rose and fell.

Still, Henry reflected, while sweeping stray leaves blown in through the entrance of the log cabin where a sturdier door would replace the old one within a few days, he was more fortunate than most settlers, with private funds at his disposal from his late father's will, supplemented by a small pension following his discharge from the service of his sovereign. He looked to the future, determined to reconcile himself to the trials of a new life without the companionship and help of the woman he loved. He was in good health. Resolved to perform the many tasks necessary to survival, he grew adept at swinging his ax, but was dismayed to find a bucket of water placed inside his cabin frozen solid overnight. There were more surprises. Milk was sold in frozen "cakes" and transported to market in boxes or baskets; sugar, produced from the boiled sap of maple trees, leaf tobacco, twisted into long ropes. Homesteaders killed the greater part of their cattle and poultry, salting and smoking them for winter storage. Five months of deep snow and sub-zero temperatures lay ahead, followed by hot, dry summers alive with pesky hordes of mosquitoes and blackfly, maddening both humans and livestock alike. Outdoor activity required the settler to cover his entire body with clothing from head to foot to protect it from bites and ticks.

Early in the spring, a settlement known as Chad's Falls, a few miles distant, consisting of a prosperous woolen mill, church, barns, farmhouses, and stables, was consumed by fire. A strong wind fanned the flames caused by a lightning strike in the forest nearby. It drove them with exceeding ferocity in the direction of the village. This tragedy was repeated often in various communities across the land, forcing the inhabitants to start over again. The path created by the fire was sufficiently wide to admit a team of oxen to clear land for crops. But it was no easy matter to control the beasts, who bucked and trampled the ground when attacked by swarms of insects.

It was time for Henry—having erected a split rail fence around a portion of his acreage, with the advice and assistance of his neighbour, Mr. Tewksley—to purchase a cow. A livestock auction held in the village of Pakenham on April 9th was conducted by a gentleman who paid four shillings for a license to sell cattle in an old converted warehouse not far from the Mississippi River. A wink of an eye, a nod of the head, or a raised finger signaled Mr. Blake a party was bidding on a particular animal. Mr. Tewksley pointed to one cow and said, "Looks like a good milker." For the sum of twenty-five pounds, Henry purchased his first cow. As the two companions journeyed homeward in the late afternoon, Henry leading his animal by a length of rope, Tewksley related the story of one of his cows developing a penchant for more exotic fodder than a mere ration of hay. To Mrs. Tewksley's annoyance, the animal devoured two full baskets of wild strawberries resting on the back of her husband's wagon while he was deep in conversation with a friend at the entrance to their modest dwelling. The cow was due to be milked shortly. Henry asked with a straight face if it produced pink milk or if the cream set aside to be churned into butter was pink also?

"No, but mebbe the ornery beast will find something else to her liking not meant for her to eat. My good wife is quite put out because the strawberries didn't produce any more milk. Please refrain from mentioning this incident to her. But let me give you some more advice, Henry. A cow and a few chickens are a necessity. When it's calving time, the cows cause trouble by ambling into the bush for hours unless you always tether them well and keep your fences in good repair. You will need to build a sturdy hen house with several nesting boxes. This little dwelling is our home. Remember what I told you about the cow. Why don't you come inside and have a drop of potato whiskey?"

Tewskley led the way into a sparsely furnished one-room cabin. A single iron bedstead stood curtained off in one corner, a rough-hewn table was placed by the stove. "Your next purchase should be a pair of oxen," he continued, as Henry sipped the whiskey placed before him by Mrs. Tewksley. "That is, if you intend to plough and sow a crop of wheat or corn. Oxen are strong, patient beasts, but getting them to move forward in the direction you wish to travel, yoked together by a heavy wooden yoke, is quite a feat. I usually find a twig and touch them gently on their heads, yelling 'Haw! Haw!' Just avoid muddy patches left by heavy rains or they will sink in, cart and all, and it's the Devil's job to get them out. Isn't that right, my dear," he said, turning to his buxom wife as she refilled the whiskey glasses.

Henry thanked his host for his good advice and the potent libation, more than ready to take leave of his garrulous friend, but loneliness and the desire for company led Tewskley to urge Henry to stay a little longer. Alice Tewksley offered Henry some cheese and a third glass of whiskey. He felt how potent the potato whiskey was, probably as good a remedy for colds as his hostess claimed. "Have you ever heard of a fellow called Philemon Wright, Henry? Well, let me tell you the story of his journey from Montreal, covering a distance of some one hundred and twenty miles during February, 1800, to a place which he founded on the north shore of the Ottawa river. He named it Hull. Wright organized a party of several families, traveling in sleighs pulled by teams of oxen and horses. For sixty miles of the journey, there was no road, or even a track through the dense bush. The river was their only guide, and but for the services of a young Indian brave, who expertly guided the exhausted immigrants across the ice, I don't think they would have survived. They were forced to abandon their sleighs on the frozen river as night fell, and made camp after a fashion." Henry rose to leave once more, but Mr. Tewksley bid him listen to his story, after refilling Henry's glass.

"A certain regiment of soldiers traveled the six hundred miles between New Brunswick and Montreal by snowshoe, sheltering at night on spruce boughs, before reaching their destination. It was truly a miracle that the men only suffered minor frostbite. Never get lost in the bush, Henry, especially after dusk and in the winter."

Henry patted his coat pocket. "I have the Reverend James Croxton's little book. I find his advice very helpful. Thank you for your warning about the bush." But for Henry, just learning to recognize animal tracks and perform daily chores occupied him from sunup to sundown. Then he had an adventure which almost cost him his life during his second winter, within a few days of Christmas. He lost his way in the bush and attempted to return to his cabin, walking along an icy creek. With an ominous crack, the ice splintered and gave way. Helpless, Henry sank to his knees. The cold, biting wind froze his wet clothing as hard as a piece of wood. He struggled to his feet, but a few yards upstream, stumbled and fell again. In great misery, with the light fast fading, Henry knew that unless he found shelter quickly, he was in mortal danger. Death alone in the woods appeared very possible. And without his compass, left behind on a shelf in the cabin, to guide him west back to safety, Henry resigned himself to his fate, resting his weary, frozen body against the bank, and closed his eyes.

CHAPTER 35:
CHEATALL'S PAWNSHOP UNCLE
CHARLES AND THE HEIR TO
ALBATROSS HALL PASS AWAY

The proprietor of the pawnshop, patronized mostly by the upper ranks of society, added a new and profitable dimension to his burgeoning clientele: Royalist emigres from France. Sailing vessels of all description were commandeered or chartered to convey aristocratic families seeking refuge on English soil across the Channel. There was such an urgency to the matter that many English sympathizers gave their approbation without question. Cheatall rubbed his plump hands together with satisfaction remembering how flustered the Duc de Louvier appeared on his premises yesterday, with his mistress, Madame Bercy, on his arm.

"It eez avec, excusez moi, how do you say triste that je suis obligez to place notre bijoux dans votre maison." Cheatall was much obliged to monsieur and madame for their patronage, making entries in a neat column on a sheet marked, "Furriners of various nationalities—Frenchies." He wrote, "Item: one ruby necklace, two diamond rings, a pouch of golden Louis d'or, minted in 1640, circulated through the reign of the ill-fated, Louis XVI, and a gold watch, still performing well after rough seas in the channel." He bowed his clients to a waiting cabriolet, a light one-horse carriage with two seats and a folding top—always a necessity in times of inclement weather. For protection during the choking, dense fogs of London, two oil lamps were mounted on each side. Cheatall assured them the cash he advanced was the most generous of any of his honourable profession in that part of London.

"Monsieur, you can do no better than come to a bloke like me," he said, placing both forefingers in his waistcoat pockets. "Best prices and best service." He wished them a long stay in their country home in Surrey—a mansion owned by an English count, Lord Devaux, landlord to many tenants and courtier to George IV, known for his pursuit of "the fair ladies", a bevy of beauties always in attendance on the king. Devaux was a favourite courtier and confidant, a dandy, sporting a gold-topped cane—which came in handy for encounters with street urchins and other despised vagrants—elegant clothes, styled in the manner of Beau Brummell, and fashionable waxed mustaches, each carefully groomed by his manservant. Brummell quarreled with the Prince Regent before his ascension to the throne; fleeing to France to escape his creditors in 1816, Brummell ended his days in an asylum for the insane. Lord Devaux supported the Bourbons, liberal in terms of lease arrangments and the modest amount of rent he required. He was a gentleman accustomed to dealings with well-bred foreigners. Beaufort Manor, furnished in the French style, would be at the disposal of Monsieur and Madame and their retinue of servants.

Louise Louvier was conveniently left behind in an establishment a mere two miles out of the port of Dover. Her wayward husband assured her this location was very convenient for a quick return to Paris should the Bourbons regain the throne. (Louis XVIII, during those critical times, was so stricken with gout and arthritis that his portly frame was confined to an iron bed-stead.) A triumphant return by Bonaparte from exile would inevitably shake the French throne. Louvier refrained from informing his wife that this arrangement served an ulterior motive. Louise would be excluded from high society, residing two day's journey from the capital. Monsieur Louvier and Madame Bercy were thus able to make the acquaintance of King George IV, bearing a letter of introduction from Count Devaux.

Cheatall resumed his seat at the counter. He found some jewels still had fragments of cotton attached, the result of being sewn into hidden pockets in

Madame Louvier's voluminous skirts to avoid detection by zealous customs officers. But despite this welcome increase in business, the pawnbroker was not in the best of humours. Some items in his stock, placed on the counter by his assistant (a mangy individual with a pockmarked face, permanently scarred by smallpox, and wearing ill-fitting clothes) were losing value. Too many jewels and too much art flooding the market! Cheatall assured his employee that he expected exemplary service, impressing upon the boy that he was but a temporary addition to the firm, replacing the absent Chicksaw and his associate, "Goldie" Finch. The pawnbroker's plans for Lord Matthew Ponsonby to redeem his family treasures at a handsome profit had undergone a severe setback, due to the foolish actions taken by his hot-headed agents. They sent a message to the pawnbroker, stating their violent attack on Matthew had been fully justified. He had produced a pistol and the pair of ruffians had acted in self-defense, since they had thought their lives in danger. Chicksaw had stabbed Ponsonby with his sword, delivering a near fatal blow to the chest. It remained to be seen whether Matthew would recover sufficiently to testify against his assailants in court, should he recognize Cheatall's agents. In which case, the pawnbroker had a plan. He would offer the presiding magistrate a substantial bribe. He was always ready to do business using any underhand method he could devise, so why not a few gold sovereigns into the hands of the man of justice?

Cheatall fixed his loupe into his right eye and scrutinized an exquisite cameo brooch, lacquered in blue and gold enamel, bearing the Ponsonby coat of arms. Next, a lustrous pearl necklace with a pendant in the form of a heart-shaped gold locket, containing a small fragment of blonde hair. The reverse showed a miniature portrait of a cherubic little boy, dressed in a blue jacket over a white ruffled shirt, clasping a tiny King Charles spaniel in his arms. The finely engraved inscription read, "To my dearest Charlotte on the birth of our son, Cecil."

Such are the trappings of the landed classes, thought Cheatall, removing his loupe. He placed the heirlooms into a secret drawer beneath the counter, carefully locking it and depositing the key into his greatcoat pocket. This faded blue woolen coat was habitually draped around the proprietor's bulky frame to compensate for lack of heat on the premises. A small brazier stood in one corner, fed only rarely from a scant supply of firewood and meager portion of coal. Cheatall held the premise that all bills must be kept to a minimum for the ultimate reward of greater profits. He glanced at his watch. A customer was expected at midday. Cheatall took a candle and ascended the dark, narrow staircase, now unsafe since the bannister was removed and put in the firewood box. He stood at the entrance to the upper floor, his view of the clerks, perched on their high stools, unimpeded. He had thoughtfully removed the old oak door. From this vantage point, the pawnbroker observed his employees. All were scratching away in large ledger books, dipping quill pens into inkstands that required frequent replenishment. Some of the leather-bound books bore the title "ACCOUNTS PAID," while others, notably the red ones set aside on a prominent desk were labelled "ACCOUNTS OVERDUE." They received the most attention. Cheatall pushed the "OVERDUE" clerk roughly to one side and ran a fat finger down a list of names all delinquent in their payments to the pawnbroker.

Cheatall junior developed a strong aversion to his father's business. With little schooling and showing interest in a seafaring way of life, he decided to run away to Plymouth at the tender age of thirteen. He made it plain to the crew of the bark Endymon, that he wished to be known by the name of Cartie. This would give him respectability, replacing the name Cheatall, surely making him the butt of ribald jokes! "Someday," he told the captain, "I would like to become a cartographer, mapping the world's coastlines as my hero, Captain James Cook, did, decades ago." Cheatall junior didn't wish to encounter any clients entered in the "OVERDUE" ledger.

Peggles was the unfortunate expected at noon, standing with an air of great humility before the pawnbroker. He discussed his account, notable for an excess of red ink. Peggles meekly proffered a small quantity of coin, emptied out of a worn leather pouch.

"Sorry, guv, but this is all the change I have. I hopes your honour will be satisfied for just a few more days. I have tried begging, but the peoples is poor like me and all I gets is a few pennies tossed into my cap."

"Well, my man," said Cheatall, counting the coins while shouting upstairs, instructing Jinks to make a second entry in the "OVERDUE" ledger. "What sort of a business do you think I run 'ere? Where would I be if customers didn't pay on time for their goods? I will give you four days. There are remedies for beggars. We are not far from the river. Good day, sir."

Peggles trembled at the thinly veiled threat that he might be subjected to a watery grave. He made his way down the street, despairing that he could ever repay his debt to such a hard, unforgiving man. His wife and small children lived in poverty in a dank, evil-smelling place. He feared for their survival as much as his own. "Times is 'ard," he muttered to himself as he turned down Prospect Street. "What a name for a fellow in my miserable state. I ain't got no prospects."

"Never did I see a creature so perilously close to having one foot in the grave. He looks sickly with tuberculosis," thought Cheatall, unlocking the drawer and removing the Ponsonby pendant to examine for any flaws in the exquisite piece of jewellery. The face of Cecil Ponsonby, heir to Albatross Hall and its estates, looked back. The heir to Albatross was now deceased. Winchester school had been caught in a virulent epidemic of measles, claiming the lives of several young scholars. Cecil had died without a murmur in Everett's arms. Cheatall replaced the pendant and climbed the stairs once more. The names of Guilbert, Masson, Deveaux, Louvier, and other French families in his ledgers drew his attention. What a pity that paintings of great value still adorned the palaces of Tuilleries and St. Cloud, prey to Republican mobs who ransacked ornately decorated rooms, even fouling the bedsheets left in King Louis's bedroom. Escape from a vengeful populace was arranged by loyal servants, donning the apparel of their masters and mistresses. Thus disguised, they travelled by coach to Calais. If questioned en route, they told a plausible story about "selecting" such costumes ransacked from the great houses of the nobility. It mattered not a whit to the pawnbroker how his new clients managed to obtain their belongings. His premises became a hive of activity, a mixture of legitimate, but mostly clandestine business.

"Matilda, kindly leave those black crepes hanging where you found them. I don't know, my girl, why you seem to dwell on such sad things. Bentinck made sure that everything was returned to the cupboard following the funerals of Charles and Cecil. I'll trouble you never to take out those things again." Mrs. Dobson scowled at her daughter. "Just you make yourself useful and fetch Lady Charlotte's breakfast tray. Molly is sick in her room in the attic. Mark you Bentinck," she continued, as the butler entered the kitchen, "I'll not be surprised if her ladyship hasn't taken any nourishment. Now she has lost her only son, and her husband is very poorly, I don't know how she will overcome her grief. So far, Lady Cynthia has been her only companion. She refuses any other visitors. The black wreath is still a hangin' on the front door. It is well that Parson Bray is coming later today. I told him not to bring Miss Gaunt. I know she wouldn't have wanted to come as she is in mourning for her brother. Mistress only brightens up when a letter from Canada arrives. But come to think of it, we have had no news of Master Henry for weeks." The housekeeper took up her rolling pin. The gamekeeper had guaranteed that there would be hare pie on the menu today. Mrs. Dobson thought her mistress was fond of Henry, although the discreet parson had not dropped so much as a hint to anyone. As Cecil was laid to rest next to his grandfather and grandmother in the family tomb, the rector had paid a warm tribute to the deceased Uncle Charles: "a devoted, affectionate uncle to his nephew, kindly and generous, with high hopes for Cecil's education, now so abruptly terminated."

Charlotte had shed tears of anguish, hidden from view underneath her heavy black veil. Life was unbearably cruel. The promise of hope for the future of Albatross Hall lay in his tiny white coffin, adorned with red roses, as his grandfather's before him.

CHAPTER 36:
MATTHEW IS MURDERED

Dr. Fortescue was, by the standard of the times, very old fashioned. Many years older than Dr. Palliser, he insisted on wearing a black tricorn hat. Underneath his long black coat, he wore a lace cravat and cambric white shirt. The buttons of his grey waistcoat, his only concession to colour, strained at their moorings as the good doctor's girth increased. To the young rascals of Bath, he was the object of unbridled merriment. A well-aimed stone at either his hat or bulging black bag caused Fortescue to stop in his tracks and shake his fist angrily as they ran away down Laura Place, sticking out tongues and yelling out that he was the angel of death. Perhaps they held this view because shortly after he departed from the house of a patient, the sick frequently departed this world. He had long ago given up delivering babies. Not many survived past the age of five.

The bells of Bath Abbey pealed out as Dr. Fortescue opened the gate to number thirteen. Greech had taken the wise precaution of muffling the clapper of the door knocker with black silk so no sound reached Matthew's chamber. The windows were firmly closed. Heavy tapestry curtains prevented any stray sunbeam casting unwanted light.

Matthew Ponsonby yet lingered a while, lapsing in and out of delirium, incoherent to those gathered around his sickbed. "Does the name 'Cheatall' bear any significance at all?" inquired Dr. Fortescue, hovering over his patient. "He repeats it whenever I am near, as if this person might be known to him. Do you think this Cheatall, whoever he is, might have something to do with Matthew's attempted murder? As his doctor, I suggest he is troubled in mind. Furthermore, I am of the opinion that if we were to send for a certain reverend gentleman, a Mr. Beck who lives on Milsom Street, Matthew might be able to unburden himself. As you know Miles, Milsom Street is within easy reach of Laura Place, just a short carriage ride down Argyle and Bridge streets."

"What a coincidence Mr. Beck should reside on the same street that Matthew stayed on when he first came to Bath, years ago. I believe it was at the Dolphin Hotel." Miles drew his chair closer to the bed, taking his friend's cold, limp hand between his own. "I hesitate to send my man to fetch Mr. Beck. Do you not think the appearance of a man of the cloth would give Matthew the impression he was about to receive extreme unction, one of the final rites of the church—that his earthly journey will soon be over? I warrant there will be time for lamentations and prayers later. On no account must we endanger Matthew's health by informing him of his son's death. Better to offer Matthew some nourishing broth rather than spiritual sustenance." Miles eased him onto some pillows and rang for Greech. "But in answer to your question, doctor, I have never heard Matthew mention a Mr. Cheatall. Yet I pride myself on an intimate knowledge of his affairs. I must confess that I feel partly responsible for the attack."

Dr. Fortescue listened to Matthew's heart and lungs. He was breathing rapidly and very feverish. "In what way Miles, do you feel any guilt for what happened outside the Harrow and Plough?"

Miles turned away, looking embarrassed. "Truth to tell, I refused him a loan when he came to me for help. It is my belief that he was troubled by debts owed to criminals. These debts were the cause of the confrontation—a matter of revenge, if you will. I really can't forgive myself. How exceedingly fortunate that Greech found him."

Matthew groaned several times and sank back on his pillows.

"He is still in great pain," observed Fortescue. "Instead of soup, I think I should give him a dose of laudanum. Tell me, has any progress been made into the investigation of the crime?" Miles shook his head.

It was a certainty that Crickshaw and Goldie Finch had made good their escape from Bath. But just in case they were arrested, Cheatall had devised a plan. It entailed bribing the presiding judge if the agents were summoned to appear in court. Any witnesses called to testify (supposing any came forward) would benefit from a tidy cash payment, discreetly delivered, on their behalf, to the landlord of the Harrow and Plough. It was a known fact the justices of the peace were not above receiving "tokens of regard" on behalf of the accused. One of a few "incorruptible" magistrates in the 17th Century was none other than Henry Fielding, author of Tom Jones. If Matthew died, as Cheatall hoped, there would be no need for his wicked scheme. He had confidence in his agents that they could be relied upon to disguise themselves, invisible to any constable …

After his rescue by his neighbour Henry, still very weak and pale, leaned for support on the rail of the new steamship, the S.S. Savanna. He thought of his earlier life on board in the company of his companion, the late Captain Billop, sailing home on the Bellerphon, full of hope, eager to forget military exploits, wounds, imprisonment, and near starvation. The Savanna was just a day out of Plymouth. It was almost three years since Henry had left England's shores for a prosperous new life in Canada. How had England fared during his absence? What was happening at Albatross Hall? Many letters destined for Henry had failed to reach him. Vessels carrying mail foundered in storms or perished on submerged rocks.

The familiar sight of Plymouth lifted Henry's spirits as the Savanna slowly nosed up the Sound, passing Drake's Island and the Hoe, where legend says he played his famous game of bowls while awaiting the Spanish Armada. The hustle and bustle at Sutton Wharf was unchanged. Porters, carters, wagons laden with sacks, seafaring mariners, one with a colourful macaw perched on his shoulder, vagrants, mercenaries, militia—such a cacophony of sights, sounds and smells. Hawkers with trays of oysters and shellfish, their shouts mingling with the clatter of carriage wheels, whose occupants demanded to be driven close to vessels about to sail for parts unknown.

Henry disembarked in search of a porter willing to carry his trunks to a stagecoach bound for the North, scarcely avoiding a dray full of live chickens in small, cramped cages heading in his direction. The driver cracked his whip and glared down.

"Watch where you're a goin guv. Nearly ran you down, I did. Move out of the way."

Henry, piqued by the drover's rudeness, elbowed his way through the crowds to Looe Street, turning the corner onto Palace Street before finding lodgings at the Crown and Anchor. It rained hard against the inn's diamond-leaded windows. He took his seat at a round oak table near a roaring fire. The waiter, sensing that Henry was a stranger in town, advised Henry of the marvelous advances in transportation as he set a large platter of mutton stew before him.

"I hopes you 'ave heard sir, since you 'ave bin away so long from these 'ere parts, that we now 'ave a railway line running up somewheres in the north from Stockton to Darlinton', opened just last year, 1825. Designed by some genius of a bloke, George Stephenson. All reported in the Plymouth Enquirer. Mind you, I don't says as everyone is 'appy. Some say that this new fanglin' creature is an infernal monster. They say it can spy into everyone's back garden, hissing and grunting by at twenty miles per hour. Still, progress is progress. S'pose it won't be long sir afore the 'ole country is crisscrossed by rails everywhere. Anythink more I can get for you, sir?"

Henry shook his head and drank from his mug of porter. Things had indeed changed. He found the handle of his mug difficult to manage, owing to the loss of three fingers to frostbite. Still, it was a small price to pay for his deliverance from certain death by farmer Tewskley and neighbours who searched the inhospitable bush for hours to find him.

A note sent by the evening's mail coach, delivered to the office by the stable boy, told Matthew and Charlotte to expect him in two or three days—depending on the next available booking.

Matthew drifted in and out of consciousness, but never mentioned Cheatall's name again. When asleep, he saw visions. A collection of dirty bottles shrouded in cobwebs; a leering image of Mr. Tweedy, mine host of the Three Jolly Rodgers, still dressed in brown leather jerkin and gaiters; the black cat snarling at a grey mouse. In his hand, Tweedy held aloft a black falcon. Matthew, terrified at these apparitions sent from the past, awoke, and feebly reached for the bell rope. He fell back, his brow bathed in sweat, trembling from head to toe as the "angel of death," Dr. Fortescue, placed a hand on his ashen face.

"It is time to send Greech for the reverend Beck," he whispered to Miles.

With great solemnity, Beck made the sign of the cross and anointed Matthew's head with holy oil, while murmuring a fervent prayer for the peaceful repose of the departing soul.

In the early hours of the morning of the 15th of June, 1825, the scion and squire of Albatross breathed his last. The legend of the black falcon had come true.

A week after Matthew's elaborate funeral, costing even more than that of his father, an important decision emerged from discussions between Henry and Charlotte in the library. It was decreed the falconry had to go. Then, on Charlotte's orders, a new inventory was written of the contents of the Hall. To his dismay, Henry found that his late brother had deliberately ignored the strictures imposed by Lord Cecil's will. An inspection of each room showed many paintings and objects of artistic value missing. Even Charlotte's jewels were not to be found, although they had been deposited in a locked case. She knew her husband alone was responsible. A loyal servant, nothing could be gained by questioning Tapper. That he was party to all transactions, Henry was certain. But where had Matthew taken them? Henry busied himself looking for clues. Perhaps the secret drawer in the library desk might contain receipts or bills? However a search of the drawer, opened by a craftily concealed spring, revealed just one souvenir from young Cecil's childhood: a brass fitting from his rocking horse.

Henry felt frustrated at this turn of events. He intended to make Charlotte his wife as soon as a respectable period set aside for mourning passed. The joyful meeting of Henry and Charlotte proved the old adage that "absence makes the heart grow fonder." Mrs. Dobson observed the happy pair walking arm in arm on the terrace, as was their custom before Henry went away. Now, visibly agitated, she entered the library unannounced. "Beggin' your pardon, Mistress and Master Henry, for the intrusion," she began, and then stopped, making a deep curtsy. "Please excuse me. I should have said Lord Henry Ponsonby, now that Your Honour has succeeded to the title of squire. I have found some old yellowing papers in my kitchen a lyin' neath the copper bath which mebbe will be of interest. Although the writin' is faded, I could read the name at the top."

"Well, go on, Mrs. D. What did it say?" asked Henry, impatient to learn all he could about Albatross affairs.

"It said 'CHEATALL, Soho Place, London.' Written underneath was a list, similar to my 'ousekeepin list. Agin, beggin' your pardon, sir," went on Mrs. Dobson, covering her head with her apron in confusion, "they wos things which used to be in this very 'ouse. There wos also some promising notes from a Mr. Thomas Coutts, banker to King George. I knows that cos I recognized the royal coat of arms—I think it meant a warrant or sichlike."

"You mean 'promissory' notes, Mrs. D. Do you perchance have them with you?" The housekeeper removed a small bundle of papers from the pocket in her apron.

Henry, accompanied by Tapper and Bentinck, approached Cheatall's shop. A plan to deal with the pawnbroker was interrupted by loud noises coming from the premises. Just as Henry and Bentinck arrived, a poor, disheveled man stumbled through the door, ejected with such force that he landed on the slippery cobblestones in front of the carriage. The two brown bays reared in fright, flailing their hooves, one catching Peggles a glancing blow on his side as he lay prostrate, unable to move.

"My dear man," said Henry. "You are trembling all over. There is a nasty gash on your forehead where you struck the pavement. Let me send you at once in my carriage to see a doctor. My coachman will drive you there."

Peggles demurred, muttering that he had no money to pay any medical man. "You see sir, I wos in the shop behind you to pay part of a debt." Peggles gasped for breath, clutching his side in pain. "The pawnbroker gave me a wicious push, sayin' he would drown me in the Thames if I didn't pay in full next time. He done this afore, and me with a wife and children to feed."

"We'll see about that later. Don't trouble yourself, I will pay the doctor his fee." Leaving Bentinck to assist Peggles into the coach, Henry strode purposefully into Cheatall's shop.

"Now sir, what have you got to say for yourself, you cowardly villain?" Cheatall retreated behind the counter. "How dare you treat a customer in such a way, giving the wretched man a violent blow sufficient to cause him injury. Let me advise you, sir, that you will pay the doctor's bill, just as you will settle my accounts with me, and to my satisfaction, you rogue."

Cheatall rubbed his hands together. "But may I 'ave the honour of knowin' your identity guv? I don't recognize you as havin' had dealin's with you afore."

"Well then," replied Henry, relishing the advantage he held over Cheatall. "I am Lord Henry Ponsonby, brother of the late Lord Matthew Ponsonby."

The proprietor turned pale, shuffling uneasily to the bottom of the staircase.

"Stay where you are you rogue," thundered Henry. "You have built a sordid business, fleecing and duping innocent people. You will pay for your crimes. Before I hand you over to the constable patrolling the street, you will return to me all heirlooms, jewellery, and paintings on your premises which belong to Albatross Hall. The law will then take its course. Customers such as Peggles will no longer be in your clutches. Goldie Finch and Chicksaw were arrested two days ago, charged with the murder of my brother. You will be very lucky if you escape the noose too."

CHAPTER 37:
LORD HENRY AND
CHARLOTTE MARRY

"Just as we were discussing after Lord Cecil's funeral, Bray, times have not changed very much. You talk about law and order. The newly formed Bow Street Runners are doing their best to apprehend criminals, but they wear such distinctive red jackets they must be easily recognized on the streets. Their job is made more difficult by an uneducated populace who mistakenly view the activities of the runners as a breach of their personal liberties. I look forward to the day when a more competent police force will be established. As a lawyer, I consider that Parliament has adopted a very foolish law, Bray. Would you believe, they decided to reward a constable with forty pounds for arresting a highwayman, while a shop thief is assessed at ten pounds! They are not paid a decent wage, so some corrupt constables have inveigled innocent people into crime and thus they claim a reward. Mark my words, England is an unruly country. It is so bad that unscrupulous men actually 'buy' back stolen goods and then sell them back to the rightful owner for a five shilling 'consultation' fee. I don't know what England is coming too. I sound a bit like Miss Gaunt, but when one magistrate, Sir Robert Baker, actually takes the view that it isn't a crime to receive back stolen goods by the practice of buying them back, then words fail me."

The two old friends Lawyer Feathers and Parson Bray were sitting in the library at the Hall. This time, however, it was to celebrate the marriage of Lady Charlotte and Lord Henry, but, as always, the topic of conversation was the deplorable state of affairs in England.

Bray sipped his glass of brandy and stretched his legs before him. He was seated in a comfortable leather chair and feeling very satisfied after a delicious wedding breakfast. He yawned, feeling the effects of numerous servings of punch. "Such a wonderful thing, Feathers, that I was able to join two loving people in matrimony today. I always knew that Henry had strong feelings about Charlotte and I know that she felt the same way. He confided his passion for her when he paid me a last visit before sailing to Canada. I think it most appropriate they will spend their honeymoon in Italy."

"But let me finish my story," broke in Feathers. "One notorious thief taker I heard of at Gray's Inn, an individual named Jonathan Wilde, lined his pocket to such a degree that his dishonest 'trade' became widespread in various quarters. It gained a reputation as a very lucrative occupation. He would buy stolen property for a pittance and then betray others who would not go along with his fraudulent scheme. I read this report in the Hue and Cry. Some years ago, Wilde was hanged for his crimes as a warning to others. Something in a more recent issue might interest you, Bray. Henry kindly brought it to my attention. It said that after his trial, Cheatall was sentenced to transportation to Tasmania. One paragraph underneath reported that both Chicksaw and Goldie Finch were given the death penalty for the murder of Lord Matthew Ponsonby."

"Justice has been served. May the Lord have mercy on their souls," replied his friend as together, arm in arm, they walked into the Great Hall to join the wedding guests dancing to the strains of music from the minstrel's gallery.

"Can I really believe my eyes, Feathers," said Parson Bray, astonished at the incredible sight of Miss Gaunt cavorting around the floor on the arm of Tapper.

"She is truly a changed woman since I buried Charles. Never distributes any religious tracts as she used to, and seems content to live out her days in peace in Bramble Cottage. Now that Henry has recovered her gold cross and chain and all the treasures belonging to the Hall, both she and Charlotte have found true happiness. Look at the way she is dancing. You know, it wouldn't surprise me if she and Tapper made a match …"

"Well, let us hope that the fortunes of the Ponsonby family take a turn for the better. A toast to my Lord and Lady."

Both gentlemen raised their glasses. On their next visit to the Hall, they would find a new portrait of Henry and Charlotte. It was painted in the studio of Pietro Batoni.

~Finis~

Printed in Canada